DON'T LET HER STAY

An unputdownable psychological thriller with a breathtaking twist

NICOLA SANDERS

AMARYLLIS

An imprint of Manjul Publishing House

AMARYLLIS
An imprint of Manjul Publishing House Pvt. Ltd.
• C-16, Sector 3, Noida, Uttar Pradesh 201301, India
Website: www.manjulindia.com
Registered Office:
• 2nd Floor, Usha Preet Complex,
42, Malviya Nagar, Bhopal 462 003 - India
Distribution Centres
Ahmedabad, Bengaluru, Chennai, Hyderabad,
Kochi, Kolkata, Mumbai, Noida, Pune

Don't Let Her Stay by Nicola Sanders

This edition first published in India in 2026
Second impression 2026

ISBN 978-93-7317-785-4

Cover design by Dissect Designs

Printed and bound in India by Repro India Ltd.

Prologue

'Don't wake up. Please don't wake up.'

Begging my four-month-old baby to sleep — or stay asleep — has never worked before. God knows I've tried. So I don't know why I think this time will be any different.

But begging is all I have.

I'm holding her so close to my chest I have to keep checking that I'm not hurting her. But I can feel her stir, a sure indication that she's about to wake up. If she wakes up, she will cry because she always does.

And if she cries, we will die.

I'm doing everything I can to get us out of here alive. I am so close. I'm at the front door. I open it and slip out as quietly and quickly as possible.

It's dark out here. So quiet that even the sound of gravel crunching under my feet gives me away. But I can't slow down now. We only have seconds. I run to the Range Rover and crouch beside the back wheel, my fingers feeling for the spare key I keep up there. When I press the button, the car flashes with a beep that may as well be the blare of a trumpet. I stop, my heart pounding, and listen. Nothing. The interior light comes on when I open the door and my hand shoots out to turn it off. I fumble to put Evie down in the baby car seat. Her eyes flick open like a doll.

Then her mouth opens. Wide.

'Please don't cry, Evie. Please, baby, please don't cry.' I hold my breath.

Evie yawns.

I close the door gently but I'm shaking so much that the key slips from my hand. I drop to the ground and feel around for it in the dark.

Please don't cry. Please don't cry. I feel the plastic square under my fingers.

Thank god. I've got it. I stand up just as light blasts out of an upstairs window, illuminating the car.

I can't help it. I turn around and look up at the house even though it costs me a second I can't spare. It's coming from the nursery. It's the only light on in the house.

My hand flies to my mouth when she appears at the window, slamming both palms flat against the glass, dark smoke rising behind her.

Our eyes meet.

I turn away, lock myself in the car, and drive.

Chapter One

Three weeks earlier.

Oscar gives a lazy bark just as I hear a van drive onto the gravel. The bark is only for show. We both know that he'd let an intruder walk right in, wag his tail at the thief and put his paws on his chest. He's an old caramel Labrador who loves everybody and everything, even the neighbour's cat.

I step away from the cot to the window. It's the postman. He walks up the steps to the front door and seconds later I hear the clank of the door flap. There's a letterbox at the gate, but when it's just me in the house — which is the case most days — I like to leave the gate wide open. It feels less lonely that way, knowing anyone could drive right up to the house without having to ring the intercom. Richard disagrees. He says it's not safe, which invariably makes me roll my eyes. This is a charming but rather sleepy village, and this gorgeous country home is like a fortress. When we first moved in, Richard was so concerned about Evie and me being isolated that he had locks installed on every window.

I look down at Evie asleep in her cot, her limbs out like a starfish, and I pull the blanket over her and kiss her soft pink cheek. She doesn't even stir. If someone had told me even a year ago that the arrival of the post would be the most exciting thing to happen to me *all day*, I would have laughed. But now, as I walk quickly down the stairs, I feel a little thrill of anticipation that there might be something for me among all the letters and bills addressed to Richard. A magazine maybe? The latest issue of *Homes & Gardens*? Now that's another one I would have laughed at a year ago. Not anymore. I could spend a good hour, maybe even two if I paced myself, in the rocking chair in the nursery, flicking through on-trend bathrooms, country conservatories — perhaps we should do that next, after the kitchen makeover. Except that I've done nothing about the kitchen makeover. The pictures I cut out are still there, their corners curling on the magnetic board I set up for the project in a spare room I've claimed as my office. Richard has his own study downstairs, a large room with an oversized oak desk, shelves that take up the entire back wall, and French doors that open onto a patio. He rarely uses his study. He doesn't like to bring work home.

My office is less grand, just a room with a desk and a filing cabinet where I keep my private documents. I decorated it with pretty wallpaper and got Simon, our gardener, to hang the large magnetic board on the wall since Richard wouldn't know which end of the hammer to hit a nail with.

I had big plans for this house back then. I was pregnant, past the nausea stage and deliriously happy from whatever hormones were coursing through me. I still believed, foolishly, that I'd have the energy to do it all and that having a baby would be a walk in the park, except that my beautiful baby doesn't sleep. I mean, she does. She takes about fifty million naps a night, and in between she wakes up and cries until she gets her feed. These days the brutal reality is that some mornings I'm too tired to wash my hair.

I bend down to pick up the post, Oscar by my side, and let out a sigh as I flick through the pile. I guess I'll have to find something else to pass the time because there's no mail for me today.

I put the bundle of mail on the console table, all neatly in order of size — *Investors Chronicle* at the bottom, bills and smaller items at the top. There's a large letter from Amsterdam which I assume is related to the conference Richard is attending in three weeks. I stick that at the bottom of the pile. A letter slips to the floor. I pick it up and turn it over in my hand. Like all the others, it's addressed to Richard, but this one is handwritten and it's pretty clear from the handwriting that it's from a woman. I flick it over, but there's no return address, no indication of who it's from. I immediately think it's from Isabella, beautiful Isabella, Richard's ex-fiancée. I know they're in touch, although why she would send him a handwritten letter is a mystery. Maybe it's an invitation to an event. A special invitation. To a special event. Just for him. No plus one, please.

Suddenly I'm dying to know. I turn it over between my fingers. I consider using the old steam trick to open it, although I suspect it doesn't work anymore.

A gust of cold air makes me jump.

'Hi, Mrs A.'

'Roxanne!' I laugh, clutching the envelope to my chest. 'You gave me a fright. Is that the time already?'

She leans her bicycle against the wall outside and walks in, closing the front door.

'Sorry for scaring you,' she says, pulling back the hood of her coat. 'I should have rung the doorbell. I thought you'd be upstairs with Evie.'

I wave a dismissive hand in the air. 'Evie is fast asleep. It's been at least fifteen minutes. I think it's a record. I was checking the post.'

'Okay, well, I'll get started then, Mrs A.'

I've asked Roxanne fifty times to call me Joanne, but she never does. I'm always Mrs A even though she must be around twenty-five, twenty-eight maybe, which makes me only five or so years older than her.

She hangs her coat in the coat room, which is a small room off the hall where we keep umbrellas, raincoats, wellies... She strides straight through the double doors that lead to the large kitchen to get the trolley of cleaning products from the pantry-slash-utility-room. I am right behind her.

'Do you want some tea before you start?' I ask this every time and more often than not, she says no. She must think I've got memory problems. Or that I'm hard of hearing.

'No, thank you,' she says. 'I'll get on with it.'

'I'm thinking of getting a bicycle,' I blurt before she has time to walk away. It's not true. What would I do with one? Stick the cot on the back wheel? But I'm dying to talk to someone. I feel like I haven't spoken to anyone in days, although that's not strictly true. I talk to Simon, although we're still in winter so he doesn't spend much time here at the moment. He only comes once or twice a week, mostly to tidy the grounds and get things ready for spring. I speak to Richard of course, every evening, but Richard works long hours and lately doesn't even come home in time for dinner. He owns a boutique investment bank and along with his managing partner, they are working on a new product, some big new finance portfolio thing. He tried to explain it to me but I didn't understand a word of it. I blamed it on baby brain.

'What do you think I should get?' I ask Roxanne.

She shrugs. 'There's a bike shop in Chertsey. You could ask them.'

I nod. 'Yes. Good idea.' I listen for Evie, and satisfied that all is quiet, I pick up the kettle and raise it in Roxanne's direction. 'You're sure?'

'I'm sure,' she says.

'Okay!' I pop a peppermint tea bag in my mug and lean back against the counter. I watch as she gets her cleaning things together. I try to think of something else to say, but my brain is like mashed potato.

Sometimes I wonder what on earth we were thinking, moving to such a big house miles away from town. I know how lucky I am, living in this beautiful home. It has six bedrooms, five bathrooms, a drawing room *and* a morning room, views for days, a basement where Richard keeps his most precious wines and that he's threatening to turn into a home cinema or something, an enormous kitchen and a pantry larger than the flat I used to live in back in London. All I ever want to do is sit in the kitchen with Evie on my lap, drink tea and chat to Roxanne. Some days I find myself following her around the house as she works, me with Evie in my arms, just to have someone to talk to.

Roxanne pops her earbuds in her ears and taps the screen on her phone. I swallow a sigh. I get the message. 'I'll leave you to get on then,' I say, even though she can't hear me. I pour the boiling water on the tea bag and walk with my mug back into the hall.

Chapter Two

Richard and I have lived in this house since I was pregnant with Evie. Our forever home. I'd overcome my reluctance to rely on Richard's money by then, at least when it came to buying a house. At the beginning of our search, every time he took me to see a property, I would baulk at the price tag. I had nowhere near the income to take on the kind of mortgage he seemed to have in mind. And those places weren't even as grand as the one we ended up buying.

'Don't worry about money, Joanne. Let's find the right home for us. Let it be my gift to you,' he'd say, kissing the top of my head.

I still remember the first time we toured the property. I couldn't believe my eyes. Richard absolutely loved it. Could this really become ours? I tried to picture the life we would have here as I gawked at every room, every cornice, every window. We talked of the parties we would host, marvelled at the mature landscaped gardens, imagined our children — and Labrador — playing on the lawn. We immediately agreed how perfect the upstairs room overlooking the rose garden was for a nursery. The kitchen was a little outdated and I excitedly told Richard I could give it an upgrade. It could be my personal project, I said.

Except it's not going the way I'd hoped. I can't make a simple decision about worktops or cupboard finishes and since I used to be an estate agent, you'd think I'd know about this stuff. I've seen many, many kitchens, and I know what layout works, what sells, what looks good.

Or I used to anyway. These days I find myself asking Roxanne questions like, 'Is this a good oven, do you think?' Or 'What's a nice kitchen style these days? Polished concrete? What about shaker? Or wait, what about this one? High-gloss white. Do you like high-gloss white?' And she would look at me, eyebrows slightly raised, and say, 'I don't know, Mrs A. It's up to you.'

That was before she started bringing her earbuds, obviously.

I first met Richard when he came with Isabella to the estate agency where I worked in Chelmsford. I'd moved there years earlier with my then-boyfriend Marc after he was given the opportunity to manage a computer hardware development company there. After Marc and I split up, he moved back to London and I stayed in the area, out of inertia, mostly.

Richard and Isabella were interested in a Georgian house that we had on our books. The property wasn't mine to show. It was assigned to my colleague Anthony — I had a bit of a crush on Anthony but that's another story — and as Anthony was away that day, I offered to show them.

It was a gorgeous house, with well-proportioned rooms and large open fireplaces, high ceilings and set on two acres of land with its own lake. *That* house was supposed to be their forever home. His and Isabella's.

I remember her well. In her forties, beautiful and tall, curly dark hair framing her gorgeous face. A lovely smile. A few days went by, and one day Richard called. He wanted to take another look at the house. We arranged a visit, but on the day Isabella was running late so I went through it all again with Richard. He asked to see the cellar. I don't like cellars, or dark places, which can be a problem in my line of work. But this was my job so I squared my shoulders and said, sure. We went down there, and a gust of wind slammed the door shut. Richard went back up to open it but it was stuck. I was shaking. My legs had turned into columns of jelly.

'Are you all right, Joanne?'

'Yes,' I lied and rested my hand against the damp wall for support.

'Don't worry. We'll be out of here in a jiffy.' He pulled out his mobile, and of course we had no reception whatsoever down there.

I started to hyperventilate.

'Now you don't worry about anything, Joanne. All right? See the window up there? I'm going to get through that window, and I'm going to go around the house and open the door.'

'*That* window?' I'd breathed. It wasn't even a window, just a gap really. A few missing bricks. Surely he wouldn't fit through *that*.

'Trust me. Everything will be fine.'

'Okay,' I whispered, with some difficulty.

He took his suit jacket off and folded it carefully on top of an empty crate. He rolled up his shirt sleeves, loosened his tie and ran his fingers through his hair. And even though I was on the verge of a panic attack, the sight of him, with his slightly crooked thick-rimmed glasses and his dark, floppy hair and his tie now askew, made me smile. He looked like Clark Kent. Or how Clark Kent would look if they'd let him get to fifty.

He brought together three more empty crates — thank god they even had those lying around — and fashioned them into some kind of staircase. 'May I put my hand on your shoulder? To steady myself?' he asked.

'Yes, sorry.' I came to stand next to him, but I had to brace one hand against the wall to stay upright. Black dots danced in front of my eyes while he somehow climbed up the crates.

It looked so awkward, the way he tried to wriggle through the gap. If I hadn't been so scared, I would have found it funny. But instead I kept wondering, what if he got stuck? What if he died up there? Jammed in that tiny window opening? Then his legs disappeared which brought a fresh round of panic.

'You're not going to run away and leave me here, are you?' I yelled nervously.

He popped his head back in. 'Wild horses couldn't keep me away,' he puffed. 'I'll be right back.'

And then he was gone.

I crouched down and let my head drop between my knees. I wondered what I'd do if he didn't come back and realised there was nothing I could do. Nothing at all. I'd just die here, alone. A rotting skeleton in a cellar.

Then the door opened wide and he ran down the stairs and helped me up.

'I feel so stupid,' I said, once we were outside.

'Not at all. You couldn't have known the cellar would lock itself.'

'I mean getting so scared.'

'It's over now. There's nothing to be scared about

anymore.' He pulled me into his arms and I started to cry. I felt so silly, sobbing all over his nice shirt, but the truth was I didn't want to pull away. I felt more safe being held protectively like that than I had in a long time.

We stayed like that for a few moments, him caressing my head and me shuddering like a child, until I pulled away and wiped my nose with my sleeve. 'Sorry. I messed up your shirt. Also you left your jacket down there.'

'I'll get it.' He handed me a handkerchief, assuring me it was clean, just as a car pulled up in front of us.

Isabella had arrived.

The following week he came to the agency and told me he wasn't going ahead with the purchase of the property because he and Isabella had separated.

'I'm so sorry,' I said as his eyes welled up.

It was five o'clock, so I took him to The Ship around the corner for a drink. He told me Isabella had left him for another man. She'd been having an affair for months and when they were looking to buy the house, she already knew she wouldn't be moving in. 'She just didn't know how to tell me.'

I've had my own experiences with betrayals in relationships. I told him about Marc, who I'd moved here for. Marc and I were together for three years. Marc didn't want children yet, then later Marc didn't want children at all. 'I'd make a terrible father,' he'd say. Then one day Marc announced over breakfast that he was leaving. He'd been having an affair with Olive from Human Resources and she was pregnant.

'They have a little boy called George now, with another one on the way.'

Richard shook his head. 'That's terrible.'

I shrugged. 'It was a while ago,' I said, as if I didn't still seethe with resentment every time I thought of it.

We talked some more, then suddenly it was closing time. I hadn't felt so comfortable with someone in a long time.

'Thank you for listening,' he said, closing the door of the cab for me.

Two months later he asked me out to dinner. Eight months later we were married.

Chapter Three

I take my mug of hot tea with me, and as I enter the hall on the way back upstairs to the nursery, I glance again at the mysterious letter on the console. I pick it up, try to remember if I've ever seen Isabella's handwriting, but if I did, I don't remember it. I wish I didn't feel so insecure, but a few months ago, Richard told me that Isabella had been in touch and that her relationship had not worked out. She was single again.

'Do you think she wants to get back with you?' I'd asked incredulously.

'No. Not at all. It's just that we were together for many years. I think she wants to talk to someone who knows her well. A shoulder to cry on.'

If Richard had meant to make me feel better, it wasn't working. After all, *I'd* been a shoulder to cry on, and look where that got us. Although back then I was slim and full of energy, a busy professional, *and* I had clean hair. Now? Now I feel so boring I can put myself to sleep just talking to myself.

I should up my game. That's what I should do. I should make him a delicious home-cooked meal. No, make that a candlelit dinner. And we haven't had sex in weeks and that's my fault. I'll wear something sexy. Do I have something sexy to wear? Something that still fits me? Something that won't make me look like salami encased in twine?

I'm about to go upstairs when the phone rings. The land-line. We have phones in just about every room in this house because the mobile reception around here is patchy at best, although Richard claims it's to save me running around looking for my mobile in case I'm nursing Evie. For some reason everybody worries about me exerting myself when I'm nursing Evie.

'Joanne, darling. How is your day going?'

'Really well!' I say brightly. 'Really good. And I'm glad you called because I was thinking of making something special for dinner tonight. What time will you be home?' Then I add, 'I've got a surprise.'

He laughs. 'What kind of surprise?'

I flick the letter between my fingers. 'Well if I tell you it won't be a surprise. But never mind. Since you ask, I thought I would make us a romantic dinner for two… And maybe, you know… dessert?'

Great. Now he's probably thinking of jelly and custard.

'Sweetheart, I'm sorry. That sounds wonderful, but the reason I'm calling is because I have to work late. We have to get the prospectus out by Monday. Geoff called for all hands on deck tonight.'

Oh, bugger Geoff. 'That's all right,' I say, trying to sound upbeat and failing. 'Another time.' I can hear Evie stir upstairs. 'I should go. It's time for Evie's feed. Will you call me later?'

'Of course, darling.'

I know it's those stupid hormones but still tears prickle. I can't help but wonder if I'm losing him. That he finds me so boring, he prefers to spend his evenings with his colleagues at his office.

I go back upstairs and check on Evie who is awake. She's lying on her back, staring at the mobile of woodland animals above her cot. She looks at me as I approach, starts to cry, and still my heart soars. I pick her up and kiss her soft hair. She stops crying and rubs her nose into my neck. I laugh. Every insecurity has vanished from my mind. My heart is full of love and happiness when I'm with my baby.

I take the bottle I prepared earlier from the little corner fridge and drop it in the warmer, then I walk around the room waiting for the ping from the machine. I'd love to be able to breastfeed my baby, but unfortunately I don't produce enough milk.

My mobile phone rings. It's my friend and ex-colleague Shelley from the agency. I wedge the phone in the crook of my neck and settle Evie on my hip.

'Shelley! Hello! How are you? Hang on, I can't hear you. I'll go outside. One sec.'

I walk to my bedroom and stand in front of the French doors that lead to the balcony. It's always a good spot for reception. 'Can you hear me now?'

'Hey, mama! There you are!'

I can hear the phones ringing in the background and feel a little pang of nostalgia.

'You sound busy,' I say.

'Always. You know how it is. How are things with you?'

'I'm so busy too! I don't have a minute to myself!'

'Sorry, Jo,' she says. 'I won't keep you, just a quick question.'

'No please keep me. I was just joking. I'm about to die of boredom here. You can talk to me all day if you like.'

She laughs. 'Surely things aren't that bad. Listen, seriously I'm in a rush, but do you remember the Berry House we did a valuation for? Then the client decided not to sell?'

'Yes, I remember.'

'He's changed his mind and he wants to see the original valuation. I can't find the file. We've looked and looked, and we've got a meeting in five.'

I bounce Evie gently on my hip. 'It's in the filing cabinet, where we keep the "call back in six months" files.'

'Oh my god, Jo, you're amazing. I completely forgot but you're right.' I hear the creak of a chair being pushed back, the sound of a drawer opening, and then, in a loud, triumphant tone Shelley yells out, 'We got it!' She must be holding the phone up because I hear a *whoohoo!* A couple of people clap, and I feel a rush of pride, as if I've saved the entire agency from instant bankruptcy.

'You're a star. You really are,' she says. 'I have to rush off but thanks, Jo. I'm trying to juggle three things at once. You know how it gets around here. We've got so many rentals now we need to open a whole new branch just to deal with those, and we lost both Terry and Kimberley.'

'What happened to Terry and Kimberley? Did they quit?'

'They certainly did. They went and got married. Didn't you know?'

'No! Well, that's great news, isn't it? I mean, maybe not for you.' An idea pops into my head. 'Wait, I was wondering, could you use some extra help? I could work from home a day or two per week if that was of any use.' I'm speaking quickly now, blurting it out as the idea takes shape in my head. 'All the documents are in the cloud. I won't be able to show prospective buyers obviously, but I could team up with one of the others, Jacklyn maybe? Or I could help with the tenancies, organise repairs, inspections, that sort of thing?'

Needless to say, the odds of Shelley giving me a job, any

job, are about as good as me winning the lottery. I live seventy-odd miles away. I haven't stepped foot in the agency for over a year. I haven't even worked at *any* job for that long. What do I know about their current listings? Do they even still use the same systems?

She is silent. Any minute now, she's going to say 'no thanks' and send me on my way.

'I tell you what,' she says finally. 'We could use the help until I get more staff, but it might not be the most interesting work, just slog, you know?'

'I love slog! Slog is my favourite thing in the world!'

She laughs, and we make plans to talk again in a day or two, after she's had time to think about it and talk to the team. I am giddy with pleasure when I hang up.

'Mummy might be going back to work,' I coo to Evie. 'Wouldn't that be something? And you can sit on my lap and help me. Would you like that?'

I don't know why, but I suddenly have the feeling that I'm being watched. I turn around, and a shadow moves in the doorway.

'Roxanne?' I poke my head out and catch sight of her rushing down the corridor. 'Roxanne?' I call out again. 'Did you need something?' But she's walking away without turning around.

I return to the nursery and settle with Evie in the armchair. Has Roxanne been watching me? Of course not. Why would Roxanne care what I'm doing? I'm just imagining things. She probably just walked past and glanced in on the way, that's all. And of course she didn't hear me. She's wearing earbuds, remember?

I shake my shoulders to dislodge the strange feeling. 'About time Mummy found something to do, don't you think?' I whisper to Evie. Another quirk I've acquired lately, talking to myself while pretending to talk to my baby. 'Otherwise, Mummy might go completely bonkers.'

Chapter Four

I fell asleep with Evie on my chest but now I'm awake. Something woke me. Roxanne? No, it couldn't be. She left hours ago.

'Joanne? It's me!'

'Richard?' I get up, put a sleepy Evie back in the cot. 'You're home!' I run down the stairs to meet him. 'But I thought you were working late tonight?'

He unbuttons his coat. 'I told Geoffrey he could do it himself if he wanted, but I was going home. I miss my girls too much.' He puts his briefcase on the floor and opens his arms.

'But you're so early!' I say, folding myself into them.

'I took the rest of the day off.' He kisses the top of my head. 'I'm sorry,' he says softly.

'What for?'

'You wanted to do something special tonight for us, and I'm a boring old man. I'm leaving you alone too much. I don't deserve you,' he says.

'I wish you'd called. I would have brushed my hair!'

He runs his hand over my head. 'Your hair is perfect.'

I pull away, glance down at my front. 'But I look a mess.' I'm wearing an old, misshapen sweatshirt and a pair of distended yoga pants. 'And I've got Evie's snot all over me.'

'And I think you look beautiful. Come on, let's open a bottle of wine.'

That is one benefit of not being able to breastfeed. I can have a glass of wine in the evenings.

'I haven't prepared anything to eat,' I say.

'Let's get something from Piccolino.' He takes my hand.

'Oh yes, let's do that,' I say. 'I could kill for a pizza.'

Later, we sit at the large wooden table in the kitchen, the baby monitor between us. Richard twirls a strand of spaghetti around his fork. His hair flops over his forehead. I should give him a haircut. I often wonder how someone like Richard, who is so intelligent and so successful, can present himself as such a nerd. Sometimes I have to stop him before he leaves the house so I can fix his shirt because he's skipped a button. Or he'll wear a pair of socks that almost match, but not quite. Or spend half an hour looking for his glasses when they are literally on his head. I sent him to the optician once to check he wasn't going blind. But no, perfectly good eyesight. He didn't even need to upgrade his glasses. It's just the way he is, and I wouldn't want him any other way. He is my own handsome, silver-templed Clark Kent, and I melt just looking at him.

'You look tired, sweetheart.'

I try to smile. 'She didn't get to sleep until two last night.'

'You should have woken me.'

'No! You have to go to work. It wouldn't be fair.'

'I could have helped. How was the little monster today?'

'She slept all day, of course. Like an angel.' I take a bite of my pizza, wipe my mouth with my napkin. 'Anyway, on another note, I've got news.'

'Oh?'

'I talked to Shelley today.'

He pours us both a glass of wine. 'Shelley….'

'From the estate agency where I used to work.'

'Shelley. Of course. And how is Shelley?'

'She's great! But honestly, they're so busy in there. She can barely breathe.' I start playing with my napkin, folding and unfolding it. 'Anyway,' I continue, 'she asked if I could help out a couple of days a week. Just working from home of course,' I add quickly, in case he thought I'd be traipsing off to Chelmsford every other day.

He frowns at me over the rim of his wine glass. 'But sweetheart, is that what you want?'

I slap an inch of butter on a piece of bread, forgetting my earlier determination to get back in shape as quickly as possible. 'Well… She needs my help, so…'

'But what about what *you* want?' He reaches for my hand. 'You're happy, aren't you? I worry about you sometimes. Did we rush into this? I know you wanted to live here, in this house, away from the city… But did we do the wrong thing?'

And that is why I felt the need to tell a little white lie. Shelley didn't ask me to work again. It's me who blurted it out and almost begged her to have me back. But as Richard reminds me, this house, this life, it's everything I wanted. I wanted lots of children and a home that I can tend to. I wanted a big kitchen with pots and pans hanging from the ceiling. I wanted to cook delicious meals every night for my family. I wanted all these things and I'm the one who has been waxing lyrical for months about how much I was looking forward to full-time motherhood and how much I wanted to fill this house with children and friends and laughter and how busy I was going to be and how fantastic life was going to be away from the bustle of work. Richard doesn't care what I want as long as I'm happy. I firmly believe Richard couldn't care less if I changed my mind or if I wanted to work part-time or not. It's not him who is disappointed in me. It's me.

'I think it might be fun. I do miss the busyness of the office.'

He takes a sip of wine. 'And will you be working with Anthony in that busy office? What about our baby? What happens to her?'

I put my hand on his. 'Firstly, I'd be working from home. When I said the busyness of the office, I meant metaphorically. Secondly, I don't even know if Anthony still works there.'

Which is a lie. Anthony *does* still work there. He messages me occasionally, just to say hello. But Anthony is a sticking point between us. We kissed, once, a few weeks before I met Richard. It was after the agency Christmas party, and he'd walked me home. After that we'd flirt at work and I kept hoping he'd ask me out, but neither of us took it any further. And then I met Richard. But I made the mistake of telling Richard about him. I think I wanted to make him feel like I was a catch. That men were lining up to date me.

'There's this guy at work, he's driving me crazy. He keeps flirting with me. It's very sweet but you know, he just won't take the hint,' I'd said once. We were in a very expensive restaurant in Mayfair. I even bought a new dress for the occasion that had cost half my month's salary.

A vein throbbed on his temple. 'Why would he do that? He knows you're attached, doesn't he?'

'Yes! Of course he does. It's just that …' I shouldn't have said it. I should have known from his tone that this wasn't going the way I'd expected, but I was stuck in my own little performance. 'We kissed, once.' I waved a hand in the air. 'I was drunk. Christmas party. Need I say more? Anyway,' I sighed theatrically. 'I think he's a little bit in love with me.'

He put his glass down very slowly. 'And you do that often? Get drunk and fuck other men?'

I gasped audibly. He motioned for the waiter. 'The bill, please.'

'What are you doing, Richard? We only just sat down!'

'I don't want to keep you from your lover. If you'd rather spend the night with him, then you should.'

I argued, explained I was just saying it to make him a little bit jealous, because I'm stupid and I would never, ever even contemplate being with anyone else. But his face was red with fury and his hands were closed into tight fists by his side. I'd never seen that side of him before and I couldn't believe his reaction. I tried to explain. It meant nothing. It was just a kiss. Anthony meant nothing to me. Only Richard. On and on we went, but he wouldn't listen. Normally I would have stayed at his place in Kensington, but instead he put me in a cab and walked away. I took a train home, sobbing all the way in my elegant new dress.

The following day he sent a dozen red roses with a note. *I'm just a silly old man who is incredibly in love with you. Please forgive me?*

I did, of course. But I was careful after that, because my slightly nerdy, slightly goofy, silver-templed Clark Kent also had a temper. I only saw him lose his cool once after that over something that happened in his office, I'm not sure what. We were at home, the conversation took place over the phone. He put his fist through a window. Well, not through the window since it didn't break. But it must have hurt.

'It's not like I'm the first person to be working from home,' I say now. 'There are a couple of people in the office who work from home one or two days a week. It's very common these days.'

'But what about Evie?' he asks.

Richard is very protective of Evie, and that's one of the things I love most about him. From the minute she was born, he has fussed over her, worried about her, protected her. He was thrilled when I said I wanted to take a long maternity leave, at the very least for the first two years. Sometimes I feel he's even more protective than I am, and that's saying something. He put as much research into choosing the right baby monitor — a fairly pedestrian object I would have thought — as he would selecting the right school.

'I'll get some help, of course. A nanny to come here and look after Evie on the days I'm working.'

'But how will you know you can trust the nanny? What if she wants Evie for herself? What if she steals our baby?'

I know he's not serious. 'Richard! There are professional nannies out there. I'll contact a reputable agency. They only deal with vetted people who come with glowing references and I won't just pick anyone off the street. I promise.' I smile and he smiles back.

'Joanne, darling, if that's what you'd like, then I think that's wonderful. Congratulations!' He raises his glass, and I do the same.

'Thank you. It means a lot.'

We chat about his day, and then he asks, 'So what else did you get up to today?'

Well, I sat with Evie all morning, I got the post which I put on the console table, which you've barely scanned through so haven't yet noticed the letter from Isabella, then I tried to chat to Roxanne but she didn't want to know and then I fell asleep with Evie, and then you came home.

'I've had a really busy day,' I say. 'I'm thinking of getting a bicycle.'

Chapter Five

It's only later when we're sitting in the living room that Richard opens his mail. I stoke the fire — that's one thing I'm good at, getting a good fire going. I do my best to look as if I'm not remotely interested in his post. I pat Oscar, wait as long as I possibly can which is a whole five minutes, then I resume my place on the sofa, tuck my feet under me and lean across as if I've only just noticed him reading the letter from Isabella.

'Who's that from?' I ask, innocent as a lamb.

'You are not going to believe this.'

'Why? Who is it?'

'It's from Chloe.'

I sit back. 'From Chloe?'

He holds up the letter in the air, a smile spreading over his handsome face. He shakes his head slowly, bewildered and happy at the same time. 'She wants to come and visit us.'

'Your *daughter* Chloe?'

'Yes!' He turns the page and keeps reading, his grin so wide it brings out a dimple on his right cheek. 'She says she doesn't want us to be angry anymore. Listen to this. "I miss you so much, Daddy. I'm sorry about everything, and I really want to meet my baby sister. I've got a semester break coming up. I could come down and stay with you if that's okay."' He looks up. 'Can you believe it?'

I almost ask if she has mentioned me and if she'd like to meet me, too, but probably not. After all, I'm the reason they fell out. I don't know why since I never laid eyes on her, but she was so upset when her father remarried that she refused point-blank to come to our wedding. She has not spoken a word to her father since, despite his many attempts, and that was eighteen months ago.

'When did you tell Chloe about Evie?' I ask. I'm pleased they've spoken, but also surprised because he kept putting it off. We had family portraits taken after Evie was born and I thought that would be perfect, suggesting he could send one to Chloe with a nice letter. But he wanted to tell her face-to-face, which considering she wouldn't even take his calls, sounded like wishful thinking to me.

'Why didn't you tell me?' I ask.

Evie starts to cry. We both stare at the monitor, trying to gauge whether she'll settle on her own or not.

'I think that's the most wonderful news,' I say, and I don't even mean that it's not from Isabella. Evie's cries recede. We both let out a breath. 'So when is she thinking of coming over?'

He laughs. 'Friday.'

'This Friday? Like, in three days?'

'Yes!' He gets up. 'I'm going to give her a call right now.' He strides out of the room. Oscar, who was asleep by the fire, raises his head and looks in the direction of the door, possibly pondering whether to follow Richard out, then thinks better of it. I scratch him between the ears and he drops his head back down, groaning with pleasure. 'Chloe is coming to meet her baby sister!' I whisper.

Great. Now I'm talking to the dog as well as the baby.

Chloe was eleven years old when her mother passed away. They were living near Reading at the time. Diane had been ill for some time, and Richard was away in Spain when she died unexpectedly. The closest neighbour was two miles away, and Chloe remained alone with her dead mother all night long, until the local grocer came early the following morning with his weekly delivery and found her.

I can't begin to fathom what that must have been like for Chloe. One minute she had an idyllic childhood, two parents who doted on her, and the next not only had she lost her mother but she had to wait alone with her for hours. Richard paid for the best professionals he could find to help Chloe, but he says she never fully recovered from the trauma. Where she used to be a happy, cheerful little girl, she became detached. Closed. She didn't speak much. Richard believes she subconsciously blamed him for being away when it happened, and he carries his own guilt.

I asked him once. 'Was it cancer?'

His eyes filled with tears. 'Jo, sweetheart. Let's not talk about the past. I hate thinking about it.'

'Of course,' I said, my heart breaking for him, and for Chloe.

They moved to London where Richard was hoping to settle Chloe into a new school, but it was hard. She was very clingy. She wouldn't leave his side and became completely dependent on him. If he left for work, she'd be hysterical. She refused to go to school. This went on for months. Richard desperately wanted her to get better, to put the past behind and be happy again, so he decided to send her to a boarding school where she could make new friends with girls her own age. He genuinely believed it was the only way for her to recover from the death of her mother and return to a normal life.

He researched the top institutions with the best reputations for academia and chose a school he thought was particularly suited to Chloe. One of the most exclusive — and most expensive, not that it mattered to Richard — international schools in Switzerland.

He said to me once he still feels guilty about it, even though deep down he believes he did the right thing, because gradually she became more confident, happier. She came home for every break, every holiday, and in summer they'd travel to Italy together, or to Paris, or wherever she wanted to go.

Then two years ago she finished high school, and now she lives in a flat Richard bought for her in London. Last I heard she was studying fashion photography at the London College of Fashion.

I've wanted to meet Chloe since before we were married, back when we were dating, but every time Richard suggested it to her, she had a reason not to. She was too busy. She had to study. She'd already made other plans.

'Is it the age difference?' I asked once. 'Does it worry her?' Richard is nineteen years older than me and maybe to Chloe that seems too much.

'I don't think so. She didn't blink when I told her. She just needs time.'

One day he told Chloe over lunch at Le Gavroche that he was going to ask me to marry him. He'd meant to reiterate that she must meet me, that he wanted her approval, but Richard told me afterwards she went white, got up, grabbed her coat, and left.

'She'll come around. You'll see,' he'd said.

I thought it was sweet he wanted her to meet me and

have her approval, but we'd been trying to do that for weeks and she didn't seem that interested.

'We have all the time in the world,' I said, although by then I was starting to wonder.

Then one day he announced he'd had enough. 'She's got her own life, and so do we. If she wants to play games, so be it.'

We got married in Kew Gardens on a beautiful spring day and it was only later, during our honeymoon — on the Greek islands, enchanting — that Richard told me Chloe had called him the morning of our wedding and said that if he went ahead with it, she'd never speak to him again. He told her that was up to her, and that he loved her very much but he wasn't going to be dictated to in such an irrational way. She hung up on him. It was the last time they spoke. Until he told her about Evie.

So for her to write now and to say she wants to come and visit us and meet her baby sister is wonderful. Chloe has been the one dark shadow in our life together, and that's finally about to change.

Richard comes back into the room.

'So? Did you speak to her?'

He nods, grinning. 'Yes. Yes I did. She'll get the train on Friday around five.'

'Oh, Richard. That's wonderful! I'm so happy for you.' I get up and wrap my arms around his neck. 'I'm going to make sure she feels really welcome. This is her home as much as ours and I'm going to make sure she knows that.' He holds me at arm's length, his eyes moist.

'Thank you, Joanne, that means everything. You're sure you don't mind if she spends a few days here? With us?'

'Mind?' I laugh. 'Apart from the fact she's family, it'll be nice to have company while you're out at work. I'm really looking forward to finally getting to know her.'

. . .

When I look back on that day, I see myself so filled with hope and joy. With Chloe in our lives our family would be complete. I couldn't wait to meet her, to show her that I was no threat, that I respected their relationship, that I would never, ever get in the way of their bond. I would be like a caring aunt. I would do everything in my power for us to get along. No, more than get along — for us to *belong*, as a family, together.

Anyway, let's just say things didn't quite work out that way.

Chapter Six

It seems only five minutes ago that Richard went to the station to pick Chloe up, and now I hear the car outside. I am so excited to finally meet her. My step-daughter! Richard and I have been talking of nothing else for the past few days. 'Tell me more about her. What is she like?' I'd ask over and over.

He'd laugh. 'You'll love her. She's really sweet. She's a really sweet girl. She just had a wobble about me marrying again but that's over now.'

Well, she's going to find out she had nothing to worry about. I've been fantasising non-stop about the two of us becoming close. I've had visions of us baking together while Richard is at work, chatting about her boyfriends, her studies, what kind of job she'd like to do. I've imagined myself as a kind of older sister to her — weird I know, but stepmother feels weird too — someone who would be there for her no matter what. Someone she could talk to, when she would have spoken to her mum if she'd still been alive.

I settle Evie in the cot. Richard calls out from downstairs. 'We're here!'

I quickly go to the top of the stairs and lean over the balustrade. At first I only see Richard, his happy face beaming up at me, and I lean over a bit more. I hear her footsteps before I see her. High heels on the tiled floor. She comes to stand next to him.

'Hi!' I blurt cheerfully and wave. 'It's so nice to meet you, Chloe! I'll be right there! I'm just putting Evie down for her nap.'

Chloe looks up at me. I am struck by how pretty she is. Her light brown hair is straight, parted in the centre, with blonde highlights. Her lashes are thick and dark, making her green eyes stand out. She has her father's eyebrows. Dark and lush and perfect.

'Hello, Joanna, it's really nice to meet you!' she says in a sing-song voice, more girlish than I'd expected for someone her age.

'And it's nice to meet you too!' I say, before realising I just said that. 'And it's Joanne.' I laugh.

'Oh! Sorry!' She clasps her hand over her mouth, like she's horrified at her own mistake.

Now I feel terrible. 'No, please. No problem at all!'

'Okay, you're sure? I wouldn't want to get off on the wrong foot!'

'Truly,' I say, eager to get off the subject. 'Absolutely no problem.'

She turns to Richard and says, 'Okay. Phew. So should we get my bags out of the car?'

'Yes, let's do that.' He looks up to me. 'See you in a minute, darling.' They both turn around and go back out the front door. I return to Evie, make sure that she's comfortable. She smiles at me, closes her eyes and does a little sigh. She looks like she is settling in for a good couple of hours. She's been great today. In fact it's been a great day all around.

. . .

I had my first work meeting this morning with Shelley and Ben, another estate agent who started after I left. I like Ben. He's a lovely man in his late thirties with a bald head and a long face. He talked me through how they've updated the system for tenancies, where they keep a log of tenants who call and need repairs, which properties are coming up vacant.

I knew all this — most of it anyway — but I was grateful for the refresher. Even Evie was happy during the meeting. She stayed on my lap, sucking on her little elephant rattle.

'I'm going to get a nanny two days a week,' I said to Shelley after Ben logged off the meeting. 'Just so you know.'

'That's great! Maybe you can come and work in the office sometimes,' Shelley had suggested. 'If you want to. Catch up with the team. I'd love to see you in the flesh.'

I laughed. 'That's not going to happen in a hurry, but it would be nice to get out of here occasionally.' I pressed my hands gently over Evie's ears. 'Before I go completely mad,' I said and made a face. Shelley cracked up.

After we logged off I scrolled through Facebook where I checked local groups for nanny recommendations. I'd already spoken with two agencies who sounded promising, so I wasn't too concerned about finding someone.

I felt so excited by the prospect of working with Shelley again that I even took another look at the kitchen refit. And then I got a call from one of the nannying agencies I'd contacted the day before.

'We have someone we think would be perfect,' the woman called Melanie had said. 'I've just emailed her CV. Her name is Paula, she's twenty-eight years old, and she is studying infant psychology.'

'Really? Let me look!' I went through the email while at the same time bombarding Melanie with questions. 'And you checked her references?' I asked, my pulse racing with excitement.

'Of course! They're excellent. I've attached them as well.'

I scanned through them. Paula had six years of experience working with two different families, and the second family also had a baby about Evie's age. Her references were positively gushing. Organised, reliable, very kind, a problem solver, the children adored her and so did the parents.

'She lives nearby, in Staines,' Melanie said.

'That's only ten minutes away!'

'She can come for an interview this afternoon. Do you have time? I'll be upfront with you, Joanne, she's going to get snapped up one way or another.'

'No! No, don't let her get snapped up! What time can she get here?'

Paula arrived precisely two hours later. Even though I knew she was only twenty-eight, I'd expected someone almost matronly. It was the references. They made her sound like a cross between Mary Poppins and Mrs Doubtfire. Instead I found myself standing face-to-face with a teenager. Or that's what she looked like anyway. Black spiky hair, a short-sleeved shirt and a tattoo that seemed to cover her entire right arm before stopping abruptly at her wrist. She smiled and extended her hand. 'I'm Paula. I'm here to interview for the position.'

Thirty minutes later, I'd given her the job. She was funny, chatty, got lots of smiles out of Evie, explained she only wanted to work two days a week as she was busy with her studies. By the time she left I felt like I was saying goodbye to a friend. So yes, a great day all around.

I can hear Richard and Chloe chatting downstairs. Evie is fast asleep. I shake my fingers through my hair and go down to join them.

Chapter Seven

I find Richard and Chloe in the living room, standing by the fireplace. They're facing each other, holding hands. Richard looks so happy. Oscar is trying to get his attention by putting his front paw on his leg, but Richard is oblivious.

'Sweetheart. Look at you. You're all grown up!'

They haven't heard me come in so I have a moment to check out Chloe. She is nothing like I expected. Granted, the photos I've seen of her are from a long time ago, mostly before her mother died, and a few from when she was in boarding school. But even in those later photographs she still looked like a child. Shy smile, light brown hair usually in a high ponytail, a fringe over her eyes.

'Would you like something to drink, Chloe sweetheart?'

'Yeah, okay. A G&T would be nice, thanks, Dad.'

Richard notices me in the doorway. 'Joanne, do we have gin? Or tonic?'

'Yes! There's gin in the bar and tonic in the fridge. I'll get it.'

'No, that's okay, I'll do it. You two get acquainted.'

He leaves the room, brushing his hands together. Chloe turns to me.

'Hello again!' I say brightly. 'Chloe! How wonderful to finally meet you!'

I cross the room with my arms extended, ready for a hug, but as I reach her, she extends her hand for me to shake.

'Yes, you said that.'

'I'm sorry?'

'You already said it was nice to meet me, like, three times.'

Her voice is different. Lower. More natural. Then, almost imperceptibly, she raises one of her gorgeous eyebrows and gives me a slow up-and-down look. I feel myself blushing. I should have brushed my hair. I look down at my front. I have a little bit of sick from Evie on my left collarbone. Then again, I always have a little sick from Evie on my left collarbone.

I release Chloe's hand to brush the stain. It doesn't come off. Now I have sick on my fingers as well as my shirt. I laugh. 'That's what a four-month-old baby will do to you!' She looks slightly disgusted. I wipe my fingers on my jeans. 'Anyway, welcome! We've been so excited about your visit.'

Richard returns with a cold bottle of tonic and some ice on a tray and puts it on the coffee table.

'Thanks for saying that, Joanne! That's really so sweet of you,' Chloe says sweetly, her voice back to that weird, childish pitch.

Richard beams. 'Did you want something to drink, Jo?'

I'm speechless for a moment. 'I…'

'Yes?'

'Sure, the same for me, thanks, Richard.'

'You're drinking?' Chloe asks.

'What do you mean?'

'Aren't you breastfeeding? Evie is what… like, three months old?'

I bristle. 'She's four months old. So yes, she's still on the bottle. But unfortunately, I haven't been able to breastfeed.'

'Why?'

What does that mean, *why?* 'Because I haven't been able to produce enough milk.'

Chloe leans forward a little. 'Is that to do with your age?'

'My age? Of course not.' I smile. Gosh, I must look more tired than I thought. 'I'm thirty-three years old.'

'Oh,' she says, and smiles back. She takes the glass Richard hands her. 'Thank you, Daddy.'

I take mine and gulp it down.

'Would you like to show Chloe to her room?' Richard says when we finish our drinks.

'Yes, good idea,' I say. 'Come this way.'

We walk through the hall and I catch a glimpse of the two of us in the tall mirror. My heart sinks. I look about a hundred years old and I do look frumpy. I make a mental note to make an appointment for a facial next weekend when Richard can look after Evie. Also I really, really should get an exercise bike. Or a treadmill. Or both.

'Anyway,' I say quickly, going up the grand staircase. 'I think you'll like your room. It overlooks the front garden and it gets the best light in the morning. And you'll be close to Evie's room, which I thought you might like.' I stop outside Evie's room, pop my head through the door. 'Would you like to see her now?' I whisper. 'She's asleep but if we're very quiet…'

'No, that's okay.'

'Oh! All right. Maybe later then.' I show her into the guest room which does look lovely. I've made sure everything is impeccable. The queen-sized bed is covered with a soft white feather-down duvet and mountains of pillows and I've put a little arrangement of snowdrops and rosemary from the garden on the dresser.

'You have your own ensuite bathroom… And there should be plenty of space for your things.' I open the wardrobe and step aside. 'You must make yourself comfortable and use anything you like.'

'Actually, would you bring my bags upstairs? I left them in the hall.'

I was smiling so widely my cheeks hurt. Somehow I stay like that even as I reply. 'I'll ask Richard to do it. Let me show you the rest of the house. How was the trip?'

'Fine.'

'Not too much traffic?'

'I took the train.'

'Of course, I knew that.'

'Are you very forgetful?'

'Excuse me?'

'You keep repeating yourself or forgetting things.'

'I'm sorry, I—'

'Can I see the other bedrooms?'

'Of course.' I show her the other two bedrooms further along the corridor, none of which are as nice as the one I chose for her.

'What's upstairs?'

'A converted attic. We don't use it, and there's no bathroom up there.'

She nods. 'It's a big house.'

'Yes. It is.'

'How much did it cost?'

I make a little gasp. 'You probably should ask your father.'

'I will. And this room?'

'That's my office.' I open the door to show her. She doesn't look impressed.

'Can I see your bedroom?'

'If you want. It's this way.'

We walk in silence to the end of the corridor. I open the door to our room. She walks right in, takes a look around, fingers the top of my dresser. She picks up a bottle of Cartier perfume, brings it close to her nose, then sprays a dash of it on the inside of her wrist.

'It's gorgeous, isn't it? Richard gave it to me for my birthday last year.'

'My mother used to wear it.'

I don't know what to say to that. Is it true? It must be. 'I'm sorry,' I say. 'I didn't know.' I pick up the bottle. 'Does it bother you that Richard bought it for me?'

She shrugs. I make a snap decision and hand it to her. 'Would you like to have it? You're very welcome to.'

'No,' she says nonchalantly, looking around the room. I put the perfume bottle down.

'Okay, well, shall we go back downstairs?' I ask.

'Can I see Evie now?'

I smile, pleased she wants to see Evie after all. 'Of course you can.' We walk back out to Evie's room. I enter slowly, my finger on my lips. We come to stand over the cot.

'There she is,' I whisper. 'Meet your little sister. Isn't she the most beautiful thing you've ever seen?'

Suddenly, without warning, Chloe bends down and scoops her up.

'Oh no, please don't,' I whisper.

'Why not?'

'Because she is…' I was going to say, *asleep*, but I don't have the time to finish my sentence because Evie starts to wail. Understandably. I'd be wailing too if I was picked up like that in the middle of my nap.

Then something strange happens. Chloe holds Evie out so she can take a good look at her. But there's something strange about her breathing. She's taking quick, shallow breaths through her nose. Also, she's not moving, just standing there, staring at my wailing baby.

I extend my arms. 'Here, I'll take her.'

Chloe turns to me and for a moment, she looks like she's not sure what I'm doing here. Then she gives a quick shake of the head.

'She's very loud,' she says, bouncing her on her shoulder.

'You don't want me to take her?' I ask nervously.

Clearly not. She shakes her a little too hard for my liking. 'There, there, there…' she says uselessly. Evie's head wobbles. Chloe keeps turning around and I keep moving with her, trying to steady Evie's head. 'If I could…'

Chloe gives me a disapproving look. 'What's wrong, Joanne?'

'You're not holding her right. If I could… please… for a minute…' At this point I'm actually considering wrestling Evie from her.

'I know how to hold a baby,' she says, walking away.

'Of course you do.' Except she clearly doesn't. 'I didn't mean…' Richard has appeared at the door. 'What are you two up to? Ah! I see that the princess has awoken.'

'I was just saying to Chloe, she is bouncing Evie a little too much.'

'I wasn't doing anything of the sort,' Chloe says. 'I'm sorry if me holding Evie is upsetting you, Joanne.'

'Of course not!' Now Chloe is barely moving at all. Just very gently rocking from side to side. Evie has stopped crying and is staring at Chloe, eyes wide.

'I didn't mean…'

'You didn't mean what?' she asks, her voice rising. 'What exactly am I doing wrong, Joanna?'

'It's Joanne, actually, but—'

'That's what I said.'

'No, you said Joanna but look, what I meant was, it's just that before Richard arrived you were…' I shake my head. 'You're not doing anything wrong, Chloe. You're doing great. I can see she loves you.'

'So why are you saying I was holding her wrong?' The pitch of her voice has gone right up and her mouth is turned down. Is she… going to cry?

'No! I didn't mean… I mean you were before… never mind. Honestly, everything is great.' But Richard is frowning at me.

'You're all right, Jo?'

'Yes of course!' My smile feels fake but other than that… I'm grand.

'Then let's go downstairs and get dinner ready.'

Chloe hands Evie to me. She stirs, opens her mouth to argue even though she doesn't know how yet.

'Would you mind, Joanne? Putting Evie to sleep?' Richard says.

'No. Of course not.'

Chloe hooks her arm into her father's. In the corridor I hear her say, 'Honestly, I have no idea what I was doing wrong. I wasn't doing anything at all. I don't know why she reacted like that.'

My jaw drops. She was actually bouncing Evie in a way that looked very uncomfortable, bordering on dangerous. I put Evie back to bed, and it takes about twenty minutes for her to go to sleep again. This time, before going downstairs, I swing by my room where I change my top, brush my hair, and highlight my face with a little blush. I take a breath and prepare myself for the evening.

Somehow, I have a feeling my relationship with Chloe is going to take a little more work than I'd thought.

Chapter Eight

I bring out the lasagne that I made earlier in the day. It's hot and steamy when I put it on the table. 'I'll serve,' I say. 'Chloe? Would you like to pass me your plate?'

'I'll open some wine,' Richard says. He walks over to the rack and selects a bottle. I put my hand out for Chloe's plate. She frowns at the lasagne like it's laced with cyanide but hands her plate anyway. Richard has returned with the wine.

'Oh, wait, there's a green salad too,' I say when I've served everyone. 'I'll go and get it.'

Richard chuckles. 'Honestly, Joanne, you'd lose your head if it wasn't screwed on.' And Chloe cracks a laugh. I laugh too, but I wish Richard wouldn't make fun of me like that, not when I'm getting to know Chloe for the first time.

When I return with the salad, Richard is asking Chloe about her studies.

'I haven't had a lot of time for studying. I've been doing a bit of modelling.' She stabs a bit of lasagne with her fork. 'Actually, quite a lot of modelling.'

'I didn't know you did modelling,' I say. But I can see why she would. She really is stunning looking although, at five foot six or seven, a little short for the catwalk I suspect. Tonight she's wearing a simple dark brown turtleneck and combined with her makeup and those heavy, beautiful eyebrows she's inherited from her father, it makes the green of her eyes pop. She shrugs but doesn't reply.

'That's very interesting,' Richard says gravely, like she's just been telling us about her paper on genetic engineering. He pours Chloe a glass of wine then tilts the bottle in my direction. 'Would you like some wine, Jo?'

'Yes, please.' I lift my glass.

Chloe turns to Richard. 'How old was Mum when she had me, Daddy?'

Richard tosses the salad, frowning at it like it's requiring all his concentration. 'Mmmm?'

'How old was Mum when she had me?' Chloe asks again.

'I believe your mother was twenty-four.'

'That's what I thought.' She puts a piece of lasagne into her mouth, her teeth clink against her fork. 'I think that's a good age to have a baby. Don't you, Daddy?'

'You know, thirty-three isn't old, Chloe. Believe me, you'll realise that one day,' I say, sounding like a hundred and thirty-three. 'Don't you agree, Richard?'

Richard, who must have realised by now a response is required, and preferably one that will defend me, says, 'Don't be ridiculous, Chloe. Jo isn't old!' He puts down the salad servers and squeezes her cheek with two fingers, chuckling. As he pulls his hand away, Chloe grabs his wrist, and there's a split second where I think she's going to kiss the palm of his hand. Which, it probably doesn't need to be said, would be very weird. But maybe I imagined it.

I put my cutlery down and help myself to more wine, since I can. 'So how are you finding London after all these years abroad?'

'It's brilliant. I love London. Don't you love London, Daddy?'

'Yes, indeed. Wonderful city.'

There's a bit of silence and I don't know how to fill it. I raise my glass. 'Well, I just want to say, I'm very happy you're here, Chloe. Welcome.'

Richard looks at me, his eyes moist. He blinks a few times and squeezes my hand over the table.

I glance at Chloe. She's got her head down and I'm sure I can see her rolling her eyes.

'That's so sweet, Jo. Isn't that sweet, Chloe?' Richard says, turning to her.

She smiles sweetly at her father, then at me. 'Yes. That's very sweet, Joanne.'

They start talking about people they know and I take the opportunity to clear the plates. 'I made a rhubarb pie and it's warming in the oven. Chloe, would you like cream with your pie?'

'I don't want any pie, thanks.'

'Oh? You don't want dessert?'

'No thank you.' She knocks back the rest of her wine.

'Are you worried about your figure, sweetheart? At your age?' Richard asks.

Why is everyone talking about age all of a sudden? Again, he pats her cheek. 'You look beautiful, sweetheart.' Then he frowns, suddenly all serious. 'But a little more meat on you wouldn't hurt.'

I've stacked the plates in my hands and a bit of tomato sauce drips onto my thumb. I lick it off, catch Chloe's disgusted look.

'Cream for you, Richard?'

He taps his stomach. 'Not for me, sweetheart. My waistline is expanding.'

What is he talking about? His waistline is not expanding.

He's in great shape. I tilt my head at him. 'But it's your favourite! And you don't have to have cream.'

'Maybe I'll have some tomorrow.'

'Okay! Then I guess it's just me.'

Chloe gives my hips a sideways glance.

'By the way, I have some great news,' I say when I return.

Richard looks up. 'Oh?'

'I found a nanny today.'

'A nanny?'

'You know how I told you about contacting agencies?' I turn to Chloe to involve her in the conversation. 'I'm going back to work part-time.'

'Really? Already?'

'Yes,' I reply. 'But working from home,' I add quickly.

'What do you do?'

'I'm an estate agent,' I say. I confess I'm a little surprised that she really doesn't know anything about me. But then Richard says,

'That's how we met. I told you.' He shakes his head, chuckling at the memory. 'Don't you remember the story I told you? About being trapped in the cellar? Poor Joanne was terrified.'

'I don't think you told me, Daddy. I think I'd remember. Sounds like a really funny story. So why are you going back to work, Joanne?'

'That's what I asked,' Richard says.

'Did you?' I frown.

'Oh sweetheart, did you forget our conversation about you going back to work?'

'No! I—'

'You'd lose your head if it wasn't screwed on,' Chloe says in a sing-song voice, and Richard laughs.

I smile, a little unsure why I'm being made fun of, but then decide it's an inside joke that only they know about and it has nothing to do with me. 'To answer your question, Chloe, let's just say I like to keep my mind active, and I think working part-time is a good way to do that.'

'Tell me about this nanny,' Richard says, frowning.

'Well, I have to say, she's wonderful.' I tell him all about Paula, and how lucky we are that she's available and that she lives nearby. I can barely contain my excitement as I wax lyrical about Paula's skills, and all I can think is *I'm going to have someone to talk to. Someone nice. Someone who doesn't stick earbuds in her ears whenever I walk into the room.*

'I could do it,' Chloe blurts.

'Do what?' I ask.

'Babysit Evie.'

'That's very sweet, Chloe, but you have college,' Richard says. 'Joanne needs someone for a few weeks, at least.'

'Actually….' Chloe twirls the stem of her glass.

Richard frowns. 'Yes?'

'I'm looking for a job. I quit college.'

'You quit?' Richard and I blurt in unison.

'I'm just taking a break, that's all. It's no big deal. I'll go back next year. I don't know. I'll see.'

'But why didn't you tell me any of this before?' Richard asks.

She shoots him a look. 'Because we haven't talked for like, years? Anyway, it only just happened. I got bored, that's all. So if you need a babysitter, I'm here. I could move in for a few months while I decide what to do next.'

Richard and I both stare at her, unsure what to say.

She tilts her head at Richard. 'Don't you trust me, Daddy?'

There's a tiny pause, so small you'd blink and miss it, before Richard scoffs. 'Don't be ridiculous! Of course I trust you.'

'You sure about that, Daddy? You don't sound sure to me.'

I have no idea what this conversation is about. I look from one to the other while Chloe waits, head tilted, still staring at her father, eyes wide with innocence. Then just as I'm about to say, *I already have a nanny, but thank you, maybe next time*, Richard's face breaks into a grin and he claps once.

'I think that's a wonderful idea!' He rubs his hands together.

'What?' I blurt. 'But Richard, I just hired someone!'

He turns to me, the grin still intact. 'When you say, hired, do you mean you actually signed a contract?'

'Well, no, but she's perfect. She lives locally—'

'But Chloe just said she'd be happy to do it. And she would live here, with us.'

I don't remember hearing the word *happy* out of Chloe's mouth, but I let it slide. 'But Paula is doing her master's in child psychology!' I whine.

Richard chuckles. 'I don't think you need a master's in child psychology to look after Evie, sweetheart.'

'No, of course not. It's just… I mean… I really like her.'

'Thanks,' Chloe says.

Richard pats her arm. 'Don't be silly. Joanne's joking.'

'No, I didn't mean that,' I blurt, even though I meant exactly that. 'It's just that I already told the agency I was going to give her the job.'

'Joanne, sweetheart, what's wrong with you? Chloe just said she'd do it. You can talk to the agency and tell them you've changed your mind. They won't care! It happens all the time.'

'I know but…' I turn to Chloe. 'Are you sure it's what you want to do? It's only two days a week, just a few hours, that's all. What will you do the rest of the time? This is a small town, a village, really. There is nothing very exciting about living here. What about your modelling work?'

'I can take the train up to London when I get a modelling gig. If you prefer, I can go there every day I'm not babysitting and be with my friends. Get out of your hair.'

Richard clicks his tongue at her. 'Sweetheart. That's not at all what Joanne meant.'

'I would like to get to know my little sister. After all, that's why I came here. But it's up to you, Joanne.'

She smiles at me. They both do, in a Stepford Wives kind of way, as they wait for an answer. I think of Paula, how well we got on, how warm and friendly she was, how great she was with Evie, and I swallow my disappointment.

I paste on my warmest smile. 'I think it's a terrific idea. I'll call the agency tomorrow and tell them I won't need their services anymore.'

Chapter Nine

'Thank you for being so kind to Chloe.' We're in bed and Richard is nuzzling my neck. 'She hasn't had an easy time. It means the world to me that she wants to spend time here, with us.'

'Of course.'

'Just be patient with her. She will need time to adjust. She hasn't always been…'

'Been what?'

He kisses my bare shoulder. 'Never mind.'

'No, tell me. She hasn't always been what?'

He sits up, his eyebrows knotted together. 'She hasn't always been *well*, is what I meant to say. With everything that happened… you understand. But she's great now. She's wonderful, right? Isn't she? And isn't it wonderful she wants to spend time with us? She wants to get to know her little sister…'

I tilt my head at him. He seems to have gone somewhere, lost in his own thoughts. I cup my hand on his cheek. 'I think it's great. I really do. I'm very happy for you.'

Suddenly I felt terrible for not *wanting* her to be the

nanny. I should be thrilled that she wants to be here with us. That's what a good stepmother would feel. Gratitude.

We spend the weekend getting Chloe settled in. I cook meals while Richard takes her for a drive. It feels right to give them time together to catch up. On Sunday I let her use my laptop so she can check her email. At dinner they talk mostly about her old school, about her friends, about her plans.

'What are you doing for your birthday?' Richard asks.

Chloe shrugs, pushes a few peas around her plate. 'I don't know, Daddy. I don't have any plans.'

'When's your birthday?' I ask.

'Next weekend.'

Richard frowns. 'And you're not doing anything with your friends?'

'No.'

'But it's your twenty-first, sweetheart!'

'I know.'

I look at Richard. 'Well, we must have a special dinner here!' I say. 'Let me know what you'd like to eat.'

'That's a terrific idea!' Richard says.

'Is there anyone special you'd like to invite?' I ask, smiling. I lean forward. 'A boyfriend maybe?'

'No,' she says. 'I mean, I could ask a couple of my girlfriends.'

'Perfect! Let me know how many and I'll organise something. We'll order a cake from the patisserie in the village. They make the best birthday cakes.'

'Okay.' Chloe shrugs with zero enthusiasm. Oh well. At least Richard looks happy. He mouths silently, *thank you.*

. . .

And now it's Monday. I call the agency and say that I am terribly sorry, I really liked Paula, but my husband's daughter is here and she wants the job. Okay, maybe I don't say it like that. I just say that since my stepdaughter is staying with us, there's no need to hire someone. 'It's nice to have family around,' I say. 'Who want to help.'

'Well, I'm happy for you but I'm sorry to hear that, Mrs Atkinson,' she replies, in a slightly clipped voice. 'I think Paula would have been a great match. But of course, I understand completely.'

I sigh. I was so looking forward to having Paula here a couple of days a week. I just know we would have got on so well. 'I'm sorry we couldn't make it work this time. Please tell Paula I wish her the very best.'

But family comes first. This is what I tell myself as I secure Evie into the car seat of my Evoque Range Rover. Evie grouses, kicks her feet up every time I tuck in the blanket around her little legs. 'God, I love you!' I whisper. I blow raspberries on her cheeks. Whenever Richard does that, she laughs hysterically. When I do it, she whines. 'I'm just going to get your buggy and put it in the boot, okay?'

Family comes first, except that family is nowhere to be found. I told Chloe earlier I would take her to the village to show her around. I check my watch. I said we'd meet down here at ten thirty and it's twenty to eleven. Maybe she lost track of time. I go up the few steps to the house to grab the buggy. 'Are you ready, Chloe?' I call out. Silence. I take the buggy outside and go through the various steps to fold it which I can never get right. I catch my finger in the hinge.

'Ouch!' I suck on the tip of my finger, shake the buggy until it finally collapses the way it's supposed to.

'Chloe!' I call out again as I close the boot more forcefully than I'd intended.

'I'm here.'

She is leaning against the passenger door, arms crossed over her chest.

'Oh!' I laugh. 'I didn't see you there.' She's wearing black jeans, black high top Converse, her black leather jacket and a huge pair of sunglasses.

Oscar waddles down the steps.

'Oscar, come on, not today. Get back inside.' But it's too late. He's already jumped onto the back seat next to Evie.

'Okay, then,' I say to no one in particular. 'Looks like Oscar's coming too. Chloe, would you mind grabbing Oscar's lead please? And pull the front door shut?'

'I don't know where his lead is,' she says, checking her fingernails.

'It's, erm… never mind. I'll get it.'

I unhook it from inside the coat room and close the front door. Chloe has settled in the passenger seat, leaving the back door of the car wide open. I chuckle to myself. She must be as absent-minded as her father. I close it and get in.

'Okay! Let's go!'

This is the first time we've been alone together and a perfect opportunity to get to know her better. I pepper her with questions. Why did she give up college? Does she know what she's going to do next? Does she have a boyfriend? I have to say, even by her standards, her responses are pretty curt: College was boring. No, and no. Maybe Chloe is naturally a very subdued person. I make a mental note to ask Richard this evening, so I can understand her better.

We spend the next five minutes in silence and I wrack my brain for something to talk about that would interest her, but whatever I come up with is met with a grunt. I must say, and I would never say this to Richard, but I wish it was easier. I wish *she* was easier, because I would love nothing less than to have a warm, loving relationship with my stepdaughter.

'I've got a shopping list for dinner, and I thought it would be a good opportunity to show you where I get the groceries,' I say.

'Doesn't look like there's a lot of options,' she replies dully.

'Well, no.' I laugh. 'We are in the country! And we must go and order your birthday cake. What day is your birthday?'

'Saturday.'

'Wonderful. Let me know how many friends, all right? By the way, do you have a driver's licence?'

'Not yet.'

'I could teach you if you like.'

She shrugs. 'Okay.'

Alleluia.

'Here we are.' I park the SUV outside the patisserie, pleased I snagged a spot there. It's the nicest part of the village, the oldest part, too, with its rows of old timber-framed shops.

I get out of the car and put the leash on Oscar, who hops off heavily. 'Chloe can you hold—' But Chloe is already walking up the street. I guess she didn't hear me. She stops outside the dress shop and stares in the window.

'Okay!' I whisper to myself. I try again. 'Can you give me a hand with the buggy, please?' I call out. And I swear I can see the slightest dropping of her shoulders. She comes back to the car and watches me get Evie out of her seat.

'Did you want to hold her while I get the buggy out?' I ask, already handing Evie over.

'No,' she replies. 'I'll get the buggy out.'

'Oh, okay then. It's actually really hard to unfold. There's probably a trick to it, but I've never—'

Chloe presses a black button on the side of the buggy. It unfolds itself gracefully.

'You must show me how to do that one day.' I laugh, settling Evie into it. I hook Oscar's lead to the handle and blow my hair out of my face. 'Okay. Let's go and order the cake.'

We tie Oscar outside the shop and go inside. Chloe selects a Black Forest cake with as much enthusiasm as if I'd asked her to choose a pumpkin. I smile broadly at the young woman serving us and say I'll call in a couple of days to confirm the numbers.

'I've got six friends who said yes so far,' Chloe says.

'Oh, nice, it will be quite the party then.' That will be nine people at least. Maybe I should have it catered.

Outside I ask her to untie Oscar. 'Next stop, the grocer. I have my list right here,' I say, pulling it out. Honestly, the way she moves, anyone would think I was asking her to chop off her own foot. We walk together up High Street, where I tell her a little bit about the village, its history, our favourite restaurants. 'We eat at the pub sometimes on Sundays, or we used to anyway!' I laugh, glancing down at Evie.

'Hi, Mrs A.' I turn around. It's Roxanne. She pulls out one earbud and I am unreasonably pleased to see she doesn't just wear them when she's around me.

'Hello, Roxanne. How are you? This is…' I was going to say, *This is my stepdaughter*, but stop myself. 'This is Chloe, Richard's daughter. She's come to visit for a few days. Weeks. Maybe longer.' I turn to Chloe. 'Roxanne comes to the house once a week to help me.'

'Doing what?' Chloe asks, frowning at Roxanne.

'I clean. I'm a cleaner.'

'Does it pay well?'

I bite my bottom lip.

'It's alright.' She shrugs. 'I'm not fussy. Plenty of work around.'

I smile. 'Well, we better get on then,' I say. 'I want to get our shopping done before it rains. Bye, Roxanne.'

'Sure. See you, Mrs A.'

Chloe follows me to the grocer with the enthusiasm of a convict being dragged to the gallows. When we get there I put her out of her misery. 'Would you like to wait outside with Oscar? I only need a few things.'

Evie whines as I push the buggy. Maybe I should have left her with Chloe. I didn't think to ask. I fill my shopping basket and I'm back outside barely ten minutes later.

Oscar's tail wags when he sees me. He is tied to a lamp post.

There's no sign of Chloe.

A drop of rain falls on my forehead.

I wait for another fifteen minutes with Oscar's lead looped around my wrist. He starts to get antsy, pulling at the lead.

'Yes, Oscar. I know. We all want to go home. But we can't leave Chloe here, can we?'

It's only raining lightly, but I fear it's about to pour so I pull the top of the buggy over Evie. She starts to cry. We start in the direction of the Range Rover. I've got one bag chock full of groceries hanging off one of the buggy's handles. It swings around as I walk, bumping against my hip. Oscar wants to check something at the base of a tree we just passed and he pulls back sharply. He may be old and slow, but he's a heavy dog, and he can be as stubborn as the best of them.

I can see in the distance that Chloe isn't near the car and I'm kicking myself for not asking for her mobile number. Did she get lost? It's pretty hard to get lost around here. The village consists of one High Street and a railway line. You'd really have to work at it.

Then I see her. She's sitting with Roxanne under the bus

shelter, eating ice cream cones. How did those two become so friendly so fast? Roxanne sees me first and pokes Chloe in the ribs with her elbow. Chloe looks up at me, says something to Roxanne and I'm sure I see Roxanne smirk. Then Chloe pops the last of her cone into her mouth and walks towards me.

'I thought we were meeting outside the grocer?' I say, trying to keep my tone even.

'No. You said to meet you at the car.'

I jerk my head in confusion. 'No I didn't. I've been looking for you everywhere.'

'You told me to meet you at the car.'

'Chloe! That is not what we said.'

'You just forgot. You do that a lot. It's no big deal, okay? Relax. I'll push the buggy if you like.'

I'm completely dumbfounded. Is she mad? Is she hard of hearing? But before I have time to argue, she's taken hold of the buggy, looped Oscar's lead around the handle and taken off in the direction of the SUV. I bite my tongue. I wouldn't have taken Oscar along if I'd known she'd just take off and do her own thing. And I wouldn't have left him on his own outside the supermarket. What if somebody took him? I look at her. She is completely at ease, pushing the buggy. Maybe it really is a misunderstanding. I certainly hope it's a misunderstanding, because it doesn't bode well if I'm to trust her with my daughter.

'You can show me what to do with Evie when we get back. Like how to feed her, all that stuff.'

I hesitate before nodding. 'Good idea.' And I'm going to give her clear instructions even if I have to write them in felt pen on the wall. There'll be no room for *misunderstandings*.

. . .

I've put Evie in the back seat. Oscar jumps in next to her and shakes his head, spraying water all over the inside of the car, most of it on Evie, who starts crying again.

'I wouldn't have taken him if I'd known…' I mutter. I kick the buggy to fold it down. It doesn't work. I grit my teeth, kicking it again. And again. And again.

'Here,' Chloe says, reaching for it.

I let go and she bends down, presses the black button. The buggy folds itself with a soft whoosh.

'Thanks,' I mutter. 'I didn't know that's how you did it. How did you know?'

She shrugs. 'There's a big button that says *press here*.'

I laugh, surprised and relieved that we can share a joke. But then she adds, 'Maybe you need glasses.'

I can't tell if she's serious or not. I tilt my head. 'Glasses?'

'It's not unusual, at your age.'

Chapter Ten

Evie is tired and grizzly when we get home. Which makes two of us. I put her in her lounger, press the little baby elephant rattle into her hand. She throws it away and starts to wail.

'She really doesn't like you much,' Chloe says.

I turn around. My jaw is pretty much on the floor. 'Excuse me?'

'I said she doesn't like her toy much.' She points to it. 'She keeps throwing it away.'

I blink a few times. I was sure I heard something different, but I don't dwell on it. I must have been mistaken. I pick up the elephant rattle. 'She loves it. My best friend Robyn gave it to her.'

Chloe makes a face, glances sideways. 'If you say so,' she mutters.

I give the elephant rattle back to Evie, who chucks it right back out.

'Okay well, never mind.'

Chloe helps me put the groceries away while I keep an eye on Evie. I'm still reeling from what she said before about needing glasses. Maybe she was joking. Not that I care whether I need glasses or not, I just find her tone so rude sometimes. Okay, often.

'What's wrong with her?' she asks, jerking her chin at Evie.

'Nothing. She's hungry, that's all. I'm going to feed her now. Do you want to come upstairs with me so I can show you?'

'Sure.'

'And can you grab a bottle for her from the fridge? They're in the door.'

'This one?' She holds it up.

'That's it.'

'Nice,' Chloe remarks, looking around the nursery. It's only one word, but it's the first time she's said something positive. I consider that progress.

'Did you decorate it?'

'Yes.'

She nods. 'It's nice.'

Well, there you go. Maybe she is beginning to accept me. She hadn't spoken to her father for eighteen months because he married me. If I want to have a relationship with her — and I do, with all my heart — then I should be more patient, more understanding.

'I'm glad you like it. I really enjoyed decorating it.' Truth is, I love being in this room. I love the large windows overlooking the rose garden. They make the room so bright and cheerful, even on an overcast day. There's a window seat long enough to lie down on — and sometimes I do just that — and one wall covered in a wallpaper scene of Alice in Wonderland. Soft, plush furniture, colourful rugs over the pale floorboards, an antique French dresser which I've painted white and use as the changing table and a cupboard shaped like a gingerbread house where I keep Evie's blankets and bed linen.

'Does she sleep in here? Or with you?' she asks.

'Most nights she sleeps in here. We have another cot in our bedroom and sometimes she sleeps there, but she wakes up so much, it's hard for Richard to get a good night's sleep so we're training her to sleep in her own room.'

She nods but doesn't say anything else. I show her how to use the bottle warmer and while we wait, I talk her through how to sterilise a fresh bottle and how to mix the formula. Then the bottle warmer beeps, indicating that it's at the right temperature.

'You sit here,' I say, pointing to the armchair. I carefully hand Evie to her, expecting Chloe to take her, but she doesn't. She just stares at her, like I'm showing off a prized fish I just reeled in.

'It's okay, she won't bite.'

She slowly takes her from me. I show her how to hold her, careful to support her head, and give her my little pink towel to catch any dribble so her T-shirt doesn't get stained. Meanwhile, Evie is getting more and more cranky and Chloe looks increasingly nervous.

'It's not you,' I say. 'She's been like that in the last few days. It's because she's teething. After you feed her, she'll be calmer.'

I hand her the bottle and show her how to keep it at an angle to get the right flow, how to gently guide Evie to suck on it.

'Perfect. I'll get some Calpol for her gums.'

There's an ensuite bathroom off the nursery. That's where I keep Evie's medications. I turn around and walk toward the door.

'Can you take her?' Chloe says behind me.

I can hear Evie suckling on the bottle. 'You're doing fine,' I say, opening the vanity door and holding the medicine bottle to the light. There's hardly any left, and then I remember I forgot to get some more from the shops earlier. I pull out my phone and text Richard.

'Can you take her?'

'One second, I'll be right there.' I type the text, *Can you pick up a bottle of baby Calpol on the way home please darling?*

'Can you take her? Now!'

I turn around. 'What's wrong?'

Chloe has stood up. Her eyes are wild, manic. She's holding Evie out to me, her hands shaking. The bottle of formula has fallen on the floor.

'What is—'

'Take her! Just take her!' Chloe shouts. She pushes Evie into my arms. Evie wails and I hold her close, her head on my shoulder, and rock her gently to calm her down.

'What on earth happened?' I ask again, but Chloe has run out of the room.

I manage to calm Evie down and pick up the bottle from the floor. I sterilise a clean one then fill it with a fresh batch. I sit down and feed Evie. When she's finished, I put her in her cot, and she falls asleep almost immediately. I clean everything up. My heart is still racing when I come out an hour later.

I find Chloe sitting on a swing chair on the back patio, pushing herself back and forth with her foot.

'Who's that guy over there?' she asks when I sit on one of the wicker chairs.

I follow her gaze. 'That's Simon. He takes care of the grounds.'

She whispers something. It sounds like *hot.*

'Can we talk about what just happened, Chloe?' I mean, Simon *is* hot, no doubt about that. He has messy, sun-kissed hair and green eyes that crinkle when he smiles. Also an incredible body. Muscles everywhere you look.

But still.

'Where does he come from?' she asks.

'What do you mean?'

'Does he live locally?'

'Yes, he lives just on the other side of the village, with his father.'

'Really? How old is he?'

'I don't know, in his thirties, I guess. His father was injured in an accident at work. His arm got mangled so Simon moved in to look after him.'

'So how did you find him?'

'He put a notice on the notice board in the church. Chloe, can we please talk about what happened back there?'

She grinds her toe on the ground. It makes the swing rotate back and forth. 'I just… I'm not used to babies, that's all.'

'But—'

'I'm just going to need practice, okay?'

This makes no sense. Everybody needs practice if they've never held, let alone fed, a baby before, but they don't run out of the room screaming.

I suck in a breath. 'You don't have to do it, you know,' I say, wondering — okay, maybe hoping — that Paula is still available. 'If you're not comfortable—'

'No!' she snaps. 'I want to do it. I'm sorry, okay? It won't happen again. Jesus, what do you want from me!' She gets up off the swing chair.

'I still don't understand…'

She looks at me. 'Do me a favour. Don't tell Dad?'

'What?'

'Don't tell him what happened, okay?'

'Why?'

'I don't want him to worry, that's all.'

'Worry?'

'That I can't do it. Don't tell him.' Her mouth moves, like she wants to say something but has great difficulty articulating it. 'Please?' she breathes.

I hesitate, but then I see an opportunity for us to bond, and for her to trust me. I nod. 'Okay. I won't.'

Just then we hear the car coming up on the gravel. I check my watch. 'Looks like he's home early.'

Chloe is already running through the French doors and back inside. Seconds later I hear her call out joyfully. 'Daddy!'

Chapter Eleven

She's got her arms around his neck and her head on his shoulder. She looks at me from under her long eyelashes.

'How are my beautiful girls?' Richard says, giving her a one-arm squeeze before kissing the top of her head. Chloe's eyes never leave mine and there's a strange spark of triumph in them.

'We had a lovely day,' I say with a smile. 'Evie's asleep, thank god. She's teething and I only had a little bit of Calpol left.'

'Ah yes, here.' Richard lets go of Chloe and pulls out a paper bag from his leather satchel.

'Oh, thank you.'

'And I've got a surprise for you!'

'For me!' Chloe says girlishly.

Richard laughs. 'Actually, I meant for Joanne.' Chloe turns her head slowly in my direction. Her face is like a mask and I can't tell what she thinks but whatever it is, I don't think it's nice. So much for our bonding moment over my promise to keep my mouth shut.

I turn to Richard and smile. 'For me?'

The front door is still open and Richard walks back outside. We follow him. He opens the boot of his Range Rover — he drives the big luxury one — and pulls out a bicycle with a big red bow around the handlebars. It's pale blue with a basket on the front, and it bounces a little when he sets it on the ground.

'For me?' I say again, and this time I'm genuinely surprised.

'You said you wanted a bicycle.'

I suppose I did. I hadn't really meant it. I was trying to make conversation with Roxanne and it was the only thing I could think of. I have a vague recollection of mentioning it to Richard that night.

I laugh. 'That's lovely, Richard, but I don't think Evie will fit in the basket!'

He tilts his head at me. 'But you don't need to put Evie in the basket. You have Chloe to look after her now. That's the point.'

I nod. After what happened this afternoon, I have no idea if Chloe will stick it out. I take the bicycle from him and lean it against the wall by the door. 'Thank you, Richard. It's perfect.'

Richard frowns at me. 'Everything all right?'

Chloe has gone back inside, unimpressed by the bicycle. She's leaning against the banister at the bottom of the staircase, waiting for us.

'Shall we get a drink, Daddy?'

'In a moment, sweetheart. Can you go upstairs and check on Evie?'

'Evie's fine,' she replies. 'She's asleep.'

But I remember that we left the baby monitor upstairs. 'Actually, Chloe, can you bring the monitor down please?'

She turns around and silently goes upstairs.

'Did something happen today?' Richard asks, his eyebrows drawn together with concern.

'Why do you ask?'

'I don't know…'

'No, not really,' I reply. We make our way into the living room, he has his arm around my shoulders. It feels so nice and I just want to lean into him.

I could tell him what happened with Evie, but a promise is a promise. 'You know… I just wonder…'

He takes my shoulders and studies my face. 'What?'

'Well, I just don't think that Chloe likes me very much.' I raise a hand to ward off any arguments. 'I know it's early days. I know I should be patient, but I just wonder, how wise it is for her to look after Evie? Is she happy here, do you think?'

'What do you mean, not like you very much?'

'Just a feeling. Did she say anything to you about me?'

Something in his face changes. He lets go of me and stands up straighter.

'Joanne! She only just got here! What do you expect? And she offered to look after Evie! I think that's really sweet, don't you?'

'Yes! Of course!'

'Maybe you're the one not being very friendly,' he says, turning away towards the bar.

I'm completely taken aback by the change in his demeanour. 'What do you mean?'

'Only that it's a really strange thing to say.'

'What did I say?'

'That you don't think Chloe likes you. Jesus! How about you trying a bit harder yourself? Do you think you could do that?'

'But I am trying! I'm just asking for your advice!'

He frowns at me. 'Are you trying? Are you really?'

'Of course I am. Why would you even ask that?'

He pulls out a bottle of Scotch. 'Well, for one thing, I think it would have been nice if you had put a bouquet of fresh flowers in her room when she got here.'

'What? What on earth brought that on? And I did! I put a bouquet of snowdrops and rosemary from the garden! We have such nice varieties. The rosemary has a lovely silvery hue this time of year. And it smells nice.'

'Exactly.' He scoffs. He pours himself a drink then turns back to me. 'I just think that a beautiful bouquet of flowers would have been appropriate. Something special.'

I am dumbfounded. 'I thought a bouquet from the garden was special.'

He sighs. 'Yes, well. You would.'

I stand with my hands on my hips. 'What does that mean?'

But I know what it means. I'm from a lower socio-economic background than he or any of his friends are. Even Isabella. And Diane came from money, lots of money. I'm just an average estate agent who didn't finish her GCSEs. I don't have the right *taste*. When I first started to date Richard, he took me to Ascot to shoot clay pigeons. I was horrified. When I told him that until I was at least sixteen, I thought shooting clay pigeons meant shooting pigeons the colour of clay, he burst out laughing.

'Were you born in a cave? How can you possibly not know what clay pigeon shooting is?'

'I was very young,' I said, sulkily. He laughed again. Although he didn't laugh when I missed every single one of them. 'The point is to try and hit it, darling,' he'd said, wearily.

And then there was the night he took me to Le Gavroche for dinner. I can still remember the way he looked at my velvet dress shirt. The next day he took me shopping at

Harrods. I can't say I minded. It was actually a kind of sexy experience having the man I was falling in love with wanting me to model beautiful dresses for him. I felt like Pretty Woman for an afternoon. But he never really stopped suggesting what clothes I should wear or what kind of dinner service we should buy. Then when I discussed refurbishing the kitchen, he told me he'd like to go over any plans. 'Just to make sure,' he'd said.

'Make sure of what?'

'That we both like it.' He kissed my forehead. I would have shown him anyway, of course. Obviously we have to both like it, but I got a sense that's not what he meant. What he meant was more like, *so you don't get the cheap stuff from Ikea.*

'Never mind. Would you like a drink?' He looks over my shoulder. 'Chloe, sweetheart. There you are. What would you like? A G&T?'

I turn around abruptly, but from the way she is leaning against the doorway, one hand in her pocket, the monitor dangling from the other, I know she's been there a while. She is smiling at me, but just from one side of her mouth. A mocking smile. And suddenly the most horrible thought pops into my head: that Richard knew she was there and that's why he gave me a lecture about me not trying hard enough. He wanted to let Chloe know he was on her side.

I shake my head, dislodge the thought from my mind. That's a terrible thing to even contemplate.

I'm getting paranoid. It worries me, how paranoid I'm becoming. It worries me a lot.

It makes me wonder if I'm just like my mother.

Chapter Twelve

After a fairly subdued dinner, I am putting leftovers in plastic containers when Richard, who has been stifling a yawn all evening, starts to stack the dishwasher.

'I'll do it!' Chloe pipes up. 'You're so tired, Daddy. You work so hard. It's not fair for you to do the dishes on top of everything else!'

'Well,' he says, 'that is kind of you, sweetheart. I am rather tired, so if you don't mind, I think I'll go upstairs.'

'Of course not, Daddy!' she sings. 'I'll help Joanne. I'm happy to.'

'Thank you, sweet girl.' He kisses the top of her head.

The moment Richard has left the room, Chloe grabs the bottle of wine from the table and fills her glass to the brim. She leans back against the counter. She's wearing a short top that exposes her midriff and I give it a sideways glance. She's very thin, and from the look of those abs, she works out. She crosses her arms and takes a sip of her drink. 'Nice drop, this.' She lifts it up to the light. 'Actually I have no idea. Hey, Joanne, is it true you can't breastfeed? Or are you just saying that so you can get sloshed every night?'

I square my shoulders. I am not going to get triggered. I am not going to take the bait. I am a paragon of self-control as I put the leftovers in the fridge.

'No, really, just curious,' she says.

'I thought you were stacking the dishwasher.'

'I just said that so Dad wouldn't have to. I can't believe you'd let him stack the dishwasher. Seriously, he works hard all day. Always has. I bet he comes home late most nights, doesn't he?'

I stiffen. 'Sometimes. He's working on a very big restructure at the moment.'

'Exactly. And then he comes home, he's clearly exhausted, and you make him stack the dishwasher?' She shakes her head. 'I don't get it. You're not exactly *busy*, Joanne. You have a cleaner, a gardener, a nanny… It's not like you have anything else to do.' She pushes herself off the kitchen counter. 'I think I'll watch some telly.'

At the doorway she grabs the doorjamb and swings herself backwards. 'And if you tell Dad I didn't stack the dishwasher, I'll deny it. Also, here's a hot tip for you. He will always choose me over you. And if you don't believe me, why don't you ask him?'

I desperately wanted to tell Richard about the conversation when I got to bed that night. I almost did. But what would I say? *I don't think she likes me very much. Really. I'm not imagining it. She's very rude to me when you're not there.* But I knew he'd probably tell me it was my fault for not trying hard enough, so I didn't.

Something wakes me up. It's late, it's dark, and Richard is asleep next to me, snoring softly.

I pick up the baby monitor and squint at it. It's completely dark. Did I turn it off accidentally? No. But there's no sound and only a dark, grainy image.

I throw the covers off me, grab my robe and fling open the door. It's pitch black in the passageway. I tiptoe across to the nursery and I'm surprised to find the door ajar, not fully open the way it usually is. Also, Evie's nightlight is off and I know that I left it on before I went to bed, the way I always do.

I push open the door slowly. A shiver runs down my spine. The light is on in the bathroom, but the door is shut. I didn't leave the light on in the bathroom. I'm sure of it. And yet I can see it under the door.

I hurry to the cot, my bare feet silent on the plush carpet. My heart is racing when I check on Evie, but she's fine. She's sleeping, her little chest rising and falling with every breath, a little bubble of saliva escaping from her lips. But then I see that her cheeks are wet. Has she been crying?

A noise in the bathroom makes me jump. My heart is thumping as I push the door open just enough to see Chloe standing at the sink with her back to me. She's holding up the bottle of Calpol up to the light.

'What the hell are you doing?'

She gasps as she turns around. The bottle slides out of her hand and smashes on the tiled floor.

'What on earth—'

'I wasn't doing anything!' she cries.

I point to the shattered glass on the floor. 'What are you doing with Evie's medicine?'

'I was just about to give her some because she was crying!'

'Give her some?'

'What the hell is going on?' Richard's voice booms behind me.

'I didn't do anything, Daddy!' Chloe wails. 'I heard Evie cry and I went to see her. I was trying to do the right thing. I thought some Calpol would help because she's teething.'

'Have you given her anything?' I cry out, shaking her wrist.

'No! I haven't yet. I was about to! Let me go!' She flings her arm free and massages her wrist.

'Why are you so upset, Joanne?' Richard asks.

'Because she wasn't crying! I would have heard her!' I turn back to Chloe. 'Why are you lying? And what were you doing with her medicine? Answer me!'

'Calm down, Jo,' Richard says gravely, his hand on my shoulder. 'Let's talk this through calmly and reasonably, all right? Like adults.'

He turns to Chloe. 'What happened, sweetheart?'

'I'm trying to tell you! Evie was crying—'

'I never asked you to give Evie her medicine!'

'What's wrong with you? Why are you being like this?' Richard says.

I ignore him and cross my arms over my chest.

'But you told me she was teething. You told me a little bit of Calpol on a finger rubbed against her gums helps. I saw you do it. I was trying to help. I wanted to do something nice because you're so stressed all the time. I wanted to look after Evie so you could get some sleep!'

Sleep would be nice, I think automatically. Meanwhile Evie is howling in the background. I turn around, walk past Richard and step on some broken glass. It digs into the sole of my foot, leaving little dots of blood on the carpet with every step.

I pick up Evie and pat her back, but I'm shaking so much that she gets even more upset.

I turn around and see Richard has taken a crying Chloe

in his arms. Her chest heaves with every sob. 'I didn't mean to do anything wrong!' she wails.

'It's all right, sweetheart. There, there.'

'It's because she hates me!' she cries, staring straight at me. 'I just can't do anything right!'

'Hate you?' I can't believe my ears. 'How can you say that when I've been trying so hard! It's you who doesn't like me.'

'That's enough!' Richard snaps. He leads a still-sobbing Chloe out the door. 'You're out of control, Jo.'

'Excuse me?'

'We'll talk in the morning,' he says over his shoulder.

'There's no need,' I snap.

'Oh yes, there is.' And he looks so angry with me, angrier than I have ever seen. I feel my eyes water with rage that he doesn't see what I see.

That he doesn't believe me.

Chapter Thirteen

I bring Evie to sleep in the smaller cot we keep in our bedroom. Since Richard won't sleep here tonight, he won't be able to complain. I close the door, even going as far as dragging an armchair against it in case Chloe decides to visit us in the middle of the night and finish the job. How does the saying go again? Just because you're paranoid doesn't mean there isn't an evil stepdaughter lurking around trying to kill your baby.

I'm still shaking when I pick up Evie to soothe her. I walk around the room but she won't calm down. Her little face is red, her fists tight against her eyelids, wet tears running down her cheeks. She opens her mouth wide to scream and I can see the tiny little white dots coming through her top gums.

'Oh sweetie, of course you're upset, poor little thing.' That's when I remember with a start her wet cheeks when I first checked on her in the nursery. Did she wake up crying and I didn't hear her? Could Chloe have been telling the truth? That she was only trying to give her some Calpol? The same Calpol that is now all over the bathroom floor?

It takes over an hour, but eventually, Evie runs out of steam and goes floppy with tiredness in my arms. I gently put her down into the cot and tuck the blanket around her. Then I sit on the edge of the bed and watch her. Did I overreact back there? Was Chloe's intention as innocent as she said it was?

I check that Evie is fast asleep, then tiptoe out, closing the door firmly behind me and return to the nursery to look for the baby monitor.

I find it on the floor with the camera facing the carpet. It looks like it got knocked over accidentally. That explains why I couldn't see or hear anything. Did I knock it earlier? I don't remember, but it's possible, I guess.

I get back into bed and lay on my side, watching Evie.

I think of my mother. When I was a baby, she would lock us up inside the house because she thought people were trying to poison me. She wouldn't even let my grandmother near me. It got so bad that Mrs Delaney next door called child services and when they saw the state of the place — my mother had been barricading every window and every door and she had no interest in cleaning anymore — I was sent to live with my grandmother for a few months while my mother recovered in hospital from what would be later diagnosed as postpartum psychosis.

Fortunately, she got better. I returned to live with her, although my grandmother would spend every second week with us, keeping an eye on things.

And now, as I relive the events of the night in my mind over and over, I can't help but wonder if I'm just like her after all.

Except I'm not. When I got pregnant with Evie, it was

Richard who suggested I talk to my GP about it. Richard knew about my mother — these are the kind of topics that come up when you get to know each other — but still, I was surprised he'd even bring it up.

'Can they do a blood test? To find out if you've inherited your mother's disease?' he'd asked gravely. 'Just to be on the safe side.'

I was mildly offended by the suggestion, but I decided he'd asked because he cared about our baby, and I couldn't resent him for that. So I did speak to my GP about it, and no, there's no test, and anyway she assured me it was highly unlikely I'd have the same disease, as Richard put it, but we would keep an eye on things. I don't need to keep an eye on things. I'm not crazy.

Technically, I don't start work till next week, but Shelley called this morning asking if I could do a video meeting with her and Ben this afternoon. They'd like to bring me up to speed and discuss how we could divide the work. She said she'd already sent me an email. I was still reeling from the night before, so I probably didn't sound as enthusiastic as she'd expected, because she said, 'You still want to work with us, right? You haven't changed your mind?'

'No! Not at all. I'll just check in with my … nanny that she's available and confirm by text, but otherwise, let's do it.'

At this point, I don't even know if Chloe wants to stay here. I didn't see her for breakfast, only Richard, so for all I know she's already packed her bags and left (hooray!).

But no such luck.

'She's having a lie-in,' Richard said sombrely, as if Chloe had just done four back-to-back twelve-hour shifts in the emergency ward. He looked at me with concern, took my hand. 'I'm sorry for everything that happened.'

'Are you? Really?'

He nodded. 'I can see how distressing it must have been to find Chloe about to administer medicine to Evie.'

This was music to my ears. 'Really? You can?'

'Of course! But you must see how you overreacted. What were you thinking?'

What *was* I thinking? I couldn't even bring myself to say it. *That she was going to poison her baby sister?*

I sat down next to him and rested my head on his shoulder. 'You're right. I'm sorry. I don't know what got into me.'

He caressed my shoulder with his thumb. 'Do you think it may be a good idea to speak to Dr Fletcher about this?'

'I don't know.' I pulled away. 'Do you?'

He rubbed his chin with his free hand. He hadn't shaved so he sported a nice stubble this morning. 'If there's any chance that you have… you know… that condition, that would explain a lot, don't you think?'

I blinked at him. 'Seriously?'

'Go and talk to Dr Fletcher about it.' Then he added, 'For me.'

I nodded. 'I'll think about it.'

Then I said I'd apologise to Chloe when she got up and he was glad of that.

But now I can't find her. I've looked for her everywhere. As far as I can tell, she's not in the house. I go outside and that's when I see her.

She's taking selfies with Simon, the gardener. Even Oscar is included in this activity. He's bouncing around them like a puppy. Simon seems amenable, if a little uncomfortable. She handles him like he's a puppet, taking his arm and wrapping it around her neck. *Click!* She taps her cheek with her finger. He laughs, kisses the spot. *Click!*

I hesitate. Should I disturb them? They seem so involved in this strange activity. I mean, if they're having fun, maybe even flirting, why not? They're both extremely attractive, single people (I think, anyway, in the case of Simon). What's the harm?

But then Simon sees me and waves enthusiastically, making me think he'd love to be rescued.

I walk across the lawn. Chloe glares at me.

'Hi!' I say when I reach them. 'You two having fun, that's nice.'

Chloe smiles at me from one side of her mouth. Simon takes off his cap and scratches his head. 'The young lady here wanted to take a photo. I was just—'

'No, that's fine, really. No problem at all. I just wanted to have a quick word with Chloe, that's all.'

'I should…' He puts his cap back on and jerks his thumb over his shoulder.

'It won't take long,' I say.

'It's all right. I've got work to do,' he says. He grins at Chloe. God, he really has got a killer smile. And clearly, I'm not the only one to think so. Chloe takes one last photo. Simon blushes.

'So what's up?' she says after Simon is gone, scrolling through the photos she just took.

'I just wanted to say…' I bite on a fingernail. She looks up, one perfect eyebrow raised.

'I'm sorry about last night. I know I overreacted. I'm … I'm not used to having another person caring for Evie, and I'm still getting used to it all myself.'

She doesn't say a word. Just waits. I guess what I did deserves more grovelling.

'So anyway, I am very sorry about the things I said and the way I treated you.'

She looks down at her wrist. There's a red mark, like a thumbprint, where I gripped it last night.

'Oh god! Did I do that?' I put my hand out to take a

closer look without going as far as actually touching it, but she pulls her hand away.

'I am so, so sorry, Chloe. That's absolutely unforgivable. I don't know what came over me. Can we please start again? On the right foot this time? Please?'

She looks up, like she's thinking about it. 'Okay,' she says.

'Thank you. That's really kind of you.' I let out a breath. 'Well. Have you had breakfast?'

'No.'

'I could make you something if you like. Would you like some eggs?'

'Umm… What about a toasted cheese sandwich? And a coffee?'

'Of course.' We walk back to the house together. 'Simon is very handsome, isn't he?'

'You think so?' she replies.

'Well. I mean, he's not my type, but I can see he's yours,' I smile.

She doesn't reply. She doesn't seem interested in pursuing the subject so I let it go.

'Do you know how many friends will be coming for your birthday dinner? Saturday is around the corner!'

'Yeah. I've got ten people who said yes so far.'

'That's great! It will be fun. Are they taking the train? I'll see if Simon can come and help pick them up from the station. Probably too many for a sit-down dinner, but we'll do a buffet style in the drawing room. Will some of them stay overnight? I can get bedrooms ready, and Roxanne will help. Would you like that?'

She shrugs. 'Whatever.'

'Oh, okay. Well, we can talk about that later.' Although not too much later, I hope, because we don't have much time. I hadn't expected ten guests when we discussed having a birthday dinner. Also, I'm sure I heard her say, *so far*, which means it could be more.

She disappears into her room while I go to the kitchen to prepare her sandwich. I thought we'd sit together and chat about the party, go over the menu together, maybe even talk about last night, but she doesn't come back down so when it's ready I go to the bottom of the stairs and call out to her. 'Chloe? Your sandwich is ready!'

Seconds later she's leaning over the balustrade, her hair framing her face. 'Can you bring it up?'

'Oh! If you like. I mean I thought we'd—'

'Thanks!' She runs back to her room.

Okay, well, this isn't quite what I'd hoped for in terms of getting things back on track, but never mind. She's very young. I remind myself of that. She's more like a teenager, really.

I knock on her door with her breakfast on a tray, a mug of coffee just the way she likes it — milk, two sugars — and cutlery. She opens the door a crack and takes the tray from me.

'Thanks.' She starts to close the door again so I put my hand against it.

'I wanted to ask you something. I have a work meeting this afternoon. Could you keep an eye on Evie while I'm working? Is that okay?'

'What time are you doing that?'

'At one thirty. It's only for an hour or so.'

'Okay.'

'Thank you. I'll make sure she's fed and changed before the meeting.'

'I can feed her.'

I tilt my head at her. 'Are you sure?'

'Sure I'm sure.'

'But what about—'

'I said I'm sure. I'd like to do it. Forget yesterday happened okay?'

I'm not even sure which *part* of yesterday she's talking about. *I'm* talking about the fact she almost threw my baby out the window in panic when I asked her to feed her.

'Okay,' I say slowly. *But I'll have the monitor on my desk to watch while you're doing it.*

Chapter Fourteen

I'm all set and ready to go. I did my makeup earlier, nicer than the usual brush of blush and slick of lipstick. And I got out of my tracksuit pants and put on a smart dark blue dress I used to wear in the office. The only reason it still fits is because it's a wraparound type. Still, I feel pretty good.

The video meeting starts.

'Did you get the chance to go over the spreadsheets?' Ben asks once we're done with the preliminaries.

'Spreadsheets?'

'I sent the links via email this morning,' Shelley says.

'They're the database of rental properties with the date of the next inspections. I thought you could coordinate all that,' Ben says.

'Oh, sorry. You did say something about an email, Shelley, but I got side-tracked. Let me have a look.'

I scramble to locate the email and it's right there in my inbox. In fact, there's a few of them, all sent around six thirty a.m.

I quickly go through the documents. Ben is tapping his pen on the desk waiting for me to finish. I am aware of Evie making noises in the background. She's not crying, not yet anyway, more of a grizzle. I glance at the monitor. She's in her cot, kicking her blankets until they're right down the bottom. There's no sign of Chloe.

'Sorry, Ben, what did you say?'

'I sent a link to the list of preferred tradesmen, for repairs. Do you have that?'

'Hang on. Let me look.' Evie's fully crying now. I lift up one finger. 'Sorry, Ben, my daughter is crying.'

'Yes, I can hear that,' he says and I'm sure there's a note of exasperation in his tone.

'I'll be right back.'

On the way to the nursery I call out for Chloe but there's no response. Evie is hungry, she really should be fed soon or this is going to degenerate into a full-blown scream-fest. The bottle is in the warmer ready to go, but there's no sign of Chloe. I put Evie's dummy into her mouth, then go out onto the landing and knock on Chloe's door. 'Chloe?'

No reply. Could she be asleep? She was awake moments ago. I knock again, hard. 'Chloe?'

Nothing.

On the landing, I lean over the balustrade. 'Chloe?'

Nothing. I hurry back into the nursery. Evie has dropped her dummy out of the cot. I grab her favourite rattle — which also got thrown out — and give it to her, shaking it in front of her face.

'There it is, baby girl, see? Look, Evie! Look!' She takes it, throws it right back out and continues wailing. I rush back to my office, pop my head round the door. Ben has his head down and is taking notes. Shelley is in profile, talking to someone off-screen. 'I'll be right there!' I shout.

Back in the nursery I rinse Evie's dummy and try that again. This time, she stops crying. I breathe out. 'You stay there and you be good, okay? Mummy will be back as soon as she can.'

I return to the office.

'Sorry about that!' I breathe as I sit back down. 'Okay, where were we?'

'Everything okay?' Shelley asks.

'It's fine. It's just Evie's hungry and I don't know where… anyway. You don't want to hear it. Let's get back to work. Where were we?'

'The list of preferred tradesmen?' Ben says.

'Ah yes, give me oooone second.'

It takes more than one second. There's the sound of someone's fingernails drumming the desk. I can feel my cheeks glow. Eventually I find the file and we discuss the best way for me to get those requests directly so I can deal with them.

'Do you think Marilyn could liaise with me?' I ask Shelley.

'Marilyn? You mean Meryl?'

'Yes. Sorry.' I shake my head. 'Did I say Marilyn? I meant Meryl.'

Evie erupts in a full-blown scream that makes me jump. 'I'll be right back.' I rush out to her. Her little face is red from crying. I pick her up and walk her around the room, bouncing her gently, patting her back until she calms down. Her dummy is still in the cot and I give it to her.

'Chloe!' I hiss between my teeth.

Silence.

The moment I put Evie back in the cot she starts up again. We do this a couple of times, me on the verge of a nervous breakdown, and in between I'm shouting over to the laptop, *Be right there, Shelley!* In the end I just give up. I take her with me and sit back down in front of the computer.

'Sorry!' I say, blowing hair off my face. 'My babysitter

has disappeared into thin air. Can you believe it?' I'm bouncing Evie on my shoulder and patting her back at the same time while rearranging my hair with my free hand. 'I don't know what's wrong with her. She was perfectly calm before.'

Shelley gives me a quick smile. 'Maybe we should catch up later.'

'It should be okay now, as long as I'm holding her,' I say.

Somehow we get through the rest of the meeting, but I'm flustered and even though I'm scribbling everything down with my free hand, I'm sure I won't be able to read myself back later. Or I'll miss something critical, like a tenant's electricity has gone off and they need it back ASAP so they can charge their pacemaker or something.

Honestly, I am going to kill Chloe if she ever turns up.

We end the meeting and I take Evie back to the nursery to feed her. When I finish, I glance out the window and see Chloe. She is wearing black wellies — are these mine? — and one of Richard's big outdoor jackets. She's walking my bicycle up the path. Her hair is wild and her cheeks are red, like she's just cycled back from somewhere.

I stand on the landing. 'Where were you?'

She looks up, that bored expression on her face. 'Out.'

'Out?' My jaw drops. 'You said you'd look after Evie while I was doing my work meeting! Evie hasn't been fed and she was crying and I was in the middle of a video call!'

She puts her things in the coat room — and yes, those wellies are mine. She swaps them for her regular shoes. 'I'm not a mind reader, Joanne. If you were going to work today you should have told me. I'm not waiting around so I can be at your beck and call. You have to give me some notice.'

My jaw is truly scrapping the floor. 'Chloe! We had this conversation like, two hours ago!'

'No we didn't.'

She walks up the stairs. 'Chloe,' I say slowly when she reaches the landing. 'We were outside your room. I brought you a toasted cheese sandwich for breakfast and I asked you to help me with Evie because I had a meeting. You even said you'd feed her, remember?'

She disappears into her room.

'Chloe?'

She comes out again, but this time with the tray, on which are her dirty plate and dirty mug. She hands it to me.

'I think you're losing your mind, Joanne. Just like your mother.'

Chapter Fifteen

Chloe closes her door and I stand there with the tray in my hand, my head spinning. Did I hear her right? Does Chloe *know* about my mother? If so, where did she get her information from?

There's only one answer to that, obviously. I spend the rest of the day with Evie *willing* Richard to come home early. I put Evie in the playpen which I've moved to my office so I can keep her close while I call Gourmet Catering, a local company that we've used before, and organise the menu for Saturday. I include vegan dishes as well as peanut-free and gluten-free ones, just in case.

'Will you need waiters?' Chris asks. 'I'll be honest with you, Mrs Atkinson, normally this would be too short notice but this weekend is slow for us, so we could accommodate you if you wanted help.'

Gosh, normally I'd say no, they can help themselves, but Richard will want everything to be perfect and he doesn't care about the cost, so I say yes. Then I call the patisserie and organise a massive Black Forest birthday cake.

Satisfied that's all done, I turn my mind to the documents Shelley sent.

I print out the spreadsheets, go through my notes, type them up. Then Richard comes home. He does his usual greeting from downstairs. 'How are my girls today?' And I close my eyes for a second, in anticipation of the argument that will follow because of course, I have to tell him what happened. Chloe cannot remain as the babysitter if she's not prepared to babysit. I don't think that's too much to ask. Also I want to know why he told her about my mother's illness, which I consider to be very personal.

I meet him downstairs.

'Hello, darling. I'll be in my study for half an hour or so. I have to make some calls. Where is Chloe?'

'She's in her room.'

'I'll go up and say hi.'

'Can I talk to you for a second first? Here give me that.' I help him take his coat and hang it on the coat rack.

'Can it wait until later?'

'No, not really.'

'I see…' He unbuttons his suit jacket and loosens his tie. I take his hand and I lead him to the living room.

'What happened?'

'What did you tell Chloe about my mother?'

He gives a little confused shake of the head. 'I don't know what you mean. Why? What happened?'

'We had a disagreement earlier. Chloe and I.'

He sighs, which I have to say is kind of annoying. It makes me feel like he's already decided it's my fault.

'What was the argument about?'

'I asked her to help me while I was in a work meeting.'

'A work meeting? Didn't you say you were starting next week?'

'I was — I am — but Shelley called this morning and asked that we have an onboarding meeting.' I shake my head. 'Look, that's beside the point. I asked Chloe to help me look after Evie. Except she was nowhere to be found and Evie was hungry and upset and the meeting was a complete disaster.'

'Really?'

'Daddy!'

We turn around. Chloe has appeared in the doorway. 'Daddy! I didn't hear you come in.' She skips up to him like a child, her arms open wide.

'Actually, Chloe, do you mind?' I say. She's literally hanging off his neck. She swivels to face me.

'What?'

'I need to have a private conversation with your father.'

'What about?'

'Joanne tells me there was a misunderstanding between you two,' Richard says gravely.

Chloe looks at me sadly. 'I'm sorry you're upset, Joanna—'

'It's Joanne.'

'—but it's not my fault.'

'What happened? Did you two get your wires crossed?' Richard asks.

I take in a sharp breath and turn to Richard. 'Unfortunately, Richard, I think it was deliberate.'

'Deliberate?' Chloe exclaims, eyes wide like saucers. 'You made a mistake, now you're going to blame *me* for it?'

'What mistake?' Richard asks.

'I didn't make—'

'She forgot to tell me about her meeting, Daddy. I had no idea she needed me to look after Evie. Otherwise, I would have gladly done it. I assumed I could do whatever I wanted.

I borrowed her bike…' She turns to me. 'I'm sorry! Okay? Is that why you're mad at me? Because I borrowed your bike?'

'Now, now,' Richard says, lips pursed and eyebrows knotted. 'I'm sure Joanne doesn't mind you borrowing her bike. As long as you asked for permission. Isn't that right, Joanne?'

I raise my hands. 'This has absolutely nothing to do with the bicycle!' I let them drop.

Chloe hooks her arm into her father's, leaning against his side. He taps her hand affectionately.

'I said to her, Daddy, I'm happy to work whenever she likes, but she has to tell me when. What am I supposed to do? Wait like a sentinel until she makes up her mind? I thought I was allowed out of the house when I wasn't working.'

I still can't believe what I'm hearing. 'That's not what happened, Chloe, and you know it.'

She opens her eyes wide and lets go of Richard. 'Hang on. Is it because of Simon you're so upset?'

'Simon?'

'Because me and Simon fooled around this morning? Oh my god! Are you *jealous*!'

Richard gives a quick jerk of the head. 'Simon?'

It's such an outrageous proposition that I find myself blushing. 'That's ridiculous,' I scoff.

'What's this about Simon?' Richard asks. His tone has cooled somewhat. Not that it was that warm before.

'Nothing! Chloe took selfies with him this morning but this has nothing to—'

He turns to Chloe. 'Selfies? With Simon?'

'Relax, Dad, we had our clothes on.'

'Anyway that's not the point,' I snap. 'Forget about Simon.' But I've lost my train of thought now and I blink a few times. 'You are the babysitter, Chloe, remember? If you're not around when I need you, then I'll need to get someone else.'

Richard turns to me. 'I don't understand. Did you organise it with Chloe or not?'

I think I'm going to scream. 'I did. I just told you.'

'But you told me you didn't have to work until next week,' Chloe says.

'But then I got a call. As you know.'

'Wait a minute. You told me you were going to work next week as well,' Richard says. 'You never said anything about working today. Could you be mistaken?'

'Mistaken? How can I possibly be mistaken about being in a video meeting for half an hour? And also I'd like to know, by the way, what did you say to her about my mother?'

'I don't know what you mean.'

'Chloe said I was forgetting things and that I was going crazy like my mother.' I glare at her.

'You did say she ended up in the loony bin, didn't you, Daddy?'

I look from one to the other. 'Excuse me?'

'You did say it,' Chloe says to Richard.

'For goodness' sake!' Richard snaps. He goes to sit down on the couch, crosses one leg over the other. 'I didn't say she ended up in the loony bin. I said she had mental problems that she had to be treated for in hospital.'

My mouth opens and closes with shock. 'Why would you say such a thing?'

'That your mother was institutionalised? Because it's true, Jo. I didn't realise it was a state secret. And anyway, it was just in passing.'

'Exactly. I didn't think it was a big deal,' Chloe says, checking her fingernails.

'In *passing*? But it's very personal to me!'

'Sweetheart. I was talking to Chloe. I was just describing

the difficult childhood that you had, that's all. There was no malicious intent.'

'But you make it sound like my mother was crazy.'

'Of course not. But you said she had problems after you were born. That you had to be taken away to your grandmother. Was that not true?'

'No! Yes!' I shake my head. 'Not like that! And anyway that's not the point.' I point at Chloe. 'I can't believe you told *her*!'

'Why?' Chloe says. 'Either it's true or it's not. I think we need to know. Because you're not being very stable yourself. It's like, something you inherit, right? I only ask because you've been acting really strange.'

She does a sideways eye roll, then goes to sit next to her father and puts her head on his shoulder. 'I'm sorry, Daddy, I really didn't know she was working today. I didn't mean to do the wrong thing, I swear, Daddy.'

He puts his arm around her and kisses the top of her head. 'I know, pumpkin. It's all right. You didn't do anything wrong.'

At this point I'm so angry I can't speak. I stomp out of the room and go to check on Evie. Her eyes are closed but her mouth is moving. She'll be awake for her last feed of the day soon.

'Joanne?'

It's Richard. His tone is soft and sheepish. He comes up behind me and puts his hands on my shoulders. 'Are you alright?'

'No. I'm not alright. How can I be alright? She's rude and unreliable. And you always take her side.'

'I don't always take her side.'

I shrug him off. 'You do, Richard. Don't gaslight me.'

'I'm not gaslighting you. Please. Talk to me.'

'Let's get out of here. I don't want to wake Evie.' I walk back downstairs then hesitate. I'm about to ask, is Chloe still in there? Because I don't want to see her right now. Then I remember that with all the tension today I'd forgotten I put a load in the dryer this morning. I make a beeline for the laundry, take out the washing and dump it into a basket.

Richard clicks his tongue behind me. 'Jo, please. I don't want to fight.'

'So trust me when I tell you something. Don't automatically take her side. It's getting ridiculous.'

'I'm sorry. I really am. I'm not used to having the two of you in the same house. I just want everyone to get along.'

He takes the basket out of my hands and puts it on the ground, then brings me close to him and I give in, let myself fall into his arms.

'I want the same thing,' I say.

'I know.'

I pull away from him, study his face and decide that he looks sufficiently contrite. 'Let me put all this away and then I'll make dinner.'

He nods, disappears into his study. I fold the laundry and take ours upstairs, leaving Chloe's in the basket. She can bring it up herself. When I pass Richard's study I hear him talking on the phone. I stop and listen, just in case it's… I don't know. Simon? Getting fired?

'Oh, did she? No, she didn't mention it to me. Thank you, Solomon. I'm sure it's nothing. She's just being nosy.'

Solomon is our family solicitor. I keep listening because it's an odd conversation, and I'm dying to know *who* is just being nosy. I'm pretty sure it's not me. I haven't spoken to Solomon in months. 'When exactly did she call you? … Yes. Please do. Thank you.'

Silence. He must have ended the call. I hear his chair

being pushed back and I quickly walk away. I can't imagine Richard would be impressed if he found me listening at the door and I can't blame him.

I take the laundry to our room and put it away, my mind going back to that strange conversation. *She's just being nosy. I'm sure it's nothing.* I wonder if they were talking about Chloe? I should ask him. I'll say I happened to walk past and overheard, which is exactly what happened. I'll skip the part where I stopped and listened.

Half an hour later I check on Evie again, but when I reach the cot she's not there. My pulse races as I dash out to the landing and lean over the railing. All I can think is, *she took her*.

'Richard?' I shriek.

I run down the stairs and find Richard in the kitchen, Evie in the crook of his elbow, staring at him unblinking while happily sucking on the bottle he is feeding her.

'Oh god! I got such a fright!' I laugh with relief.

'Really? Why?'

I place my hand on my chest. 'I went to get her and she was gone.'

'I called out. You mustn't have heard me.'

A sound behind me makes me stop. I turn around. Chloe is leaning against the wall, her arms crossed over her chest. I hadn't seen her there when I came in, but the look on her face as she stares at Evie makes my blood run cold.

It's a look of pure hatred.

'I don't think Chloe should be the nanny anymore.'

I've held my tongue all the way through dinner and now Richard and I are upstairs in our bedroom. I'm plumping the pillows. Punching them, more like. 'I'm sorry, but I've made up my mind. And I don't think she wants to do it anyway.'

'Of course she does.'

'She can stay here as long as she likes,' I say, not really meaning it. 'But I don't want her to be Evie's nanny.' *I don't want her anywhere near Evie.*

Richard raises his eyes to the ceiling, in a 'here we go again' manner. 'Is this about the misunderstanding today?'

'There was no misunderstanding, Richard, okay? I just don't trust her.'

'Jesus, Jo! What is the matter with you? Chloe loves Evie! It's why she came here! Because of her little sister!'

Somehow, those words send a shiver down my spine. 'I'm sorry, Richard, but I've made up my mind.'

'And I'm asking you to give her a chance. I know you think she's been unfriendly to you, but she's just a child.'

'She's not a child.'

'Joanne, listen.' He takes my hands. 'She's a sweet girl, she's happy to be here, she's doing so well. You just need to get to know her better and you'll see. She's really sweet. She's a great kid.'

'She's not a kid. She just acts like one so you'll believe whatever she says. She's manipulating you.'

'How dare you!'

It's so sudden, this change in him, it makes me pause. He moves his bottom jaw back and forth. He has gripped my hands so tightly his knuckles are white.

'You're hurting me!'

After a second or two of glaring at me, he lets go and yanks his pillow out of my hands. 'It's you who's being ridiculous. You're the one who's jealous. I expected better from you.'

'Where are you going?'

'I'm going to sleep in the other room.'

'Don't walk away from me!' I plead, just as he opens the door. And not even three feet away is Chloe, her face expressionless and as creepy as hell. And I bet she's been listening to us the whole time.

As I lie alone in the dark, I remember something Richard said, something that jarred a bit.

She's doing so well.

What does that mean?

Chapter Sixteen

Evie slept like a dream. She only woke up twice for her feed. I had to go to the nursery to get her bottle ready and when I went to the bathroom to wash my hands, I stepped on a bit of glass. I'd cleaned the floor thoroughly but I must have missed that bit.

I picked it up and held it up to the light. What *had* Chloe been doing that night with Evie's medicine? Was it really as innocent as she'd made out?

What if it wasn't?

It's still early. I prepare breakfast for Richard. Not a peep out of Chloe as usual. She never gets up early. I'm not complaining. I'm more focused on Richard.

'I can't believe you said those things about Chloe last night,' he says. He has dark rings under his eyes. He looks like he's aged ten years.

'I'm sorry, Richard. Like I said, she's welcome to stay as long as she likes, but I don't want her to look after Evie.'

'And I said she can stay on as Evie's nanny, therefore that's what's going to happen. Do I make myself clear?'

'Why are you doing this? Why won't you trust my judgment?'

'I think you know why.' He leaves his plate near the sink.

'What does that mean?'

'I think you should see Dr Fletcher. The sooner the better. I think you're overreacting to things, that you've been forgetful. I think you're …'

'What? Just say it!'

'Obsessively distrustful.'

'You mean paranoid. Like my mother.'

'You said it, not me.'

Richard leaves for work without kissing me goodbye.

I'm going to go mad, if I'm not already. It's like I'm the only one who sees the truth and he won't believe me. And what if it's more serious than that? Richard thinks I'm being paranoid, but what if I'm not?

What if Chloe really has some malicious intent?

I shudder. I have to know. I can't keep second-guessing myself like this. In the end I decide I need to talk to someone.

I call Robyn.

I've known Robyn forever. Well, since secondary school. From the day we met, we became instant best friends. I used to spend more time at her house than I did at my own. My house felt sad and lonely, neglected. My mother might have recovered from her post-natal trauma, but she was always a bit dreamy, a bit lost. Housekeeping wasn't a big deal in my house. Neither was homework, nutritious meals, or getting outside and playing sports. But all those things were front and centre at Robyn's house and I loved going there after school, knowing her mum would be baking lemon cupcakes or red velvet cakes or something equally amazing. On Saturday afternoons her dad would take us to ride our bikes around the village or kick a ball in the park. Later, she went to university to study law and I got a job as a home care assistant while I figured out what to do with my life. But we never stopped being besties. Now Robyn is a lawyer for a big firm in the City and the mother of twin boys.

'I have a question for you,' I say, after we've done our hellos.

'Shoot.'

'If you wanted to test the contents of a bottle, a bottle of medicine, how would you go about it?'

She doesn't reply right away. 'Testing for something specific?'

'I mean you wanted to make sure whatever is in the bottle is what the label says. Are there places that do that?'

'There are. We had a case once. A health supplement manufacturer had accused a competitor of lying about the contents of their products. Our client maintained they couldn't sell it that cheap unless they were lying.'

'That sounds like exactly what I'm after. Can they run tests if there's only a trace of the product on bits of broken glass?'

'I don't know, I assume so. I'll send you the details of the company we used.' Then after a pause, she says, 'Can I ask why?'

'Erm… just curious,' I reply, unconvincingly.

'You okay, Jo?'

'Yes! I'm very well, thank you. Just really busy. You know how it is.' She doesn't, now that I think of it. Robyn juggles two children under five with a full-time career as a corporate lawyer and she does it all standing on her head. I just have Evie to worry about.

'Okay,' she says slowly. 'I'll send you a couple of links. But keep me posted. You sure you're okay?'

'Absolutely.' I mean I could tell her, she's my best friend, but I think it's wise to find out whether my stepdaughter really is a psychopath before I tell the world about it.

'*Yes* would have been a comfort.' She says. '*Absolutely*, not so much.'

I laugh. This is a line from one of our favourite movies, *The English Patient.* We must have watched that movie a hundred times, tears streaming down our faces, our mouths stuffed with caramel popcorn.

'Yes,' I say. 'Yes, I'm okay.'

True to her word, Robyn texts a link to a company that analyses pharmaceutical raw materials. I call them from the nursery and explain what I'm after. I want to know if it really was CALPOL Infant Suspension in that bottle and nothing else. No problem, they say. Apparently, you can run tests on minute traces of liquid. I pay extra for fast-tracking. A courier will come to pick up the sample later today.

When I cleaned the bathroom floor the other night, I shoved the broken pieces in the bin to empty later. I go upstairs now, check on Evie who is awake but content, and lock myself in the nursery bathroom. I use a pair of tweezers to carefully pick up the pieces of glass and drop them in a Ziplock bag. When I've picked up as much as I can find, I wrap the Ziplock bag into clean white sheets of paper. Then back downstairs I stick the whole thing in a small cardboard box and add crumpled newspaper to make it fit snugly. There. Done. I hide it under the sink. That's one place I can be confident Chloe won't go snooping.

The courier won't be here until this afternoon, and there's one more thing I need. Video cameras. If Chloe is up to something, the easiest way to find out is to spy on her. I may as well go and buy them now. There's an Argos at the shopping centre in Staines. They'll have what I need.

I've put Evie in the car seat. I've got my coat on and I'm about to close the front door when she shows up.

'Are you going out?'

I jump. 'Chloe! You scared me! How long have you been up?'

'Not long. Are you going out?'

'Yes.'

'Where?'

'For a drive.'

She frowns at me. We both know that's unlikely so I add, 'I'm going to the shops. There's plenty of food in the fridge for lunch. You'll be all right on your own, won't you?'

'Sure,' she says, chewing on a fingernail. 'Are you taking Evie with you?'

'Yes. Of course.'

'You want me to come too?'

'You'll be bored, Chloe. Anyway I have to go to the council. I have an appointment.'

'What for?'

I hesitate, but only for a second. 'It's to do with the house. I want to add French doors that open to the patio.' Which is true, I was thinking of doing that. Just not lately. 'I could be a while.'

'So why not leave Evie here with me? It will so much easier for you. I'll look after her while you have fun at the shops or at the council or whatever.'

'Maybe next time,' I say with a tight smile.

She turns on her heels and stomps upstairs without another word.

Chapter Seventeen

I find exactly what I'm after: small, unobtrusive wireless cameras that run on batteries. They're square, white, easy to set up and easy to hide. They have five of them in the shop and I buy them all.

On the way home I stop in the village to shop for tonight's dinner. I want to make something special for Richard to make up for last night. I know he loves my sweet potato, feta, and caramelised onion quiche, so I settle on that.

I park the car across the road from the supermarket and it's only when I get out that I see Chloe. She is leaning against a brick wall beside the butcher's shop, smoking a cigarette. Standing next to her is Roxanne, her shoulder against a lamppost. They turn to me in unison and I raise my hand in a half wave, but neither of them acknowledges me. It's like they don't see me. Chloe drops her cigarette on the pavement and grinds it with the tip of her boot, and then they walk off in the opposite direction. What on earth was that? Didn't she see me? How could she not see me? She looked right at me, she knows the car. Maybe she was worried I'd ask her to help me with the shopping.

I put Evie in the buggy and get my groceries. Back home I notice my bicycle is gone from where I left it, which explains how Chloe got to the village.

I take Evie upstairs for her nap. She's happy and sweet, gives me lots of smiles. She hasn't been this content for days. Maybe I should take her out more. Maybe I'll ask Richard to let her sleep in our room. He'll grumble, but he'll say yes, I know he will. He won't even put up much of a fight.

As I walk past Chloe's door, I hesitate. It's just me here for once and suddenly I'm dying to take a peek. Of course, if she comes home and finds me in there, she'll tell Richard and I won't hear the end of it. I could be quick. Or, even better, there's still a pile of her clean clothes in the laundry which I asked her to take to her room, but she hasn't. I run down to the laundry, fold it neatly and take it upstairs. After all, since she treats me like a maid, she won't think anything of it. I'll say it's all part of the service.

I stand in front of her closed door and knock twice, in case she did come back and I missed her on the road, but there's no answer. I push the door gently and my jaw drops. I can't believe my eyes. The room is a total mess. The bed isn't just unmade, it's crumpled like she's picked up the linen, rolled it into a big messy ball and dropped it from a great height. Her clothes are strewn everywhere. Her suitcases are still on the floor, their contents spilling out. There's a ton of makeup on top of the dresser. The bouquet of snowdrops I'd left is well and truly dead. I walk in gingerly, put her clean clothes on the only clutter-free corner of the bed, and take a look around. My eyes land on the open suitcase on the floor. I gently go through the contents, not that she'd notice if anything was out of place since everything is already out of place.

My fingers brush against something. I pick it up. It's a photo of a grinning baby lying on its stomach, its head to the camera. It's creased and frayed around the edges. It looks old, although it's impossible to tell how old.

'What the fuck are you doing in my room?'

I'm still crouched on the floor and I fumble to put the photo back, but her hand seems to dive from somewhere above me and next thing I know she's snatched it out of my hand.

'How dare you touch my stuff.'

'I'm sorry,' I say, getting up, brushing my knees. 'I came up to drop off your clean laundry. Here.' I point to the corner of the bed.

She lifts her chin. 'So what are you doing in my stuff?'

'I saw the photo stick out. I was just being curious.'

'Surely you mean nosy.'

I try to smile. 'Okay, you got me. Who is it?'

She crosses her arms over her chest. 'It's me.'

'Oh! That's nice. You always carry a baby photo of yourself?'

She hesitates for a second. 'I wanted to see if Evie looked like me when I was a baby.'

I tilt my head at her. 'Really?'

'So? What about it?'

'Nothing. Can I take another look?'

'No. You can't. Did you tell my dad I had to leave?'

'What? No!'

'You did, didn't you?'

'You don't have to leave. You can stay as long as you like.'

'That's not what I was asking. I know I can stay as long as I like. My dad bought this house, remember? Did you, or didn't you tell him you wanted me gone.'

I take a breath. 'No. I didn't. But…'

'But what?'

'But I think it would be best if we got someone else to look after Evie. And yes, I've had that conversation with your father.'

'Why?'

'Well, for one thing, you disappeared when I needed you.'

'But that was your mistake.'

'Come on, Chloe. It's just you and me here. We both know it wasn't a mistake.'

She narrows her eyes at me, taps her index finger on her chin. 'Hey, I know!' She points her finger at me. 'Maybe *you* should leave. And take your baby with you.'

I am so shocked by her boldness, I can't speak for a second. 'Excuse me?'

'Maybe you should move out.' She raises an eyebrow. 'Or you can stay but you know, I like this place. I'm staying here, forever. This is my house.' She glances down at her baby photo. 'You will never be rid of me. Would you like that?'

'Well....'

'Exactly. Think about it. That's all I'm asking.'

'Think about what?'

'Leaving.'

I scoff in disbelief. 'I live here, Chloe. I'm not going anywhere.' I brush strands of hair out of my face with one hand, pick up my empty washing basket and start walking toward the door.

'Tell Dad you've changed your mind and you want me to babysit, okay?'

'That's between me and your father.'

'Wait.' She picks up her phone, her finger quickly flicking across the screen. When she finds what she wants she thrusts the phone into my face. I pull back, squinting.

'What's this?'

'What does it look like?'

My stomach clenches. It's a photo of me, taken outdoors. I've got my sunglasses on and my hair is windswept. Also, I'm kissing Simon's cheek while he's grinning at the camera.

'What the hell is this?' I've never kissed Simon's cheek, or any other part of Simon for that matter. I have no idea where that photo came from. But then it comes to me. The *me* part was taken on a holiday Richard and I took last year to Brittany, before Evie was born. But Simon wasn't on the holiday. That photo, the real one, the one that doesn't include Simon, is of me kissing Richard's cheek.

'I don't understand.'

She takes the phone back. 'Just a little Photoshopping. I got the photo of you from Dad's phone. I deleted the original by the way, so there's no way to compare the two. The photo of Simon is from yesterday. So what I'm thinking is, you tell Dad you've changed your mind and I get to stay and look after Evie. What do you say?'

I stare at her face. Is she joking? Is it some kind of prank? 'I thought you wanted Evie to leave?'

'You and Evie, yes. But if you won't, then I'm the babysitter.'

'But why?' I shriek. 'You want to hurt her? Is that it?'

'No! Jesus, Joanne. Don't be so dramatic. I just want to hang out with my sister, that's all. I'm not going to hurt Evie. I love Evie.'

'Do you?'

'Yes.'

'You're going to show Richard that photo?'

'Only if you don't let me babysit Evie.'

'This is insane. He'll never believe it!'

'Won't he?' She tilts her head at me. 'I could tell you stories, you know. Maybe I was only eleven when my mum died, but I still remember the jealous rows he used to have with her. And judging from your face, you know exactly what

I'm talking about. So I'm asking again. You sure he won't believe it?'

My heart is bouncing around my chest, like a fireball of outrage. I can't let her get away with this. But then she has a point about Richard. He does have a jealous streak, and the way things are between us at the moment…

I bite the knuckle of my thumb. I wish I could take another look, see if there are any obvious flaws in her work, like the Photoshop fails you see on Instagram of influencers who tried to narrow their waist and ended up making the sea behind them look like it's about to have a tsunami.

The thing is, he might not believe it, but he'll wonder. And he'll definitely fire Simon, just to be on the safe side, and Simon is caring for his father and he needs this job.

'Great,' she says. 'I see we have a deal.'

'That's just… evil.'

'Let's not get carried away. We're negotiating, that's all.'

I can barely stand. My legs are like columns of jelly. I have to think. I have to find a way out of this mess. I turn around to leave.

'Hang on a sec.'

God, what now? I turn around. She's picking up swathes of dirty clothes from the floor and she dumps them in my basket. 'Then you wouldn't have done the trip for nothing,' she says. She goes to sit at the dresser and starts brushing her hair. 'By the way I saw you at the shops earlier. What's for dinner?'

I'm still reeling from everything. I look at her in the mirror. She's got one eyebrow raised, like this is a completely valid question.

'Erm…' I rub my fingers on my forehead. 'I'm making a quiche,' I say.

'A quiche?'

'Your dad's favourite with feta and sweet potato.'

'Cool.'

When I reach the door she says, 'Don't tell Dad.'

'Don't tell Dad what?' I ask, one hand on the doorknob. There are so many things I am not to tell Dad, I've lost track.

'About my baby photo.'

'Why would he care?'

She narrows her eyes at me. 'He doesn't like to talk about the past, okay?'

'But this is just a baby photo.'

'Oh my god! Joanne! Where have you been? He still misses our family, he misses my mum, don't you get it? He's still in love with her!'

Chapter Eighteen

My head is spinning, trying to grasp all the horrible things Chloe has said. Including the bit about Richard still being in love with Diane. Is it true? He never gave me that impression. And I can't stop thinking about the photo of me and Simon. Why would she do such a thing? She's insane, that's why. Would Richard believe it? I try to imagine his reaction if she showed it to him and I honestly don't know what he would think. And why this obsession with being Evie's nanny? We told her she could stay as long as she wants, although now the thought of it makes me shudder. I can't believe she wants *me* to leave. I mean, she had a point. Could I put up with a lifetime of having her around? Only if we get a much bigger house. One with outbuildings and acres between us where we can exist without ever laying eyes on each other.

Then I hear a car drive up. I'd completely forgotten about the courier. Suddenly I wish I'd asked them to meet me at the gate, but it's too late now.

I rush to the door before they have a chance to ring the doorbell. I give the driver my package and he takes his time, handing me a docket to sign. As I take the pen from him I see Simon raking the leaves near the hedge.

'Hello!' he yells out cheerily. And even though he has nothing to do with the photo and the photo isn't real anyway, I still feel a stab of embarrassment. I put up my hand and do a kind of half-wave. Finally the driver gets back into his van and leaves.

I quickly close the door after him.

I spend the rest of the afternoon in the nursery, almost glued to Evie. I hear Chloe going down the stairs, then doors opening and closing. I think she's in the kitchen and I can't stop wondering what she's doing down there. Making herself a snack? I know she's had lunch; I could tell from the way she put the ham back in the fridge without wrapping it properly and, in case that wasn't enough, she left her dirty plate and dirty glass on the kitchen table.

At five o'clock, I go downstairs to get everything ready for the quiche. The first thing I notice is a sprinkling of powdered chocolate on the table. I wipe it clean then open the fridge to reach for the eggs, but they're not there. I rummage around, moving things out of the way in case they got pushed down the back.

No eggs.

'Evie's awake.'

I turn around abruptly. Chloe reaches for a glass in the top cupboard. 'Did you hear what I said?' she asks. She turns on the tap.

My stomach churns. I glance at the baby monitor. Evie is indeed awake.

'Is she crying?' I ask.

'No. She's just awake.'

'Okay.' I think the best thing here is to act normal until I figure out what to do about the stupid photo. I wipe my hands on a tea towel. 'By the way, I bought some eggs this afternoon. Do you know where they are?'

She takes two or three sips of water before wiping her mouth with the back of her hand. 'I was hungry. I made an omelette.'

'When?'

'An hour ago.'

'You're kidding.'

'No, why?'

'You used all six of them?'

She leans back against the sink. 'Like I said. I was hungry.'

I close my eyes briefly. 'I wish you'd asked me. I would have made you something else.'

'You said I could help myself to whatever I wanted,' she says.

'I know but… I needed the eggs to make the quiche for dinner this evening.' I flip open the door of the freezer and pull out the drawer, loudly rummaging around for something to eat.

'Well sorry. I guess I'm still not a mind reader. My bad.'

I'm about to say something back, something snappy, but I'm interrupted by Richard's voice coming from the hall.

'Hello! How are my girls today?'

'Never mind,' I say.

Richard seems more stressed than usual, or maybe that's just the atmosphere in the house. I serve reheated chicken casserole for dinner. Richard will wonder what I do all day if I can't even get a nice home-cooked meal on the table.

'So what did you two get up to today?' he asks.

'Not much, I went shopping.'

'I went for a bike ride,' Chloe says.

'That's nice,' he says. 'To the village?'

'Yeah, Joanne wasn't here and I was lonely by myself.'

Richard looks at me with raised eyebrows.

'I had errands to run.'

'Errands?'

'Yes, errands. Shopping, that sort of thing.'

'Joanne went to the council to discuss stuff about the house,' Chloe says.

'Oh? What was that?'

I touch my hair. 'You know, nothing, generic things, for the plans we want to submit for the renovations.'

'How interesting! I didn't know you were going to do that!' He sits back, looking pleased. 'Which part?'

'Yeah,' Chloe joins in. 'Which part?'

'The extension to the kitchen, with the north wall opening onto the patio.'

'But why didn't you tell me?' Richard asks. He seems equal part surprised and delighted.

Chloe drapes an arm over the back of her chair and smirks. 'Yes, Joanne, why didn't you tell us about your planned visit to the council?'

She knows. I feel my cheeks grow hot. I'm probably looking like a beetroot right now. Richard frowns at her, and her smirk morphs into a sweet smile.

'And you took Evie with you?' Richard asks.

'Yes.'

'I think that's terrific. It's good that you get out with Evie. She wasn't a handful at the council chambers, I hope.'

He's right. I never go out with Evie unless absolutely necessary. I find the whole experience of loading and unloading the buggy and associated baby paraphernalia nerve-wracking. That I would voluntarily take her to a boring meeting at the council makes no sense.

'I offered to babysit so Joanne could go on her own,' Chloe says.

'That's kind of you, sweetheart,' Richard says. As if Chloe offering to babysit was a favour rather than her job. Her paid job. The one she insisted on getting and he insisted on giving her. The one she's now blackmailing me into keeping.

'I'm surprised you didn't take Chloe up on it, Jo, if she offered.'

I really am going mad. 'Because I felt like taking Evie with me.'

Richard nods. Seeing everyone has finished eating, I pick up the plates and stack them, glad of the diversion. Then I notice Richard gives Chloe a small nod and Chloe pushes her chair back.

'I'm going to get something. I'll be right back.'

She disappears into the pantry — I say pantry, but it's more of a second kitchen. It's big enough for a table and a chest freezer. And that's with wall-to-wall shelving.

Richard is smiling to himself, gazing in the direction of where Chloe was just now.

'She ate all the eggs,' I say.

'Excuse me?'

'I wanted to make the quiche you love so much. I went to the village and shopped for everything. And then when I came down to prepare dinner they were gone. She ate them. All six of them. Because she was hungry.'

'Are you all right?'

'Yes! I mean, not really. I just wish she'd asked, you know?' I shake my head.

'Surprise!' Chloe says.

I turn around. 'What is this?'

'It's a cake!' she says. And so it is. A chocolate cake. 'That's why I used the eggs, Joanne. I'm sorry about that, I didn't know you needed them. I mean I assumed you'd have some spares. I meant well. I swear to god.'

'You made a cake?'

'That's right, Joanne.' Richard says. 'Chloe made a cake. For you.'

Why on earth would she make me a cake? They're both looking at me expectantly. 'You should have told me. I would have got enough eggs for both the quiche and the cake.'

'I didn't know you needed them!' she says.

'But I told you about the quiche!'

'No, you didn't.'

'Excuse me?'

'I mean I had no idea you needed the eggs. You did say something about a ... what was it? A quiche? Is that French? I don't know what it is. Do you know what it is, Daddy?'

'Yes,' Richard replies gravely. As if this was a completely normal question.

'Did you know it required a hundred eggs?'

'Not a hundred, Chloe, but yes, I knew that.'

'Huh. Well I didn't. I've never had one, and I didn't know, and I'm sorry. I'm sorry, okay? Really, really, really sorry.' She drops the cake on the table, her mouth turned down, her eyes filling with water.

'But I said—'

'For Christ's sake!' Richard barks. 'Enough about the quiche! What is the matter with you?'

'I'm sorry, I—'

'I just can't put a foot right with you, can I?' Chloe wails. 'I was trying to do something nice, but it doesn't matter because you don't like me and you don't want me here. Maybe I should leave. Maybe that's what you really want. Maybe that'll make you happy.'

Richard has stood up abruptly. 'Sweetheart, come here.'

He puts his arms around her and she sobs in his chest while he pats her back and makes noises of comfort.

'I'm just going upstairs for a minute, Daddy,' she says between sobs. 'Wash my face, okay?'

He takes her face in his hands. 'I'm sorry sweetheart. You go upstairs, and I'll come and see you in a minute.' He pulls out his handkerchief and dabs at her eyes.

'Okay,' she says in a tiny, tiny voice. But before she disappears she grabs the plate with the cake and shoves it in the bin, then almost throws the plate in the sink and runs out the door with a strangled sob.

'My god, Jo! What the hell is wrong with you?'

I raise an eyebrow. 'Has she ever considered a career in acting? Because, truly, give the *child* a BAFTA. She's earned it.'

'Are you completely out of your mind?'

I sigh. 'She's manipulating you. She knew I bought the eggs to make a quiche. We had a conversation about it. She knew I wanted to make it for you because it's your favourite. That's why she used up the eggs. She wants to make herself look good and make me look bad.'

He doesn't say anything. When I look up at him, his mouth is opened.

'I don't know what to say anymore. You're insane. You really are.'

I take a sip of wine. 'I'm telling you the truth.'

'Do you know that Chloe believes you dislike her profoundly? Are you aware of that? Because I think maybe she's right.'

'Is there something wrong with her?'

'What?'

'With Chloe? Is she, you know, mentally unstable?'

He looks at me with real concern on his face. 'She made

a cake, for Christ's sake! And now you're talking about Chloe being mentally unstable?'

'You didn't answer me.'

He shakes his head slowly. 'Chloe called me at the office this afternoon. She told me that she wanted to make a cake as a surprise for you because she upset you last night. It was her way of saying sorry. Then she asked me, would Joanne like that? And I said yes. Joanne would really like that. It's a very sweet gesture. Very considerate. But now I see that every time Chloe tries to do something nice, you go out of your way to ruin it. You really don't like her, do you?'

There's no point. I see that now. And if I push, she's going to show Richard the picture. And then? I don't know. Maybe he'll divorce me, because right now he's convinced his precious little girl is an angel and I'm the jealous stepmother. If she shows him the photo, he'll think to top it all off, I've been having it off with the gardener.

My eyes prickle as I realise I'm never going to win this argument. Chloe wanted to make me look bad, and she did. She laid a trap for me and I dived head-first into it.

I should have said thank you and eaten the fricking cake.

'I'm sorry,' I mumble.

'Don't say it to me, Jo. Say it to Chloe.'

Hardly, but I nod anyway. 'I will. I'm really sorry.'

Richard gets up, goes to the sideboard and opens another bottle of wine. I get up to clear the table. He pours himself a glass and doesn't ask me if I want one.

'I'm going to check on my daughter,' he says. For a split second, I thought he meant he was going to check on Evie before realising he meant to check on his twenty-year-old psycho daughter.

I swallow a sigh and nod. Then something moves on the edge of the doorway. A shadow. It's gone now.

Chloe. It was her. I'm sure of it. She was standing there,

listening to every word of our argument and probably relishing every second of it.

Later, when I go upstairs, I hear them talking in her bedroom and I stop for a second outside the door. The floorboards creak. I wince as I hold my breath.

'I don't know what else I can do, Daddy! I just can't do anything right!'

'Shhh. Sweetheart. It will be all right,' Richard soothes.

'No it won't! I don't know how to make her like me! Every day she asks me how long I'm going to stay! Every day! But you said I could say as long as I wanted and I really want to get to know my sister, you know? Do I have to leave, Daddy? Can't I stay and spend time with my baby sister?'

What a lying little cow. Richard responds with a stern, angry voice. 'She said that? Well! Don't you worry about that, sweetheart. I'll have a word with her.'

I think I'm going to be sick. I take Evie to our bedroom because whether he likes it or not, she's sleeping with us. But it doesn't matter in the end because for the second night in a row, Richard takes his pillow without a word and goes to sleep in one of the guest rooms.

Chapter Nineteen

I have to put the cameras up around the house and I have to do it tonight. My only problem is that this house creaks. Loudly. I need a good excuse in case either Chloe or Richard get up to investigate.

As it happens, I have one right here.

I look down at my sleeping baby, sit on the edge of my bed, and wait. Then, a few minutes after midnight, Evie wakes for her feed. I give her her bottle, but then instead of putting her back in the cot, I get up with her in my arms and bounce her gently on my hip.

'We're going for a little walk, okay, sweetie?' She rubs her eyes with her little fists. I bet she'd go right back to sleep if I let her, which ordinarily would make me weep with gratitude.

But not this time. 'We're going on a little adventure. What do you say?'

She makes a little whimper as I shove my phone in the pocket of my robe. I open the bedroom door a crack. Silence. With Evie firmly wedged on my hip, I walk softly along the corridor to the nursery. I keep one eye to the door as I rummage through the cupboard and grab the cameras from where I'd hidden them behind her baby blankets. I've already decided the best place to hide one in this room will be inside the teddy bear. I really thought long and hard about this. It's not ideal, since that's what they always do in movies, so surely that's the first place anyone would look, but I can't think of anything else. The teddy is far too big for her, so it just sits on the top of the cupboard gathering dust.

I set Evie down in her cot while I cut open the poor teddy, pull out the white stuffing material, push the camera in, and shove the stuffing back in.

I hear a noise behind me. Or maybe I'm imagining it. I hold my breath, my eyes trained on the door. If anyone walked in right now, there is no way I could come up with a reasonable explanation for what I'm doing.

Silence. I let out a breath and return to my task. Poor teddy looks a bit bedraggled by the time I sit him back on its shelf and point the camera straight at the cot, checking that the angle is right on my iPhone app. Then I put the other four cameras in a big blue cotton tote bag I use to carry baby things when we go to the shops. I shove them under packets of nappies, hoist the bag on my shoulder, pick up Evie who had just gone back to sleep, and walk out.

Next stop, the living room.

The sound I make walking down the steps is so loud I keep having to stop every second step, my heart beating in my throat.

Oscar waits for us at the bottom of the stairs. He knows he's not allowed to go upstairs and he's very obedient that way. But now he bounces around us, his tail threatening to knock off a vase or two along the way. Maybe this was a bad idea, doing this now. Evie is laughing because Oscar is jumping on me. If no one was awake before, they will be any minute now.

First stop, the pantry. If Chloe wants to poison us, that's where she'll do it. How hard can it be to drop rat poison into a jar of coffee? Maybe it's lucky I didn't eat the chocolate cake.

I set Evie down on a blanket, on her stomach, then stand on my toes to hide a camera between packets of flour and quinoa. The packages are all more or less white and I'm hoping that the camera won't stand out too much. It takes a few tries to make it as invisible as I can while still getting a good angle, but I get there, or close enough.

Next stop, living room. I pick up Evie, shove her blanket back in the bag and step back to admire my handiwork.

'What on earth is going on here?'

My breath catches as I turn around. Richard is standing there, in his blue and white striped pyjamas, his hair sticking out on one side.

'I—' I search his face, my heart beating in my throat, trying to work out how much he has seen. But his eyes don't leave mine as he waits for an answer. He doesn't look up towards the shelves, towards the camera I've just hidden.

'She wouldn't get to sleep. I tried everything. I took her downstairs so she wouldn't wake you up.'

'Well, I'm awake now. You've been stomping around the house all night.'

'Did I? I'm sorry. I …' Evie rests her head on my shoulder. Her eyelids are fluttering. She is seconds away from sleep.

'Finally!' I say with an exaggerated eye roll.

Richard sighs. 'Can we all go to bed now, please?'

'Yes.' I say. 'I guess we can.' I'm about to pick up the tote bag but I hesitate. I wasn't careful when I put the blanket back and I can clearly see one of the cameras sticking out. He'll want to know what it is, and what it's for. He turns around. 'You're coming?'

'Yes, I'm coming.' I push the bag with my foot and slide it out of sight, under the bottom shelf. I'll just pick it up later.

I follow him up the stairs. I half expect him to come back with me to our room, but when we reach the landing he turns left, leaving me to turn right. It seems I am not forgiven.

I put Evie back to sleep and slide into my own bed, checking the camera app.

I've done it. I've put two cameras where they matter most. I set both to record to the cloud and finally go to sleep.

Chapter Twenty

'We need to talk,' I say.

Richard briskly flicks his wrist and glances at his watch. These are the first words I've said to him since he marched me back to my room last night. I'm surprised to find him up and dressed in the kitchen. It's not even seven in the morning. I turn on the coffee machine and pour ground beans into the dispenser.

'I can't. I have to go to work. I'll see you later this afternoon.'

'But you haven't had any breakfast.'

'I'll get something in the city.'

If I thought he was angry with me yesterday, this is a whole new level. He won't even look at me. 'We really need to talk, Richard.' What I want to say is, we really need to talk about Chloe, because last night, I decided to tell him everything. I'm going to tell him about the photo she fabricated; I'll even enlist Simon to testify the photo is a fake. I'm going to tell him she asked *me* to leave this house and take my baby with me. I'm going to say something isn't right with her, I think you know it, and she needs to go.

'What time will you be home?'

'I'll try and be back by four. Are we all set with the dinner party this evening?'

My face is a blank. 'What dinner party?'

He was already leaving the room, his back to me, his expensive leather satchel in one hand and pulling at his tie with the other. 'Please don't tell me you forgot!'

'The *birthday* party? It's tomorrow,' I blurt.

'Tomorrow?' He tilts his head. 'Is this a joke? Joanne! It's tonight!'

I burst into tears.

'Chloe?' I say softly, knocking on her door. I'm still shaky from how angry Richard was with me just now. 'You better sort it out, I swear to god,' he'd barked.

She opens the door. 'What.'

'Your birthday party, it's tomorrow, isn't it?' I can't help but grimace as I ask.

'Tomorrow?' she shrieks. 'No! It's tonight! Why?'

'But you told me it was Saturday!'

'Oh my god. It's like you have no brain. I've been saying Friday ever since I got here. Ask my dad.'

I bite my bottom lip. 'Yes, that's what he said.' I want to argue, I really do, I know she said Saturday and I know she's setting me up. She wants me to fail. She wants to show her father what a horrible stepmother I am, who couldn't be bothered putting together a simple party for a dozen people for her stepdaughter's twenty-first. In fact, if Richard hadn't mentioned it, her guests would have arrived and there would have been no party. Just me holding a dish of olives in one hand and a bottle of rosé in the other.

I figure I have two choices here. I argue my point and cause World War Three, knowing full well Richard will take her side, or I rescue the situation and whip up a birthday party for thirteen people — that's got to be an omen, surely — with less than twelve hours to go.

Option two it is.

Chloe narrows her eyes at me. 'Does that mean we ordered everything for the wrong day? Like, my friends are coming and there'll be nothing to eat or drink or anything?'

'No, no. It's all under control.'

'It better be,' she snaps, before slamming the door.

I sit down at my desk and call Chris at Gourmet Catering. I explain the misunderstanding and ask if we can do it tonight, waiters including.

'Unfortunately, Mrs Atkinson, there's no way I can cater for your party this evening. We're already fully booked.'

I bit my bottom lip. 'That's too bad.'

'Will you be cancelling tomorrow's order?' he asks. 'Because there's a full charge if you cancel less than forty-eight hours ahead. It's on our website.'

'I see. That can't be helped, I guess.'

'I'm afraid not, Mrs Atkinson.'

I hang up and call other caterers, each one increasingly further away and more expensive. Finally I find a company that will do it for eight hundred pounds more than I'd budgeted. At this point I'm so relieved I almost cry as she reels off a proposed menu, which, I have to say, sounds perfect. She mentions names of wines, something about champagne, cocktails… 'Would that work?' she asks.

'Yes!' I say. 'Yes, that would work! All of it! Thank you so much. You're a lifesaver!'

She laughs. 'Don't worry, Mrs Atkinson. It happens a lot. We'll see you at four o'clock this afternoon.'

Next I call the patisserie and explain the situation.

'I'm sorry, but there's no way I can get the cake ready in time.'

'I understand,' I say, still high on my previous win. I cancel tomorrow's order — only fifty percent penalty, bargain — and search for a Black Forest cake recipe online.

I spent all morning shopping with Evie in the buggy and most of the afternoon making that cake with Evie in the playpen in the kitchen. I moved her to the morning room while I put out nice linen on the table and arranged chairs and sofas. In between I fed her, changed her nappies, put her to sleep.

Chloe was nowhere to be seen.

Simon helped — I asked him to come over so he could pick Chloe's friends up from the station. It's almost four, and at this point I still have no idea how many people, when, or what their names are.

'You're doing a nice party for Chloe,' Simon says, putting down champagne glasses on the table.

'Thank you. I hope she'll be happy,' I say. And she better be. I've left nothing to chance.

At three minutes to four the caterers arrive. They get everything organised while I go upstairs and change, Evie on my hip. I am literally not leaving her side, nor she mine. Meanwhile, still no sign of Chloe. At fifteen minutes past four Richard comes home, joins me upstairs.

'Everything looks wonderful sweetheart,' he says. 'You included.' I fall into his arms. I'm so relieved I could cry. I have Chloe's birthday present right here – we agreed that a two-hundred-fifty-pound gift card from Harrods would be the best thing to do, that way she can choose what she likes.

'Where's the birthday girl?' he asks.

'No idea.'

Richard goes in search of Chloe while I finish getting ready. At five p.m. I am back downstairs. Evie is asleep in her cot in my room.

'I hope nothing has happened,' Richard says, looking worried. He's been leaving her messages but she hasn't returned his calls.

'There she is.' I point at the window. Chloe is pushing my bicycle up the path, looking dishevelled. We meet her in the hall.

'What's going on?' Richard asks. 'What time are your guests coming?'

'My guests?' Her bottom lip wobbles. Her eyes are red from crying. She points a shaking finger at me. '*She* got the wrong day! And I had to call all my friends and tell them not to come! I've never been so *embarrassed* in my life!'

My jaw drops. 'What? But I—'

'What are you talking about!' Richard says. 'Joanne fixed everything. The party is ready to go in the drawing room!'

She takes off her jacket with angry, sharp movements and throws it on the floor. 'Well she didn't tell me that. She said the party was off because she got the wrong day.'

'No, I didn't,' I blurt, already bracing myself for Richard's angry stare.

But instead, he frowns at Chloe. 'Joanne spent all day getting the party ready for you.'

'Well I didn't know that. Nobody told me.'

'Are you saying that nobody's coming?' I ask, incredulous.

'You can't be serious, Chloe!' Richard snaps. 'Joanne has gone to a lot of trouble and you're acting very spoiled right now.'

She shoots him a look of pure hatred, but quickly catches

herself. She cracks a sob, a big one that makes her shoulders quake. Then she flings her arm over her eyes, lets out a strangled, 'I hate you!' and runs upstairs, sobbing loudly.

Evie starts to cry.

The two waiters stand in the doorway leading to the morning room, each holding a tray of champagne glasses.

'Oh bugger it,' I mutter, and walk across, helping myself to two of them.

'You really went all out,' Richard said, laughing. I'm so happy he's on my side, for the first time lately, that I have the best evening since Chloe showed up.

Chloe sulked and refused to come out of her room no matter how hard Richard tried to coax her. We sent the waiters home and dined on minted lamb koftas with yogurt dressing and Italian arancini balls with bacon. We gave Simon the plates of Prosciutto-wrapped pear with rocket and pomegranate jam because they wouldn't keep, along with cold meats and cheeses, a whole salmon and god knows what else. We put what we could in the freezer then I gorged myself on Black Forest cake and champagne.

That night Richard returned to the bedroom with me. He didn't even argue when I said I wanted to keep Evie in the cot with us. 'She sleeps so much better here,' I said. Which was the truth, although I didn't say the real reason was that I was afraid to leave her alone in the nursery. I nestled into his arms.

'I guess it was just a misunderstanding on her part,' he whispered.

I knew it wouldn't last forever, but still, I didn't expect him to turn so quickly. I swallowed a sigh and let it go. I'd had such a good night, it may as well have been my birthday, and I wasn't going to spoil it.

Chapter Twenty-One

'She did it on purpose,' I say to Richard. It's the following morning and I'm still over the moon that for once Richard took my side. When we got up and went downstairs, we found the Harrods gift card where we'd left it on the mantelpiece. She'd cut it up into little pieces and put it back inside its envelope. I didn't know whether to laugh or shudder.

'She's so fucking spoiled,' Richard muttered when I showed him. I was shocked at his reaction. Richard very rarely swears.

It's a lovely crisp day and we're walking in the gardens, Evie in the pram, Oscar walking by Richard's side.

I love these walks Richard and I take around the grounds. I'm always incredulous that it all belongs to us. There seems to be so much of it. Two acres of green lush lawns, beautiful flower beds, chestnut trees, views for days. We stop by the fishpond while Richard digs into his pocket and sprinkles some food for the fish. Normally he'd call them, by their names. Yes, my goofy, wonderful husband named our fish when we first got them and assures me the right one comes when called, which makes me laugh since they all look the same.

But he doesn't call them today. That doesn't stop them from rushing to the surface and snapping up whatever food there is.

'She did what on purpose?'

I bump his shoulder. 'You know what. Tell me the wrong day! That it was today!' I open my eyes wide. 'Can you imagine if you hadn't brought it up yesterday morning? The drama? A dozen people showing up for a party I did absolutely nothing to prepare for? That's what she wanted, you know. To humiliate me. She really does hate me.' Then I wonder, does she even have a dozen friends? Or ten? Or *any*?

I turn to look at Richard. A vein throbs on the side of his neck.

'So what you are saying is that you think Chloe *deliberately* told you the wrong day.' His tone is icy. His words have come out through gritted teeth. That's exactly what I'm saying. I thought I was pretty clear.

But maybe I shouldn't have said anything. Anyway, it's too late now. I square my shoulders.

'I'm afraid so. Just like that time when she accused me of not telling her I needed her help with Evie while I worked. Or when we arranged to meet outside the grocer and she went to the car instead, then insisted that's what I'd said. Or the time when—'

He stops walking. 'What the hell is wrong with you? You've been forgetting things, Joanne. And that's fine, these things happen, but I think you need to take responsibility, don't you? It's a little childish and vindictive frankly, to blame Chloe for your mistakes. Including that you got the wrong day for the birthday party. It was childish of Chloe to make a song and dance about it, I agree, but you can't keep blaming her for *your* mistakes.'

'But what I mean is—'

'I don't care what you mean,' he snaps, turning around. He had picked up another stick for Oscar but he throws it angrily to the side. He takes a stride toward the house but I hold him back, my hand on his arm.

'Wait! Richard, please!'

He turns around and takes my face in his hands. 'It's not like you. I'm starting to get very worried about you.'

My eyes prickle with tears. 'You don't know what it's like. She—'

But he doesn't let me finish. 'What? What's what like? I provide you with everything you desire. I don't ask anything in return, except this one thing!' He shakes a finger near my face. 'Make my daughter feel welcome and at home. But you keep accusing her of sabotage! And that's just wrong!'

He narrows his eyes at me. 'You're tired, Joanne. All the time. You're not thinking straight, that's the problem. You should let Chloe take more of the load. She says you don't trust her with Evie. Is that true?'

I'm astonished he's asking me that question, considering I've been saying exactly that for days. *I don't trust her with Evie.* I close my eyes and lean into his chest. *You tell Dad you've changed your mind and I get to stay and look after Evie, okay? Or else…*

'No, it's fine. I trust her,' I say.

Later I check the camera application. I've locked myself in my bathroom and I'm sitting on the edge of the bathtub. I jump straight to the point where the camera identifies movement. There's a lot of it, obviously. We all live in and move around this house. I've reviewed it all before so I speed through the recordings of me and Richard, many of me coming into the nursery, two of them when Richard went to change her. I fast-forward, and then I sit up abruptly. Something I've missed, from yesterday. Chloe came into the nursery when Richard and I were downstairs. I take Evie with me at night — I have for the last few nights — but until I go to bed, I leave her in the nursery. I check the timestamp. It was at 6:32 p.m. Richard and I were in the morning room, sipping champagne and piling small plates high with finger food. I must've been looking away from the monitor at that exact moment.

I watch with horror as Chloe reaches down into the cot. I know it's irrational since of course I've been with Evie almost non-stop since then, so I know she's fine, but I can't help it. As I watch the footage, my hand flies over my mouth. For a terrible moment, I think she's reaching for her throat.

'There, there, sweet little baby girl,' Chloe says softly. She picks her up out of the cot and gently holds her against her shoulder, walking her around the room as Evie buries her face into Chloe's neck. She's not crying, just grizzly. At this point it's usually best to leave her and wait.

I can't stop watching, as Chloe holds her so tenderly, so gently, it's almost a shock. She sings a lullaby to her. I strain to hear. 'There were ten in the bed and the little one said…' I recognise it as the one Richard often sings to Evie. She quickly settles down.

Chloe gently lowers her back into the cot and brings the blanket up to her shoulders. She waits a few minutes, caressing Evie's head softly, then she leaves the room. The whole scene takes no longer than five minutes.

I have no idea what's going on anymore.

Chapter Twenty-Two

It's Monday, which means I'm working today. Chloe even mentioned it over breakfast and I could feel Richard's gaze on me.

'So I'll be looking after Evie today, is that right?' she asked. I was about to reply when she added, 'I wouldn't want to get the wrong date.'

I swallow a sigh. 'Yes, that's right,' I said. 'I'll need you to look after Evie for a few hours.' There was nothing else I could say, especially since I'd received the results back from the lab this morning. The email popped up on my phone at seven o'clock while Richard was in the shower. I was sitting up in bed, staring at my phone, which was something I'd been doing all night anyway, going back over the footage that had been recorded to date. There's some of Richard feeding Evie in the living room and it's so beautiful I had to replay it about twenty times. He looks at her with such love it made my eyes water. Then I spent hours re-watching the scene in the nursery with Chloe. I'd be lying if I didn't admit that I wanted to find something, something I'd missed before. Something I could show Richard that would make him see the real Chloe. But no matter how hard I tried, I couldn't find anything. She was just sweet, tender, and caring.

I know it's not me who's going mad, but if Chloe hadn't shown me that stupid doctored photo, I would definitely be thinking I need my head examined. My grandmother used to tell me my mother started by getting suspicious about the smallest things. She'd walk around the neighbourhood holding me tight, her eyes darting everywhere like she was expecting people to jump from behind tree trunks and snatch me out of her arms. If it hadn't been for the doctored photo, I'd think I was going the same way.

I opened the report with my heart beating in my throat and read through a list of ingredients that meant absolutely nothing to me. *Sorbitol, propylene glycol, methyl parahydroxybenzoate* … and I wanted to scream at the screen, *But which one is the poison?*

Then, at the end of the summary, one line: *All contents consistent with the product branded as CALPOL Infant Suspension.*

Brilliant. So it *is* me. I really am going mad.

After breakfast I let Chloe change Evie's nappy under my watchful gaze and I have to admit she does a great job. She's gentle and at ease, and Evie can't take her adoring eyes off her. Chloe snaps the nappy into place and Evie giggles with pure joy at her. Then after her feed she goes straight to sleep — unheard of — and I get ready for work.

'How are you this morning, Jo?' Shelley asks from the screen. Ben hasn't joined us yet, he's running late apparently, and Shelley just wants to run me through a couple of things.

'I'm well, thanks, and you?'

She frowns at me, leaning slightly into the screen, like she wants to get a closer look at me. 'You really okay?'

'Yes,' I say brightly. 'Why do you ask?'

She tilts her head. 'You look a bit pale.' Which is a polite way to say I look terrible. I tried to get rid of the dark rings under my eyes this morning by slapping on makeup, but I think I just made it worse.

Suddenly Ben comes on, and Shelley gives me a quick rundown of instructions, which I listen to with only one ear because Evie has woken up. Shelley leaves the meeting, and Ben more or less repeats what she said. I position my phone with the app loaded so I can keep an eye on Evie. Then Chloe walks into the room.

'Is everything all right, Joanne?' Ben asks.

I look up abruptly. 'Yes! Why?'

'You haven't answered my question.'

'Sorry. Yes. Give me a sec.' I frantically try to remember the question. Something about the valuer. Would I be able to liaise directly with them? Yes. That was it.

'You want me to talk to the valuer for the Dennis Street property. That's no problem.'

'Good.'

Ben keeps talking and I pretend to make notes so I can look away and at my phone. I can't stop staring. I can feel Ben growing annoyed with me, but there's nothing I can do. Chloe has picked Evie up. I have the sound right down, but I can still hear her humming to Evie. That same nursery rhyme again. *There were ten in the bed, and the little one said…*

'Joanne?'

Still humming, Chloe turns around, patting Evie's back. There's a split second where she looks right at the camera, right at me.

I draw back.

'You still with me, Joanne?'

'Yes, one sec.'

Does Chloe know I've put a camera there? It was only fleeting. Maybe she just happened to look at the teddy bear, that's all. Meanwhile Evie has calmed down and now lays her head on Chloe's shoulder. She puts Evie back in her cot and leaves the nursery. Evie goes to sleep and still I can't stop watching even as Ben tries to get my attention. He's getting irritated with me. I'm not concentrating. I'm not on the job.

Finally, we end the video meeting and I rush to the nursery. Evie is fast asleep, her little eyes fluttering with whatever dream she's having. I kiss her cheek and let out a long breath.

That night at dinner — beef Bourguignon followed by lemon tart, I should have been working but I ended up cooking all afternoon — Richard is in an especially good mood, chatting to Chloe who has gone back to her girly happy self, at least when she's around her father.

I bring out the lemon tart.

'And what about you, Jo?' Richard says. 'Tell me about your day.'

'It was very good, thank you. Busy.'

'They are very lucky to have you,' he says gravely. 'What would Shelley have done if you hadn't been available?'

I cut a piece of tart for Richard, put it on his plate. 'They would have hired someone else, probably.'

'But you're the one who asked for the job, didn't you?' Chloe pipes up.

I stare at her. 'What do you mean?'

But Richard replies to her. 'Shelley was desperate for staff. She asked Joanne to work two days a week to help them out.'

I cut another piece of tart for Chloe.

'Huh! That's not what Roxanne says.' She takes the plate from me.

I'm so shocked for a moment I can't speak. 'Why would Roxanne tell you that?' I say when I find my voice again.

'I don't know. She was just making conversation.'

'Making conversation? What does that mean? Are you two talking about me behind my back?'

Richard's head jerks back. 'Joanne!'

Chloe tilts her head at me. 'Are you all right, Joanna? Did I say the wrong thing?'

'It's—'

'I'm sorry if I said the wrong thing, but Roxanne was asking me what prompted you to move out here since you always act so bored out of your mind.'

My jaw drops. 'Bored?'

'Well, aren't you? She says you never do anything but watch her clean. I told her Dad keeps saying this is your dream house and your dream life and you love it out here, or that's what Dad says anyway. She said she heard you tell your old boss you wanted your old job back because you were going crazy with boredom out here.'

'She said that?'

Richard frowns at me. 'Is that true?'

'No! I mean, not exactly! I didn't say *that*!' But my face feels hot, and I bet I look like a beetroot right now. I remember that day. Roxanne was here. She must have overheard even with those earbuds plugged into her ears. Why did I feel the need to lie to Richard? Why didn't I just tell him I'd like a bit of work now and then, keep my brain engaged? He wouldn't have cared either way. He just wants me to be happy.

Chloe carefully cuts her lemon tart. 'I mean, I was surprised. Because I don't think Dad wants this life, do you, Dad?'

'What are you saying?' I ask.

'After everything that happened, it must be horrible to live out here in a big house like this. I know you're unhappy, Daddy. I can see it. Maybe she can't, but I can.'

'That's not true,' Richard says, frowning, although not as forcefully as I would have liked.

'It must be unbearable,' she says, popping a forkful of tart into her mouth.

'Unbearable?' I blurt.

'I know you're fond of Evie, Daddy. We all are. But you didn't want another kid, did you, Daddy? I know you didn't. Not after everything that happened.'

'*Fond of* Evie?'

She turns to me. 'I know it's not what you want to hear, Joanna—'

'Actually it's—'

'—but he's my dad, and I'm just trying to look out for him. Because it's just not fair. It's not personal, is what I'm trying to say.'

'Chloe, sweetheart. That's enough.'

'How can you live like this after what happened with Mum?' Chloe says.

'What happened with your Mum?' I ask.

She looks at me, genuine surprise on her face. 'You don't know?'

Richard looks ill. He drags his hands down his face.

'You didn't tell her? Oh, wow. I really think you should tell her, Daddy.'

'Tell me what?'

'It's too much for you. It's not fair that you should sacrifice yourself like that, for her.'

'Can somebody please tell me what's going on?'

'Chloe, sweetheart. Can you get some icing sugar from the pantry, please?' Richard says.

I turn to him. 'That's all you have to say? You want icing sugar?'

Richard puts his hand on my arm. 'It's on the top shelf,

isn't it? Go and have a look, sweetheart. I'm sure you'll find it.'

Chloe pushes her chair back and leaves the room.

'What are you doing?' I ask.

'I want Chloe out of the room for a moment. She's a very emotional girl. Always has been.' He pauses, rakes his fingers through his hair. 'There are some things I haven't told you.'

'Like what?'

Chloe appears in the doorway. She's holding a small white cube in her hand.

'What's this?'

I close my eyes.

Chapter Twenty-Three

'You've been spying on us?' Richard bellows.

I don't think I've ever seen him so angry. Not even when I told him about kissing Anthony at that Christmas party.

He pounds the table with his fist. 'Answer me!'

Chloe is smirking in the background.

I take a breath. 'I was just being cautious because of Evie and I being alone out here most of the time,' I say. After all, Richard was the one who always insisted on the extra security. I remind him of that now.

He turns to Chloe. 'Can you wait for me in your room, please?'

She hesitates for a moment. Her face has gone back to that mask-like expression. I have no idea how she feels about the cameras around the house, or even if she feels at all.

In fact, I wonder if she always knew.

She leaves the room and Richard sits back down heavily, dropping his forehead in his hands.

'I'm sorry,' I say. 'I didn't mean…'

He narrows his eyes at me. 'You're always sorry, Joanne!

You are so paranoid that you've been spying on us, in my own house! You think sorry is going cut it?'

'I wasn't spying on you.'

He shakes his head at me. 'You should be ashamed of yourself.'

'I was worried!' I glance towards the door for moving shadows. 'I thought she wanted to harm Evie,' I whisper.

'Harm Evie? Again? What is wrong with you? How long have you had them up? How many?'

'Not long,' I mumble. 'I only just put them up.'

He grabs a glass from the table and smashes it against the wall. I jump in my chair.

'You've been spying on my daughter in my own house? Where are they? The cameras you've been hiding?'

I tell him where the one is in the nursery. He grabs a bin liner from the kitchen drawer and angrily drops the one Chloe found into it.

'What are you doing?'

'What does it look like I'm doing. These are going in the bin.'

I follow him as he stomps up the stairs.

'Please don't wake Evie,' I plead.

But it's like he doesn't hear me. He's mumbling to himself. 'Spying on my own daughter, in my own house. You should be ashamed of yourself.' He tears open the teddy bear and throws it on the floor. Evie's eyes snap open and sure enough, her mouth distorts and she starts to wail.

'Chloe?' I call out as we walk past her closed door. 'Can you help with Evie, please?'

'Oh, now you want Chloe to help!' Richard snaps.

Chloe opens her door. 'That's okay, I'll do it.'

'How dare you?' Richard mumbles as he runs down the stairs. I run after him. When he reaches the bottom, he turns to me and puts out his hand.

'Your phone.'

'What for?' I whine.

'I want to see the app. I want to check if you've lied to me about how many cameras you've put up.'

I go into the kitchen and hand him my phone. I'm shaking. 'I didn't lie,' I say.

'Like hell you haven't,' he snaps. 'I can't trust anything you say. I don't even know who you are anymore.' He stabs at my screen and hands my phone back. 'I've deleted it. If you ever do that again, if you ever hide cameras around this house without discussing it with me first, I ....' He runs his fingers through his hair. 'I don't know what I'll do, Jo. I really don't.'

Then he goes outside and shoves the bag into the bin.

Later, after he has calmed down, we sit at the kitchen table. I'm still shaking. I wipe my nose with a napkin.

'You must see that she hates me.'

'Hates you?' He looks at me like I've got two heads. 'How can you say that? She doesn't hate you! She's really fond of you!'

Oh god. 'You say that, but you heard her this evening! She's trying to put a wedge between us. Accusing you of not wanting to be here, not wanting to have another baby... What did she mean about Diane? You said there were things you haven't told me. What things?'

He rubs his cheeks, looks up at the ceiling. 'Officially, they ruled Diane's death as suicide.'

My jaw drops. 'Suicide? But you told me she died of cancer!'

'I certainly did not. You made that assumption.'

'But you said she was ill, that she died after a long illness.'

'Yes, because she was. She was very depressed. She was drinking too much. It had been going on for a while.'

'I can't believe what I'm hearing. Why didn't you tell me this?'

He rubs two fingers over his eyes. 'Because I don't like to talk about it. Is that so difficult for you to comprehend?'

I twist my ring around my finger, trying to make sense of what he just said. 'How *did* she die?'

'The house where we lived had a full-height galleried entrance hall. Diane fell over the third-floor balustrade. She landed head-first on the tiled floor below. She died on impact.'

'Oh my god.'

His eyes fill with tears. 'I knew she was unwell; I knew she was drinking. I had to go away to this conference but I called every day, at least twice a day. I wanted to make sure everything was all right, you see? I called that day. I called multiple times but Diane didn't answer. I assumed they'd gone out. I should have called one of the neighbours, asked them to drive over and make sure.'

'You couldn't have known.' Now I feel terrible for making him bring it all up again. I hold his hand and we sit quietly for a moment. 'It must have been shockingly horrible for Chloe,' I say softly.

'It was.' He squeezes my hand. 'Chloe is a good girl, she really is. I wish you could see that.'

I sigh. 'You heard her at dinner. She was begging you to admit you never wanted another child. At least she conceded you're fond of Evie,' I add, wryly.

He turns to me and studies my face. 'It was a very strange thing to do, Jo. Hiding cameras around the house to spy on her. I just don't understand how you could do that.'

'Look, I'm very sorry for what Chloe went through. I really am. Especially since I had no idea and frankly, I wish you'd told me. But she's an adult now.' I drop my voice. 'She told me I should leave this house and that she would stay forever and do everything she could to make my life hell.'

'Okay. That's it.' He stands up abruptly. 'I want you to see Dr Fletcher.' Something in his tone tells me he's not joking.

'I'm not making it up, Richard. I'm not …. like that.'

'You think you're not, but you are!' he barks. 'You don't know what you're saying!' From the way he looks at me, for a moment I wonder if he wouldn't do to me what our neighbour Mrs Delaney did to my mother: start a process that resulted in my mother being sectioned. Which would be outrageous. I mean, Mrs Delaney meant well, and she did the right thing. Whereas I'm not crazy.

Right?

Chapter Twenty-Four

That night Richard and I are lying in bed, in the dark. I'm wide awake, staring at the ceiling. We've barely spoken since our argument earlier. I thought he'd gone to sleep when he says, 'Maybe Chloe is a bit jealous that I've remarried.'

Honestly at this point it feels like I've been crawling in the desert for days and he's just handed me a bottle of water. The gratitude I feel is overwhelming.

'A bit?' I say, trying to keep my tone light. 'She wants you to admit you are miserable as hell in this marriage. Are you miserable as hell, Richard?'

'She didn't mean that.'

Well, that didn't last long. 'Are you?'

He props himself on one elbow. 'Look into my eyes, Joanne. I love you, I love my family, I love my life with you. You've made me happier than I've been in years. Decades.'

'So you don't miss Isabella?'

He flinches. 'Isabella? What the hell does she have to do with anything?'

I pick at the blanket. 'I know she regrets ending things with you.'

'So? That's her problem.'

'So you don't miss her?'

'God no.'

'You don't see her?'

'No! What on earth brought that on? I haven't seen Isabella since she ended things between us.' He rests his head on the palm of his hand. 'Why are you so worried about Isabella all of a sudden?'

'I don't know. I'm not really, it's just…' I let out a sigh. 'Chloe told me you still loved Diane. That you still miss her.'

'Wait a minute. I thought it was Isabella I was pining for.'

'Do you? Still love Diane?'

'Jo, sweetheart, listen to me. I love you. Only you.'

'That's not an answer.'

'Fine. I don't miss Diane. I don't still love Diane. I can't imagine Chloe would say such a thing.'

'I didn't make it up—'

'I've spoiled Chloe in the past, that's true. I've tried to make up for what happened to her when she was little. She never expected me to marry again, let alone start another family, but that's not the point. The point is, she wouldn't touch a hair on Evie's head. You have to know that.'

I nod. 'I do. I've seen her with Evie. She's very sweet to her.'

He lets out a breath. 'You say that now, but considering you put up cameras around the house, and the scene in the bathroom the other night when you accused her of …' He sighs. 'It's a lot, Jo.'

'I know.'

'Tell me you don't believe Chloe would poison Evie. I need to hear you say it.'

'I don't believe Chloe would poison Evie.'

'Promise me you'll see Dr Fletcher.'

I raise my eyes to the ceiling.

'Promise me.'

'I promise.'

Dr Caroline Fletcher can't see me until the following Thursday morning. When I tell Richard, he is pleased.

'And I'll take the day off work to look after Evie while you're gone.'

'Really? I was going to bring her with me. It's only up the road.'

He takes my face in his hands. He looks so much older even than yesterday. A whole lot of new grey hair seems to have sprouted overnight.

'I don't want you to worry. I want you to know I'm here and I will care for Evie.'

'Thank you.' I nod into his chest. 'The whole day?'

'Yes.'

'In that case, would you mind if I went to London? I need to do some shopping. And I could have lunch with Robyn if she's free.'

'I think that's an excellent idea,' he says.

For the next three days, I do my best to be nice to Chloe. Partly to appease Richard, partly because now that I know what happened to her when she was little, I can't help but feel it's not *all* her fault, that she's so screwed up.

I ask her if she'd like to feed Evie, then I tell her what a great job she's doing. On Wednesday Roxanne calls to says she can't make it and that she'll come on Friday instead. I tell her that's no problem. After lunch Chloe takes off on my bicycle, without asking, and doesn't return until dark. That's no problem, I tell her, but she's already gone upstairs. Over dinner Richard asks Chloe what she got up to today, and she mumbles something about going to the village, to see a *friend*, she adds pointedly. Then she looks at me, her bottom lip wobbling. Richard shoots me a look, like he's caught me drowning puppies.

I remind myself they're both a little broken and I need to be patient.

When Dr Fletcher asks me what the problem is, I tell her I've been feeling anxious lately. She asks me a few questions to clarify if anything brought that on. I mention my husband's daughter is staying with us for a few weeks. It's a big deal, I explain, since they haven't spoken in almost two years. I don't mention that apparently that's my fault, even though I never said or did anything to her. 'We're all getting to know each other,' I say.

Dr Fletcher nods. 'Look, everything you describe is perfectly normal,' she says. 'It sounds like having your step-daughter staying with you is a big disruption, and to Evie's routine too, no doubt. I wouldn't worry about it. How long is she staying for?'

'I'm not sure. Indefinitely?' As I say the word, my stomach drops. How long is indefinitely anyway? A month? A year?

Forever?

My throat constricts. Dr Fletcher frowns. 'I'll prescribe something to ease the anxiety.' She scribbles on her notepad.

'Thank you,' I say. At least I'll be able to show Richard when I get home. See? I'm taking something for my condition, whatever that is.

'Anything else you want to discuss?' she asks as she hands me the prescription.

'No,' I say.

. . .

As I drive to the station for my lunch date with Robyn, I'm almost tempted to turn around and go home to check on Evie.

But I don't. Richard has it all under control. I do call, check everything is fine. When Richard picks up I can hear Evie giggling in the background.

'Have fun,' he says. 'And say hi to Robyn for me.'

Chapter Twenty-Five

Robyn and I chat about everything and nothing while we wait for our food. Robyn asks to see up-to-the-minute videos of Evie, and we both coo and ahh over my phone.

'There she is! Oh look at her! She's become even more adorable! My favourite goddaughter!'

'Your only goddaughter,' I say. She smiles, still watching the screen. It's only when the waiter brings our salads that she passes the phone back to me.

'So how's everything? You look tired. Is Evie still not sleeping?'

'On and off. You know how it is.'

'I remember only too well,' she says. 'Hang in there. It'll be over soon. Then you'll have a whole new set of problems.' She laughs. 'And how is your stepdaughter?'

I bite my bottom lip. 'I'm worried, Rob.'

'Why? What happened?'

It's like the floodgates have opened inside my mouth. I tell her all about Chloe, her rudeness, the way she is with me. I can't stop talking. 'She treats me like I'm the evil step-mother who took her dad away from her. She can't stand me, seriously. Whenever I point out that since she's the babysitter, maybe she should babysit, she looks at me like I've just asked her to scrub the floor with a toothbrush. Richard says I'm paranoid. That's because every time Richard is around, she's as sweet as pie.'

I tell Robyn about the birthday party, how she told me the wrong date and if Richard hadn't brought it up that morning, it would have been an even worse disaster. 'That's the only time he acknowledged she's a bit spoiled.' I roll my eyes. 'And he still doesn't believe she did it on purpose. Everything is a misunderstanding as far as he's concerned. He's such an indulgent father. I understand he's thrilled to have her back in his life but still, she's twenty-one years old. She's an adult, although you'd never know it. She behaves like daddy's twelve-year-old little girl when he's around. So he thinks the problem is with me. That I see the worst in her. He actually thinks I might be paranoid like my mother.'

'Did he say that?'

'Let's just say he hints strongly at it.' I lean forward, conspiratorially. 'She's very good. Very cunning. You know what she did the other day? She Photoshopped a photo of me and Simon—'

'Simon?'

'The gardener. To make it look like I was kissing him.'

'What?' Robyn drops her fork. 'Did you tell Richard?'

I rub my forehead. 'Well, no. Not yet. You know what Richard can be like. I need to find the right moment.'

She's about to say something but I interrupt her.

'And there's something else. The first time she held Evie, she completely freaked out. She wanted me to take her back right away. She acted like she was terrified of her.'

'What?'

'And she didn't want me to tell Richard about it. So I didn't. But then a few days later, I found her in the middle of the night in the little bathroom off the nursery doing god knows what with bottles of Calpol because Evie was crying.'

'Oh my god! Jo! Is that what you had analysed?'

'Yes! But it was fine, it was just Calpol.'

'This is scary. I think she needs to move out pronto,' Robyn says.

'Well, yes, that would be nice. But it's not going to happen. Richard wants her to stay.'

She shakes her head. 'You have to convince him.'

'I'd like to, but I can't. And then Richard told me that Diane committed suicide. All this time I thought she'd died of cancer.'

'What? My god! How did she die?'

I shudder. 'They lived in a big old house, three storeys high, with a big central full-height hall and galleries running all the way around on each floor. Richard was away on a conference in Spain, and Diane jumped from one of the upper landings. She died instantly.'

'Oh god. That's horrible. How old was Chloe?'

'Eleven. But that's not even the worst of it.'

'There's more?'

I nod. 'They were living miles from anyone else. So she sat with her dead mother for hours before someone found them.'

Robyn clasps her hand over her mouth. 'Why didn't she call someone? The police? Anyone? They must have had a phone, surely.'

'I don't know. She was in shock, I guess.' We both stay silent for a moment. 'I know she's been through a lot. I can see why she would be possessive of her father, but still.' I shake my head. 'I'm trying to be more understanding, but it's hard.'

'She sounds unhinged, Jo.'

'I know, but somehow I'm the one who always looks bad.'

I tell her about Chloe finding the camera I'd hidden in the pantry. 'Richard was livid, as you can imagine. He made me take them all down and throw them away.'

'But did you see anything? When they were up?' she breathes.

'You know what's funny? I've seen the footage of Chloe when she's alone with Evie in the nursery, and she couldn't be sweeter. She's very gentle with her.'

"You don't think she knew you put them up?'

'I don't think so.'

She puts her hand out. 'Can I see?'

'Richard deleted the app.' But then I think of Chloe's gaze falling on the teddy and staying there just a second longer than necessary. Could she have known? Has she been so sweet to Evie because she knew I was watching?

'I don't know what to do, Rob.'

'You have to get her out. That's all there is to it.'

I feel my eyes water.

'What? What did I say?'

'It's just that you're the only person who is listening to me. You're the only one who understands.' I wipe a tear with my fingers. 'And you know what else?' I tell her about the baby photo I found in Chloe's suitcase. 'Not of Evie, thank god. That would be seriously weird. She says it's a photo of herself. Don't you think that's odd? Who carries a baby photo of themselves around like that?'

Robyn shakes her head. 'Something is very wrong.'

'Exactly. But Richard—'

'Oh, screw Richard. Trust your instincts. Remember Lucille from school?'

'Of course I do.' Lucille was a friend of ours from the same class.

'Remember that day we waited for her after school and she didn't show? And we waited and waited and I wanted to go home. I'd had enough. I thought she'd gone already. Remember that?'

I nod.

'But you had a feeling. You wouldn't budge. You thought something was wrong. That's what you said. Something isn't right, I have a bad feeling. So we went looking for her and it turned out she got herself locked in the fire escape. On a Friday afternoon. Remember that?'

'Of course.' Poor Lucille. She was in a complete state of panic. She thought she'd be stuck until Monday, and she probably would have been. She was sure she'd starve to death and die before she was found.

'You've got good instincts, Jo. You always have done. Trust them. Do what you have to, to get her out of your house.'

'But how?'

'I don't know, Jo. But you'll figure it out. I know you will.'

Chapter Twenty-Six

Richard is feeding Evie in the living room when I get back. They're staring at each other with complete adoration, so much so that they don't hear me come in until Oscar approaches me, his tail wagging against the bookcase.

Richard looks up. 'How did it go?'

'Good. It was good.' I mumble something about getting a prescription, then something else about lunch with Robyn. 'Where's Chloe?'

'Out, with her friend.'

'Roxanne?'

'Yes, that's the one. Tell me what the doctor said.'

'She gave me something to take. To help with the anxiety.' I show him the tablets I picked up from the chemist on the way home.

He nods gravely. 'Good, good. Why don't you take one and have a lie-down?'

Why would I have a lie-down? I don't want a lie-down. I've been thinking about what Robyn said all the way home: *Trust your instincts, Jo. And get her out of your house.*

I stand up from the couch. 'Dr Fletcher gave me some

meditation videos to look up,' I lie. 'I'm going to do that now. Then I'll have a rest.'

'Good idea,' Richard says. 'While you do that, I'm going to spend time with my little angel until she needs her nap.' He holds Evie up so she's standing on his thighs. She laughs and does a little shuffle on the spot.

'I love you,' I say, kissing his head.

He smiles warmly at me. 'I love you too, Jo. We'll be fine, you'll see. You'll get well again soon.'

At my computer, I open a browser window and type in Diane's name. The first article I find is an item on a local news website published the week after her death in November 2013. It doesn't have much information, just that a woman had fallen from a third-floor balcony in her house near Basildon and died instantly.

I'd never seen pictures of the house before. It's stunning. There's a picture of the three-storey, cathedral-style hall, clearly taken from an estate agent's website. It's a shock to see just how big the hall was.

Essex woman, 35, dies after fall from balcony.

A 35-year-old woman has died in her home after falling from a third-floor balcony. The accident happened while the woman's husband was in Madrid, Spain. Present was the couple's only daughter, aged eleven. The woman was not found until early the following morning, approximately nine hours after her fall, when a local grocer arrived at the house with a delivery.

Police say the woman's death is being treated as suspicious.

I sit back. Suspicious? That's the first I've heard of it. First Richard said Diane's death was after a long illness, then it was suicide. He certainly never mentioned it was suspicious.

The article ends there, but I find another one published four months later in the same paper. That one says that initially, the police thought there might have been an intruder because that's what the young daughter had said. She'd heard someone else in the house, and she thought she'd seen a man dressed in black in the upper balcony just before her mother fell, although she wasn't completely sure. However, after an investigation revealed no evidence of another person in the house, including reviewing footage from outside security cameras and the fact that the doors were locked from the inside, this, coupled with the young age and the state of shock of the witness, led police to dismiss the allegation.

An inquest at Essex Coroner's Court following a report from the post-mortem examination recorded the death as suicide.

The thing that bothers me reading this is: why would Diane do this when she was alone with her daughter? She must have known she was condemning her to a lifetime of grief. If she was really determined to kill herself, she should have done it so Richard found her, not her little girl.

But that's nothing compared to what comes next. I am so shocked by what I learn that I don't hear Richard come in.

'I've just put Evie down,' he says behind me. 'She was so tired, poor little mite.'

I turn around, feeling the blood drain from my face.

'Why didn't you tell me?'

'Tell you what?'

'That you and Diane had another baby?'

Chapter Twenty-Seven

'Why didn't you tell me?'

We're in the living room. Richard has returned from the basement with a bottle of red wine and two large glasses. I am shocked to see how tired he looks. I wonder if it's because of Evie. Anyone would look that tired after a day with Evie.

Richard doesn't ask me if I want some wine. He just pours and hands me a glass. 'I know you're not meant to drink while you're on your medication…'

I didn't take any, but I don't tell him that. I take the glass. 'Thank you.'

He stands at the window, looking out. 'Why are you trawling through my past, Joanne?'

His icy tone makes my throat constrict. I swallow. 'I'm not trawling. I'm trying to understand more about Chloe.' Which in one way is the truth, but probably not in the way he thinks. 'I'm trying to get to know her better so we can grow closer and have a better relationship. And anyway, couples tell each other everything, don't they? I told you about growing up with a single mother, and you told Chloe.

Which is fine, by the way, but Chloe knows more about me than I do about you.'

'Was that your doctor's idea? This sudden need to understand Chloe?'

'You haven't answered me,' I say, sidestepping the question. 'You had another child who died. I can't believe you never told me.'

He hesitates for a moment, then sits on the couch next to me. 'Can't you? Jo, my love.' He is no longer angry. He kisses the palm of my hand. 'Why would I tell you? It's the saddest part of my life. And it was a long time ago. I don't like thinking about it. And when you got pregnant with Evie, it wouldn't have occurred to me to tell you. Would you really have wanted to know then that I'd lost a daughter?'

'Yes. If the roles were reversed and I'd lost a baby, wouldn't you want to know?'

'Honestly? No. If you were over it, and it was a long time ago, I wouldn't need to know.'

I find that very hard to believe. But maybe this is a case of men being from Mars and women being from Venus. I know Richard doesn't have the same need to share that I have. I like to tell Richard everything. Well, I used to anyway. Before I started to leave things out, like getting bottles of Calpol tested for deadly poisons.

I rearrange myself on the sofa so I'm leaning back against the armrest and facing him.

'What was her name?'

He stares into his glass. 'Sophie.'

'Sophie,' I repeat. 'That's a pretty name.'

Richard takes a sip of his drink.

'The article said that it was a cot death.'

'Yes. It was very sudden, as these things are.'

I take his hand and give it a squeeze. 'I'm sorry. How old was she?'

'Three months old.'

'Oh my god! I just assumed…'

'What?'

'That she was much younger when she died. Just a few days old.'

'Do you think that would have made it any easier?' he asks through gritted teeth.

'No, of course not.'

He lets go of my hand and rubs his eyes with two fingers. 'Do you see why I didn't tell you? Why would I bring this nightmare into our lives? We have our own happy, healthy baby. There's no need to go back over the past.'

'There's another argument here, Richard. Maybe it would have been wise to tell me. So I could make sure, you know….'

'That it doesn't happen to Evie? You don't think I've thought of that?'

I understand now why he is so protective of Evie, why he put such care into choosing the right baby monitor, why he checks in on her day and night.

He shifts in his seat. 'Cot deaths are very rare these days. I didn't want you to worry. I worry enough for the two of us.'

'I'm so sorry, Richard. I still wish you'd told me. Especially with Chloe coming here. How old was she when it happened?'

'Didn't the article tell you?' he asks dryly.

'I don't know. You came in before I got to the end.'

'Chloe was eleven years old.'

'Eleven?' I try to make sense of what he's saying. 'You mean…'

'That's right. Sophie died not long before Diane. Just two months before in fact.'

'Oh god, how awful!'

He nods, staring into his glass.

'So that's quite a gap between the two girls. Ten years at least.'

'Sophie was a happy accident. Diane hadn't wanted another child and she was on birth control, but we turned out to be a statistic. The moment she found out she was pregnant, she was over the moon. We both were. But the pregnancy was difficult and Diane found it hard to cope. It only got worse after Sophie was born.'

'Worse how?'

He pinches the bridge of his nose. 'I was really busy, I was setting up my firm at that point, so I was away a lot. Diane became increasingly angry, short-tempered. She complained incessantly about Chloe, which was very unfair. She said Chloe wasn't adjusting to the new baby, even though Chloe clearly adored Sophie.'

'What did Chloe do, according to Diane?'

'Diane said that if she picked up Sophie, Chloe would scream at the top of her lungs and would not stop until Diane put Sophie down.'

'Oh wow. So how did Diane manage? I mean she had to pick up her baby! She could hardly let her starve in her dirty nappies!'

'Chloe went to school during the day and when I was at home, Chloe liked spending time with me. She would sit quietly in my office while I worked. But like I said, I never saw the behaviour that Diane described.'

Then he smiles to himself, like he's remembered something. 'There was this one time Chloe threw all of Sophie's toys and clothes into the bin. That did happen.'

'Wow, Richard, that actually sounds quite serious. It sounds more extreme than your usual sibling rivalry situation.'

'Diane was over-tired, that's all. You know what it's like.

She had a short fuse with Chloe.' He rakes his hand through his hair. I have to resist the urge to pat it back down.

'Maybe Diane was telling the truth,' I say softly. 'Maybe in front of you, Chloe was on her best behaviour. It sounds vaguely familiar,' I mumble.

He flashes me a look full of anger, but it dissipates almost immediately. He pats my hand. 'I'm not saying Chloe was a little angel, but you don't know what Diane was like. She found motherhood difficult. And then when Sophie died.... Well, you can imagine. Diane just couldn't deal with it. She couldn't get out of bed. It was like she'd given up on life. After about six or seven weeks, she started to get a little bit better. That conference was the first time I'd been away from them for more than a few hours.'

I put my hand on his cheek. 'It's not your fault, Richard.'

His eyes are suddenly full of anger. 'Of course it's my fault. I should never have left them alone. It was too early. I will never forgive myself. Never.'

I wonder suddenly if the fact that Richard never told me about Sophie has more to do with his guilt than his insistence that the past belongs in the past.

'There was nothing you could have done,' I say. 'You had to be away some time. You couldn't have guessed what was going to happen.'

'Couldn't I?' He knocks back the rest of his glass.

'No, Richard. You couldn't.'

'If you say so. Anyway, does that help you understand Chloe any better?'

I ignore the sarcasm in his tone and nod. 'She's had a traumatic childhood. Even more traumatic than I'd realised.'

'Exactly. You understand why I have to be gentle with her. You never recover from this kind of trauma. God knows we've tried. We did so much family therapy, me and her, but she never went back to her normal self. Not until she'd spent a couple of years at boarding school.'

'What are you guys talking about?'

We were so absorbed in our conversation that we didn't hear Chloe return. She is standing in the doorway, her hands deep in her pockets, leaning against the doorjamb. I smile at her. She doesn't smile back.

'We were just chatting,' I say. I turn to Richard. He's gone pale. He gives her a quivering smile.

I look at Chloe again. She's staring at her father, eyes narrowed. Richard disentangles himself from me.

'Would you like a glass of wine, sweetheart?' His tone is all wrong. It sounds forced, overly cheerful, and he won't meet my eye.

He knows. He knows what she's like, but he pretends he doesn't. Or maybe he is so much in denial that he can't bring himself to admit it. But one thing is suddenly very clear: he doesn't want to provoke her.

Chapter Twenty-Eight

Later, before we go to bed, I go back to my office and finish reading the article.

Just like Richard said, little Sophie died when she was three months old. Sophie's sudden death was the main reason the court cited when ruling Diane's death as suicide.

I sit back in my chair. Maybe I have been too harsh on Chloe. She's been through so much. First the death of her little sister, then the death of her mother in the most horrible circumstances. I can't believe Richard sent her to boarding school after all that, even if she was clingy or difficult, or whatever else. I understand he wanted her to have more friends, but she must have felt abandoned by the last remaining person in her life.

I make a decision. I'm going to get closer to Chloe. I'm going to show her that she has nothing to fear, that she is loved, and she has a place to live, a place to call home, for as long as she wants. She's had a hard time and there's a lot of work ahead of us, but I'm going to turn that young woman around. I'm going to make sure she's happy and well-adjusted, even if it kills me.

. . .

Roxanne has arrived for her cleaning day. I've got Evie in my arms with her little coat and beanie on, and I was about to go downstairs when Chloe meets Roxanne in the hall. She must have come from the living room.

'Let's go upstairs for a bit. You can clean later,' Chloe says.

'But what about Mrs A?' Roxanne asks.

'She won't care. She won't even know.'

'Know what?' I ask, even though I heard very well. I walk down the stairs. 'Chloe, I'm going to the farmers' market. Would you like to come with me? It's a lovely market. They have lots of locally made crafts you might like. You know, candles, scarves, that sort of thing.'

She looks at me for a moment, without expression. But I can see the bewilderment in her eyes. *Crafts? Candles? What?*

'You can go,' she says. 'I'll stay here with Evie.' She reaches for her, and Evie stretches her little arms, leaning toward her sister.

But I am determined. I bounce Evie in my arms. 'I'm taking Evie with me to the shops. Come with me, please. I'll buy you a coffee.'

'What for?'

'You know, just so us girls can have a nice chat.'

'Right, no thanks.' She turns back to Roxanne.

'I need your help with Evie then. While we're at the market.'

She does a little eye roll in Roxanne's direction. Roxanne pulls out her earbuds from her backpack and sticks them in her ears.

Twenty minutes later, because that's how long it takes to get out the door in this house, the three of us plus Oscar are in the car.

'Your dad was telling me about your mother,' I say. 'What was she like?'

She snaps her head around so fast, it's a miracle she stopped in time, before doing a full three-sixty turn.

'What do you care?'

'I'd like to know more about her. What was she like?'

She looks away, drags the tip of her finger on the window. 'She was normal. She was my mum. She was happy, and then she was sad. And then she died.'

'I'm sorry that happened, Chloe. I'm especially sorry you were there. It must have been very hard.'

'Yeah well, shit happens.'

If that had happened to me, I don't know that I would have classified the suicide of my mother and the fact that I was stuck with her dead body all night as *shit happens*, but then again, I didn't suffer like Chloe did. I'm sure she's had to come up with all sorts of ways to cope with her tragic past.

'You must miss her terribly.'

'Not really. And you know what? I don't really want to talk about my mum with you, okay?'

'I can understand that. So the photo that you have in your suitcase. The baby photo. It's not you, is it? It must be Sophie.'

I can feel the tension rise in the car. It's like the air has electrified. Anything could happen. I plough on. 'You must miss Sophie too.'

'How would I miss her? She was only three months old when she died. I don't even remember her. And what do you care, anyway?'

'I just don't know much about you, that's all.'

'So let's keep it that way.'

I swallow a sigh. 'Okay.'

'Rocket Man' by Elton John comes on through the speakers. I turn up the volume to show her that I don't mind. The conversation, for now, is over.

Chloe picks up my phone from where it sits between us. 'Sorry, but lame and I'm changing that. What's your passcode?'

I glance sideways at her.

'Passcode?'

'Yes.' She points to the speakers. 'So I can change the playlist.'

'We're only a few minutes away.'

'Exactly.'

I shake my head and turn down the volume. 'Seriously, Chloe. We don't have that far to go.' Also I'm not giving her my passcode.

'If you let me change the music, then we can talk about whatever you like,' she says.

'One five oh one.'

Her finger flicks around the screen and the music changes to some hip-hop song. Lil Wayne, according to the dashboard screen.

'Tell me about Sophie,' I ask over the noise.

She shifts in her seat. 'How about I ask you a few questions first?'

'Okay. Fair enough. Ask away.'

She lowers the volume. 'How did you meet my dad?'

I tell her about the house that he and Isabella almost bought.

'So when you met him, he was with someone else?'

'Yes.'

'Huh. Interesting. So what was she like, Isabella?'

'I don't know. I only met her twice.'

'Is she pretty?'

I feel my face flush. 'Yes.'

'What does she do?'

'She was a dancer. I think she has a dance studio now.'

'Wow. So she must have a hot body. What does she look like?'

I swallow a sigh. I don't really want to talk about Isabella, and I don't know why we are, but she's waiting for me to say something, with a mocking little smile on her lips.

'She has thick, dark curly hair, down to her shoulders.' I say briskly, shaking my fingers through my own thin hair to fluff it up a bit.

'Does she have nice skin?'

'Yes, she has nice skin. Peachy.' I think of my own skin, permanently grey from being tired all the time.

'So she's pretty?'

'Yes, I said that already. She's very pretty. I don't know what else to say, Chloe.'

'So why did he ditch her for you, then?'

'He didn't ditch her for me. She left him.'

'So do you love him?'

'Your dad? What kind of question is that? Of course I love him.'

'Like, really? You really *really* love him?'

'Yes, Chloe! I really *really* love him.'

'So you're never going to leave him?'

This time it's me who snaps my head around. 'Wait a second. I thought you wanted me to leave. Now you sound worried that I might.'

She smirks. 'No, I can't say that I'm worried.'

'Well, I'm not, never. Okay? I'm never ever leaving him. So deal with it.'

'You know he's having an affair, right?'

'Excuse me?'

'He's never home. He's always working. What does that tell you?'

'He has a very strong work ethic. And sometimes that requires him to travel.'

'But he comes home late every night.'

'No, he doesn't. And anyway, he's been home right after work every day you've been here, so I don't know what you're talking about.'

'And before I came?'

I blink a few times, scratch the tip of my nose. 'They're doing a big restructure at the office. He is very much in demand at the moment.'

'He's cheating on you, Joanne. My dad doesn't love you. Anybody can see that, except you.'

'Why the hell would you say such a thing? How would you know if he's having an affair?'

She snorts a laugh. 'For one, look at you! You're fat—'

'No, I'm not!'

'You're boring, you're sad, you're bored as well as boring. And you might tell yourself that he loves Evie but there's no way Dad wanted another baby.'

I slam on the brakes. I'm so angry I get out of the car and slam my door. Needless to say, Evie erupts into an ear-splintering wail. Chloe gets out with a smirk on her face that I feel like slapping off.

'Your father works very hard. But you know that already. He worked very hard when he was with your mother too. He was never home then either.'

She tilts her head at me. 'You don't know shit, Joanne. He's having an affair. She looks like a supermodel. She's tall and she's got really long legs and straight blonde hair and she's way younger than you.'

'Oh really! And I suppose you have photos to prove it?' I ask through my teeth.

'I just know, okay?'

'I don't believe you.'

'Well, it's a free country, so you do you.'

'Okay. You know what? You can make your own way home.'

We're in the village but I can't leave the car right here, so I get back in and drive it into the parking spot ten feet ahead then get out again.

I grab the buggy out of the boot and shake it the way I always do. And just like last time, it doesn't budge. Chloe reaches for it, but this time I yank it out of her reach.

'I've got it.' I press the button and the buggy gracefully unfolds itself. Meanwhile, Chloe stands there with her hands deep in her pockets. I ignore her and stick Evie in the buggy. She's still crying, reaching for Chloe, arms outstretched. I push her arms down.

I can't be bothered with the farmers' market. I stride across the road to the grocer and grab the first couple of things I see without even thinking about it. Which means I'm making something with cauliflower and green beans and cheese for dinner.

When I get back to the car, Chloe is leaning against it, smoking a cigarette.

'I thought you were walking home?' I snap.

'I never said that. You said that.'

'Exactly. I said that and I'm the one driving, so you better get going.'

'What, you want me to walk the six miles home?'

'That's what happens when you are rude to people, Chloe. There are consequences. I guess nobody explained that to you before.'

'Wow, you can be a real bitch sometimes.' She flicks her cigarette to the ground without bothering to stamp it out. 'You want me to walk home, get there at like ten o'clock tonight and tell my dad that you made me?'

She waits, one eyebrow raised. I purse my lips together.

'Get in the car.'

Chapter Twenty-Nine

I don't see Chloe for the rest of the day. I know that after Roxanne finished cleaning they locked themselves in Chloe's bedroom for the rest of the afternoon. I could hear them laughing in there before falling ominously silent and I wondered what they were plotting.

I can't wait for Richard to come home. I can't wait to tell him what his precious daughter said. It's all still boiling inside me when I call Shelley. She picks up on the first ring.

'Jo! Hi! What's up?' Her tone is snappy, professional. She sounds busy.

'Hi, I won't keep you…'

'No problem. Do you need something? Ben is around here somewhere… Can he help you with anything?'

'I wasn't calling about work... well, actually, I was, I am.'

'What's up?'

'Shelley, I'm sorry but things have changed here and I won't be able to continue doing the work at this time,' I say in one breath.

'You're kidding? Why?'

'I'm just having difficulties with the babysitter. I'm really sorry.'

'Oh! Okay, well, I'm sorry to hear it.'

I'm surprised she's taking it so well. Maybe she was dreading me working back with the agency, considering the stellar performance I've displayed so far. She's probably relieved.

'Thanks, Shelley. I know I'm letting you down...'

'Oh don't worry, Jo, it's always mad around here, you know that. Maybe when you find another babysitter we can try again.'

I'm in the nursery with a crying Evie in my arms when I see Roxanne take off on her bicycle. Then Richard sends a text saying he'll be late and he'll do his best to get home for dinner, but that we shouldn't wait for him, that I should have dinner with Chloe and he'll get something when he gets home.

Truly, I can't think of anything worse than having dinner alone with Chloe.

Richard comes home at about half past eight. I'm still in the nursery although thankfully Evie has calmed down. I walk out onto the landing with Evie in my arms just as Chloe comes bouncing down the stairs.

'Daddy! You're home!'

It's like some kind of ritual. She throws her arms around his neck like she hasn't seen him in days, and he laughs with pleasure. He looks up at me, still smiling as Chloe rests her head on his shoulder. I should be walking down the stairs, greeting my husband, but I can't move. I'm so angry with Chloe, and I'm upset about what she said about Richard having an affair. I know it's not true, since nothing Chloe says is true, but I want to tell Richard what she said. I want him to *know* what a nasty little thing she really is, behind that sweet display of affection. And then she can show him her fake picture of me and Simon and it won't have any currency, since Richard will know what an unremitting liar she is.

'Hi, Joanne,' Richard says, still smiling. Then his expression darkens. 'Everything okay? You look upset.'

I know how this looks. Not good. I'm standing at the top of the stairs, looking down at them, looking like the jealous second wife holding the crying baby. Anyone would look at us and think the problem is with me.

I force a smile. 'Everything is fine. Just a little tired.'

'Why are you tired, Joanne?' Chloe asks innocently, nestling closer to Richard. 'It's not like you've done anything today, except go to the shops.'

I bite my tongue and fake another smile. 'You're right.'

Richard takes off his coat. He's about to hang it but Chloe takes it from him. 'I'll do it, Daddy. You've been working all day. Go and relax in the living room.'

He smiles adoringly at her and kisses the top of her head. 'Thank you, sweetheart. Have you had dinner yet?'

'No,' she replies, then turns to me. 'Have you, Joanne?'

She knows very well I haven't. I fake a third smile. At least I'm getting good at smiling on cue, although I don't know if anybody buys it. 'I thought we'd wait for you, Richard. It's warming on the stove.'

Richard rubs his hands together. 'Great! I'm starving.'

I put Evie in the highchair. She really should be asleep but now that Richard is home, she won't want to. I'll try again in half an hour or so.

At the dinner table, Chloe sits close to Richard and nestles her head on his shoulder. She tells him about her day, her voice girly and high-pitched. 'And then I went with Joanne to the village, to help with Evie.'

Richard asks if we had fun. Which is one way of putting it, I guess. I am so close to telling him the truth; that we didn't have fun, that his daughter is a brat and also mentally unstable and truly I wanted to get close to her, but I have my limits.

'It was just grocery shopping,' I say. 'Nothing special.'

They both tilt their heads at me, smiling but also slightly puzzled as if I should say more. A phone rings in the next room. It's not mine. Chloe jumps up and runs out of the room. 'I'll get it!'

I lean forward. 'Do you have any idea what she said to me today?'

His shoulders drop. 'What did she say now?' he asks through gritted teeth.

'Apparently, you're having an affair.' I sit back, waiting for the shock to register on his face.

He chuckles to himself. 'Who with?'

I can hear Chloe chatting in the other room. 'A tall, blonde, young, beautiful woman with very long legs.'

He rubs his chin. 'I see. You know she was joking, don't you?'

I raise my hands in the air and let them fall back. 'She wasn't joking.'

'No, of course not. Because as you can imagine, young, tall, beautiful women with long legs are beating down the door to have an affair with me. I've often been told I'm the spitting image of Brad Pitt, but better looking and in better shape.'

'She wasn't joking, Richard.' Evie throws her empty cup on the floor. I pick it up and hand her the rattle instead. 'She was quite fascinated to hear about all your ex-lovers. She kept asking me questions about Isabella. Then she told me again you don't love me.'

He sighs like he has the weight of the world on his shoulders. 'Joanne, please. It's getting tedious, and frankly, it doesn't sound like Chloe at all. I just don't believe it.'

That's when it occurs to me that I've fallen right into the trap she set for me. She made up this story about Richard having an affair because she *wanted* me to tell him about it, so I would sound like the jealous, insecure wife stuck at home. And he's right. I mean, I love my husband madly, but the idea that he's having it off with a supermodel is, well, unlikely.

'I don't know what you have against Chloe all the time. I didn't think you were that kind of woman. I really didn't.'

'What kind of woman is that?'

'The kind who can't accept that a father is close to his daughter from another marriage. All I hear from you these days are complaints. Chloe has been so sweet to you. She's always striving to be helpful. I don't know why you are so stubborn about her.'

'Richard. I hate to tell you this, again, but I don't think you know her very well.'

He drops his fork with a clank. 'Don't you dare speak to me like that.'

'She's a nasty little brat. She's completely obsessed with you. She hates anyone who comes between you and her.'

'Nobody can come between me and Chloe.'

'But she *thinks* they can. And that includes me and that includes Evie. And the sooner she is out of his house the better.'

Just then Chloe bounces back into the room, skipping like a little girl. She bends down to kiss Evie's cheek making her grin with pleasure.

'There were ten in the bed and the little one said, "Roll

over! Roll over!"' Chloe sings happily, her hands between her thighs as she looks right at Evie. Evie is beside herself with giggles. Brilliant. Another Oscar-worthy performance. And it's working, too. Richard is gazing at them adoringly, his eyes moist with emotion. It occurs to me he must have sung it to Chloe when she was little, just like he sings it to Evie now.

'So they all rolled over and one fell out!' Chloe says, then finishes with a kiss on Evie's head before skipping over to sit next to her father. He puts a protective arm around her shoulders, glaring at me like I'm the devil incarnate.

'So… I've been trying to work out what to do next,' Chloe says.

'What do you mean, sweetheart?'

'Yes,' I say. 'What do you mean, sweetheart?'

She gives me a sideways glance and a little half-smile. It sends a shiver down my spine.

'The thing is, I'm just so bored.'

Richard clicks his tongue. 'I'm sorry, sweetheart. I know there's not much to keep you entertained around here.'

'Exactly. Which is why I'm thinking of leaving.'

Richard shoots me a look of horror, implying that somehow it's my fault. I try not to show my happiness as my heart does a little dance. In fact, it takes all my willpower not to jump up with joy.

'Sweetheart! Why?' he exclaims. 'This is your home! Don't you feel welcome here?'

'Well…' She toys with the food on her plate.

'But why so soon?' he asks.

'Richard,' I jump in. 'Let her leave if she wants to. If Chloe is bored, then she should go back to her friends. It's not fair on her.'

He frowns at me. 'But how will you manage?'

I smile. 'Same as I always did, darling.'

'But what about your job?'

'Oh I don't think that will be a problem,' Chloe says. 'Will it, Joanne?' I feel myself growing hot. I can tell from the way she's smiling that she already knows I quit. She must have been eavesdropping on my phone call.

'What happened?' Richard asks.

I've been watching Evie leaning sideways in her high-chair, trying to reach for her father, but he ignores her which is completely unlike him. Evie grows impatient and chucks her baby elephant toy on the floor. I pick it up, blow on it, shake it in the air and give it back to her. She throws it right back. Richard does such a good job of pretending not to notice, it's like Evie isn't in the room. I bet that's because Chloe is here. I've noticed he doesn't like to show Evie too much attention when Chloe is around. Or he doesn't *anymore*, because he used to, so that tells me he's noticed something. I think of the way Chloe looked at Evie when Richard was feeding her, like she resented her, and I wonder if maybe Richard noticed it too.

'What happened to your job?' Richard says again.

I sit back down. 'Unfortunately, they didn't have as much work as they expected.' I stare right at Chloe when I say that, daring her to contradict me.

'That's too bad,' Richard says. 'But maybe it's for the best.'

'That way you'll have more time to do the renovations on this house,' Chloe says with a smile. 'Anyway, since I'm not needed anymore, I may as well go back to London.'

'I think that makes perfect sense,' I say. I can sense Richard is about to argue.

'But I'm going away Wednesday next week. Will you still be here then? I'll be back on Friday night.'

Chloe looks up at him. 'You're going away? Where?'

'To Amsterdam for the Venture Capital Summit.'

'I'll be fine, Richard,' I say through tight lips.

'Maybe I could stay until Dad gets back,' Chloe chimes.

'Thank you but really. I'm used to being alone with Evie.'

'I think it's better if I stay.'

'You'll just create more work for me. Really. You go.'

'I think I should stay. What do you think, Daddy?'

Richard smiles proudly at his daughter. 'I tell you what. I'll take time off work when I get back from my trip, and we can spend some quality time together. Just you and me. I should have done that already.'

'That's okay, Daddy. You have to work, to pay for all these nice things.' She extends an arm vaguely around the room. 'And you have to support Joanna too.'

I'm so tired of this charade, I find myself raising my hand. 'Actually, it's Joanne.'

She turns to Richard. 'That's what I said!'

Richard shushes her gently.

'Also,' I continue, 'I've never asked your father for money. Your father bought this house, yes, it's true—'

'And everything in it,' she says dully.

'Chloe. Please,' Richard admonishes gently.

'And everything in it, yes, but I leave these decisions to him.' Which is not strictly true, but I'm beyond nit-picking at this point. 'I can look after myself,' I say stiffly.

Chloe tilts her head. 'Really? How?'

I brush my hair back. 'Well, for instance, I pay for my own clothes.'

She gives me a sideways up-and-down look. 'You don't say,' she mutters.

'And you may not know this, Chloe, but I have my own money.'

'Well, excuse me, I thought you were an estate agent. I didn't know you were an heiress. That's so cool!'

Did Richard just chuckle? He turns to me, suddenly

grave, eyebrows knotted. 'It's true. Joanne has her own little nest egg.'

'Interesting,' Chloe says. 'So how'd you do it? Did you have another rich husband before Dad?' She leans forward, wide-eyed. 'Did you kill him for his money?'

'Chloe, please,' Richard says.

'I was just kidding, Daddy.'

'I know, but still.'

I stare right into Chloe's eyes. 'I don't care about your father's money. I'm here because I love him. You might not believe it, but that says more about you than about me.'

The silence feels like it's going on for days. Chloe is the first to speak. 'Anyway, since you want me to stay, Daddy, I'm happy to stay until you get back.

Richard kisses the top of her head. 'Thank you.'

I give it one last try. 'Truly, I'll be fine on my own. I'm used to it. There's no need for you to stay.'

Chloe's chin starts to wobble. 'I just can't get anything right with you, can I? I'm only trying to help, you know.' Her eyes suddenly fill with water, like she's turned on some invisible tap. She brushes her cheek with the tip of her fingers. 'I don't know what else to do for you to like me, Joanne. I really don't.' She turns to Richard, bottom lip quivering. 'What am I doing wrong, Daddy?'

I think I'm going to scream. Richard takes my hand and he's squeezing it so hard his knuckles are white. 'Of course you're not doing anything wrong, sweetie. Joanne would love to have you while I'm away. Wouldn't you, Joanne?'

He doesn't let go. I'm not going to win this battle. He wants to believe every word that comes out of his precious daughter's mouth and nothing I can say or do will convince him otherwise.

'And this is your home as much as ours. Isn't that right, Jo?'

'Of course. This is your home, Chloe.'

Richard gives my hand another squeeze, gentler this time.

'And you're welcome to stay while Richard is away. It's only for two days anyway.'

Wrong thing to say. I know it the moment the words are out of my mouth. 'But please stay for as long as you like after that. It is your home as much as ours.'

She sits back in her chair. 'Okay. I think I will.'

That night, I download the video app again on my phone. Richard, needless to say, has retreated to the spare bedroom.

I'm not sure if the videos are still available for me to watch, but since I didn't cancel the subscription — I didn't even think of it — I hope that once I log in the videos will still be there.

And they are.

I go back over them. All of them. There must be something I can show Richard, something that demonstrates Chloe is not as innocent as he thinks. I have to find it before she gives him the doctored photograph. I don't know for sure that she will give it to him, but I don't see why she wouldn't. And even if Richard believes me, which I doubt very much since that would imply his precious daughter is a liar, he would still fire Simon.

Better safe than sorry.

I watch and watch till my eyes feel like they're encased in sand, and I find nothing, at least nothing I haven't seen before, so I watch again. Because something is not right about that girl, and I'm going to find it. I don't care how long it takes.

Two hours and fifty-five minutes. That's how long it takes before I find something that makes me sit up in bed.

It's dark, late evening. Evie asleep in the nursery. We must have been downstairs. At one point there's movement. Evie's little nightlight wasn't on, but if you squint, you can see a shadow against the far wall.

Chloe. She's crouched in the corner of the room. Then Evie starts to cry and literally one second later the shadow slips out of the room.

I sit up, my hand over my mouth. Richard comes into the nursery. He turns on the night light, picks up Evie and soothes her, starts to fiddle with the bottle warmer.

Nothing happens after that. Just me coming in two hours later and picking up Evie to take her to my room. But I watch every second of footage after that, with my heart in my throat. Because I have no idea what Chloe was doing there, crouched in the dark.

But I'm genuinely frightened.

Chapter Thirty

Chloe is up early. Unusual. Especially for a Saturday. I'm upstairs in my bedroom with Evie wedged on my hip. I'm sipping my coffee and gazing out the window. Richard and Chloe are standing in the garden. They have their backs to me. Richard shields his eyes and looks around. When he turns to face me, I am so shocked that I step away, my heart thumping.

He is carrying his shotgun, the one he uses for clay shooting. It's open, and safely wedged in the crook of his arm, but still. I hate that thing.

I put Evie down and run outside.

'What are you doing?'

Chloe is holding it now. Closed. She aims at me.

'Sweetheart. Please,' Richard says, gently pushing the barrel down.

'I was just joking.'

'I know, but it's not funny.'

'Are you teaching Chloe to shoot?' I ask, fists firmly on hips.

'Please don't overreact, Joanne. It's not loaded.'

'Don't overreact?' Great. My stepdaughter is a nutter and her father is teaching her to shoot. And I'm the one who's overreacting.

'I'm taking Chloe clay pigeon shooting when I get back from Amsterdam. I thought I'd show her how to handle a shotgun.'

'At Ascot?' I blurt, as if that made any difference.

'Not this time. We're going to Brookwood.' He squeezes her shoulder affectionately.

'Well that's wonderful,' I snap, crossing my arms. Meanwhile Chloe is aiming the shotgun at whatever, the sky, the dog, me. Every time she moves to a new target she does a little 'pow!'

Richard takes the shotgun from Chloe and opens it, carries it in the crook of his arm again, wrapping his other arm around Chloe's shoulders.

'Can you *please* put this away? Under lock and key?'

Chloe shoots me a look, like I'm the Grinch that stole Christmas.

'It's always under lock and key, Joanne,' Richard says dryly. Which is true. It lives in a locked cupboard in his study and his study is locked most of the time.

'Well, it's not under lock and key now,' I snap.

'Was that necessary? To show Chloe your shotgun?' I ask later when Richard comes back inside.

'I don't know why you overreact all the time, Jo. Truly. I told you it wasn't loaded. Why are you being like this?'

'How about because Chloe was hiding in the nursery the other night,' I blurt.

He blinks a few times. 'Hiding?'

'I saw her.'

He closes his eyes briefly. 'Joanne. Please.'

'I'm telling you the truth.'

'Are you doing this because I spent a moment with Chloe? Enjoying some father-daughter time alone? Is that it?'

Before I have a chance to argue, he walks out.

I put Evie down in her cot, grab the monitor, and tiptoe down the corridor to my office. This is what it's come to, me tiptoeing in my own house because I don't want Chloe to know where I am. Is she really going to leave after next weekend? God, that would be so wonderful. I long to be alone with Richard and Evie. I'll never ever complain about being lonely again. Ever. But was Chloe telling the truth about that? That would mean she'd given up on her plan to break us up or make me leave or whatever she's been plotting, and somehow I find that hard to believe.

I don't trust her. I was prepared to give her the benefit of the doubt, to recognise that considering her tragic childhood, it's no wonder she's … strange, and to try and build bridges with her. But what if she had *something* to do with her tragic childhood? What if… God. I can't even bear to think about it, but at the same time, I think I have to.

If Chloe was as jealous of her baby sister as Diane claimed to Richard she was, is it possible she had something to do with her death?

I close the door after me and fire up the computer. I go back to the online articles from the Essex paper. Both stories were written by the same journalist, a Jim Preston. I type his name on the search bar and find a number of other stories with his byline, all published in the same local paper. He must have been assigned to crime news because that's all he wrote about. That and fatal car accidents. The last story with his name attached is dated April 15, 2014, then nothing.

I sit back, tap my finger against my chin. I wish I could talk to this Jim Preston, find out if he knows anything about Chloe. Was there ever any speculation about Sophie's death? Any rumours of Chloe's involvement?

I click on the website's Contact Us page, expecting to find some social media links and maybe a form or an email address, so I'm surprised to find a few phone numbers for various departments like Sales or Advertising, even for the complaints department.

I'll try Jeff Stubbs, content editor, because I don't think the sales people will know what I'm talking about. I thought I'd have to wait until Monday but then notice it's a mobile number, as they all seem to be. I guess people work remotely these days.

'Who?' Jeff Stubbs asks. He doesn't seem fussed at all that I called him on a Saturday, just puzzled. I repeat my question. I've made up a little white lie that I have a local story but I only want to give it to Jim Preston because I've had dealings with him in the past. It's a crime story, I say. True crime. Very dark. Jeff Stubbs still has no idea who I'm talking about. I mention the *Essex Woman Found Dead After Fall From Balcony* story. I hear the sound of typing.

'Ah yes, got him. Jim Preston. I think he retired from the news business.'

'Oh.' I feel a stab of disappointment. If he retired in 2014, is the man even alive? 'Do you have a number for him? It's really important.'

Nobody in their right mind would reel off a number to a total stranger. Surely my best hope is that he'll suggest he calls Jim Preston and passes on a message.

'One sec.' More typing. 'You have a pen?' I'm so shocked that I scramble for one but he's already telling me the number and I have to make him repeat it. When I look out the window, I see Chloe taking off on my bicycle. I quash the feeling of annoyance that she always takes it without asking. After all, if I'm going to call this Jim Preston, this is a perfect time. But what am I going to say to him? That I suspect my husband's daughter to be a borderline psychopath, I'm concerned for my baby's welfare, and does he have any tips?

I remind myself of what Robyn said. *Trust your instincts.* My instincts are screaming right now. They're saying that something is very, very wrong with this young woman and that if I don't figure out what it is, somebody is going to get hurt.

I call the number. A male voice answers on the second ring.

'Mr Preston? My name is Joanne Atkinson.'

For the next ten minutes I ramble on, making no sense whatsoever because I did not prepare for this conversation. At least Jim remembers the case well.

'It was an unusual story. Very dramatic, as you can imagine. But I don't know how I can help you. All the information about Mrs Atkinson's death is publicly available.'

I hate the way he says, *Mrs Atkinson's death.* It feels like a premonition, since I am, after all, Mrs Atkinson. 'Well… as I said earlier, my stepdaughter has come to live with us, but she is very withdrawn, very shy, and I wonder how I can help her fit in.' Clearly, I'm making this up as I go. 'I'm trying to understand what happened from her perspective. In the article, the second one, you said there might have been an intruder. But then the police dismissed it. Do you know why they dismissed it?'

'Because there wasn't an intruder.'

'But how do you know?'

'Because she changed her mind. I spoke with the police at the time. They told me she changed her story once they put it to her that none of the neighbours saw a car drive by that day. You see, while the neighbours are miles away, they all live off the one road. These people notice whenever a car drives up. But that night, nobody heard or saw a car. The intruder, if he exists and who presumably would have been there to steal something, would have arrived on foot. And the front gate of the property was locked, as it always was. The only fingerprints on that door were the grocer's, Richard and Diane Atkinson's and Chloe's. But that's not all. Mr Atkinson had set the internal security system before he left. That means there were cameras all around the property. The police reviewed the footage, and nobody had come to the house on that day. Only the grocer the following morning. Also there was no sign of forced entry. Once the police put all this to Chloe, she changed her story. She said maybe she'd been mistaken and there was no intruder. And I'll tell you this for free, I've had my doubts about that girl's story myself.'

'What doubts?'

'I think she made up the intruder to take the investigation away from herself until she realised it was a waste of time.'

I clasp my hand over my mouth. I knew there was something not right about Chloe, but I never thought… Her mother? No. No way.

My eyes are trained on the window. Chloe is on her way back. Right now she's a small dot in the distance, but she'll be here soon. And even though she's nowhere close, I find myself whispering. 'I really need to know. I have a baby, my husband is away a lot…'

'And that young woman lives with you?'

'Yes.'

'Then don't stand too close to any balustrades, Mrs Atkinson.'

Jim Preston doesn't want to say any more over the phone. 'I'm free for lunch on Monday. There's a South American place near St Paul's. I'll text you the address.'

Chapter Thirty-One

Monday couldn't come soon enough. I've got Evie snug in a sling across my chest, my backpack laden with nappies and cartons of ready-made formula since there's no way I can drive into London with the traffic. It would take hours and I'd never get parking near St Paul's.

Normally, an hour-long train trip with Evie would give me spasms of anxiety, but today I can't wait to get out of the house and away from Chloe. And I can't wait to hear what Jim Preston has to say.

I leave a note on the kitchen table to say I'd be out all day and I am tiptoeing to the front door hoping to sneak us out of the house without alerting Chloe, when Evie starts to wail. Possibly because I've wrapped her in so many layers of clothing, she looks like a papoose.

'Where are you going?' Chloe asks. She has appeared at the double doors that lead to the living room. I can hear the TV in there. She bites into an apple.

'Out,' I say, trying to sound light and breezy, which is hard to do with a screaming baby strapped to my chest.

'Yeah, I got that, but where?'

What is it with this obsession to know where I am and where I'm going at all times?

'I'm going into London.'

'Why?'

'I've got an appointment with my—' I was going to say, doctor, but she knows my doctor is not far from here. She'll want to know why I took so long. Honestly, living with a potential psychopath is exhausting. You have to think of everything.

'A specialist,' I say.

She frowns. 'What kind of specialist?'

'A medical specialist.' I glance at my watch. 'I really should get going.'

'You can leave her here if you like.' She points her chin at Evie who immediately stops crying. 'I don't mind'

I shudder. 'There's no need. I'll be catching up with my friend Robyn again and she's dying to see Evie so we'll be having lunch together.'

'That's really nice. So you'll be having lunch with a friend and maybe doing a bit of shopping while you're there.'

'Yes. Maybe I will.'

'I miss the city, being stuck out here.' She sighs theatrically. 'Hey, I know! I'll come with you!'

'No! I mean… I don't know how long I will be with the specialist. Sometimes they take hours.'

'That's okay, I have loads of shopping I want to do. I can meet you after and go to lunch with you and your friend!' She hands me her apple core. 'I'll go get my bag.'

'Look, Chloe, it's just that I haven't seen Robyn in ages and I—'

She's already halfway up the flight of stairs. She turns around. 'Your friend Robyn? But you had lunch with her last week.'

I rub my finger over my eyebrow. 'I just wanted to spend time…'

'Doing what? It's just lunch with a friend you see all the time, isn't it? Or should I tell my dad you hate my company so much you wouldn't even introduce me to your friend? That you insisted on leaving me alone all day long. Is that what you want me to tell my dad?'

As if Richard needed any more excuses to believe I am the original evil stepmother.

'Actually, it looks like it might rain. Maybe I won't go. Like you said, it's just lunch…'

'But Joanne, you're forgetting your doctor's appointment.'

I bite my bottom lip. 'Look. I have a lot to do in town and a lot on my mind. I'd really rather be alone.'

The corners of her mouth turn down and her chin wobbles.

'You're not seriously going to cry, are you?'

She waves her hand. 'Nah, just kidding. Okay fine, have it your way.'

I almost drop my head with relief. I turn around, walk quickly towards the door before she changes her mind.

'Not everything is what it seems, you know.'

I stop. She's leaning against the wall, casually checking her fingernails.

'What does that mean?'

'You're going to have to figure it out sooner or later.' She turns to go up the rest of the stairs. 'Sooner would be better.'

I'm only a few minutes late for my lunch date.

'Joanne?'

The man that is smiling expectantly at me looks to be in his early forties at the most, dark hair with a few grey ones showing up, big ears sticking out and a wide smile full of teeth. He's wearing a dark suit.

He gets up to shake my hand. 'Jim Preston. How are you?'

I shake my head. 'I'm sorry. I expected someone older. I thought you'd retired. That's what they said when I got your phone number.'

'Did they?' He pulls out a chair for me while I shake off my backpack. A waitress brings a highchair to the table. I release Evie from the sling. She looks so happy, grinning at Jim Preston who waves his fingers at her.

Maybe we should go out more.

'Retired from writing about car crashes and small-town drug issues, you mean,' Jim says, sitting down again. 'When I was younger, I had dreams of breaking big stories, maybe winning some journalism award, but I just ended up doing local news. Then my wife and I had a baby…' He smiles at Evie then looks back at me. 'Hey, I don't need to tell you. I needed a real job, one with benefits. I'm a data analyst now. I work near here for one of the big banks.'

'Oh, my husband's in finance too.'

He nods. 'Yes, I remember that. Has he retired?'

'Retired? God no. He's not that old.' I smile.

'I didn't mean… I just remember something about his firm back then, they were shutting shop or something.'

I shake my head. 'I'm not sure. He runs his own boutique investment firm now.'

The waitress arrives. Jim orders a dish of grilled marinated chicken and rice. I do the same.

'Anyway,' he says when she's gone. 'That's not what you're here to talk about. How can I help?'

'I'm worried about having Chloe in the house. Her behaviour has been very strange, especially towards Evie.'

We both glance at her. I take a breath. 'I'm very worried, Jim. Is it okay if I call you Jim?'

'Sure. And I don't blame you, Joanne. I'd be worried too, in your shoes.'

'You said she recanted her original story to the police. Can you expand on that? You made it sound like she was lying.'

He scratches the stubble on his chin. 'From what the police told me, she originally said there had been someone in the house and that she'd heard her mother argue with someone before she fell. When it was put to her how difficult it was to corroborate that, she got flustered. She said she was mistaken, maybe she didn't hear anyone, just her mother. Every time she opened her mouth she contradicted what she'd said minutes before. That's when her father stepped in. He got a lawyer, a good one too, and they put a stop to any more interviews. He said it was too upsetting for her but I knew the detective in charge well and he let it slip they thought she was lying.'

The waitress puts the dishes down in front of us. I'm going to be sick. 'Do you think she pushed her mother?' I blurt.

He doesn't reply.

'You never said that the police thought she was lying in your article.'

'Nobody could prove it, and what if I was wrong? Maybe she was in shock and genuinely confused.' He shrugs.

'But you don't believe that she was confused.'

'Put it this way. Don't you think it strange that she waited with her dead mother all day? She was eleven years old, not three. She could have plugged one of the phones back in and called for help. She didn't. When—'

I raise my hand. 'Hang on. Go back. Plugged the phones back in?'

'Ah yes, that didn't make the article either. All the phones throughout the house were unplugged from their sockets. All of them. Apparently this was a game that Chloe liked to play: unplugging all the phones when her parents were both home, so they wouldn't ring. She'd done it again, but for some reason…' He raises his knife and fork. 'She forgot.'

'She forgot?'

'That she'd done it. Yes.' He leans forward. 'She might have saved her mother's life if she'd called 999.'

'What?' I cried out a little too loud and Evie let go of her bottle. I lower my voice. 'But she died on impact.'

'No, she didn't. Nobody knows exactly how long she took to die, but it might have been as long as twenty minutes.'

My free hand flies to my mouth.

'And I'll tell you another thing that didn't make it to the article. They were renovating that house.'

'They were?'

He nods. 'They were in the process of replacing all the balustrades. On the third floor, half had already been dismantled. Anyone leaning against that railing would have been taking their life into their own hands. Literally.' He raises a hand. 'I know, I know, she'd had a drink. I saw the autopsy report.'

I rub my hand over my forehead. 'I think it was a few drinks,' I say, playing devil's advocate. 'She was depressed. She was suicidal.'

'She put a dash of rum in her coffee that afternoon. She wasn't legless. The whole story was fishy as hell. Later I tried to access her medical records from her stay in the mental health unit but you know, there are laws against that.'

'So you must know how unwell Diane was,' I say, still playing devil's advocate. 'You don't go to a mental health unit unless you have very serious issues.'

'I wasn't talking about Mrs Atkinson. I was talking about the little girl.'

My jaw drops. 'Mental health unit? For Chloe?'

'I followed up the story, you see, a year later. Call it professional curiosity. I didn't write about it, but I found out that Chloe had been referred to a psychiatric hospital for children and she'd gone there after her mother died. I tracked down Mr Atkinson to ask about it, but he wouldn't return my calls. Between you and me, I think he pulled some strings. I think there was a definite suspicion that Chloe had something to do with her mother's death. I think he made a kind of a deal. That if she went to get some help, the authorities would not pursue it any further.'

'He could do that?'

'He had connections, and he had money. I'm not saying that he did, mind you. I'm just guessing here.'

Evie pushes her bottle away. I put it down, glance at my plate. There's no way I could eat something now. 'I know they had another daughter, Sophie, who died when she was just a few months old.'

He nods. 'Yes, cot death. It came up during the investigation. It pointed to Mrs Atkinson's state of mind.'

'Do you think Chloe had anything to do with that?' I bite my bottom lip.

He thinks about it. 'I don't know, and that's the truth. Do I think it's possible? Yes. Do I think she killed her mother? I don't know, but there are too many questions to rule it out. But I'll tell you something else. I saw Mr Atkinson and Chloe together once when I came to the house to speak to him for my article. He quickly sent her out of the room, but I saw the way she looked at him, and it was cold. Like she was dead inside. It gave me the shivers. Then I caught the look on Mr Atkinson's face and believe me, Joanne, he was scared of her. That man was afraid of his eleven-year-old daughter.'

Chapter Thirty-Two

'Bad news, then?'

Chloe stands in the doorway to the nursery. She pops a grape into her mouth.

I shudder. 'Why do you say that?' I ask innocently as I put Evie down onto the change table.

'Just that you were there for ages. So the test results were that bad, huh?'

Test results. 'No, I mean, yes, bad results. Bad news. I don't want to talk about it.'

'What's wrong with you anyway?' she asks.

'I told you. I just needed some tests, that's all.' I caress Evie's cheek. Her eyes are fluttering like she's about to fall asleep. 'As I said, Chloe, I don't want to talk about it right now.'

She pushes herself off the doorjamb. 'Whatever.'

After she leaves I go mentally over what Jim told me. I'm living with a deranged young woman who very likely killed her baby sister *and* her mother.

Is Richard afraid of her? Is that why he always takes her side? That's what Jim said, but I don't know that I agree. I've learned a lot today, and I suspect Richard is so deeply in denial that he will do or say anything to convince himself that Chloe is a normal, sweet, great kid, whatever, because the other option is simply unthinkable.

Richard comes home early and I tell him that I had a referral from my GP for a specialist in London, someone who can run tests to see if I've inherited my mother's condition. I hate lying to him. It makes me feel like we're drifting apart, and if things keep going that way I will lose him.

'Why didn't you tell me?' he asks.

'I didn't want to worry you.'

'So what did they say?'

'They don't know yet. They're running blood tests.'

Later I'm putting Evie in her cot in the bedroom — she'll be sleeping with me forever at this rate — when Richard walks in and takes his suitcase from the walk-in closet.

'It's tomorrow,' I blurt. 'You're going tomorrow.' For some reason I thought we had an extra day.

He looks at me sadly, eyebrows knotted. 'Don't tell me you—'

'No, I didn't forget.' I close the door and lean back against it.

'You never said anything about Chloe being locked up in a mental asylum.'

He whips his head around. I'm trying to read his expression. Is he confused? Surprised?

'Where did you hear that?'

'Please don't change the subject, Richard.'

He brings out two ties and studies them. 'She wasn't locked up. She went through a traumatic experience and I got her help. I made sure she had a few sessions with a professional. What about it?'

I cross my arms over my chest. 'Why did you hide this from me?' But suddenly I'm not feeling as confident as I was earlier. When Jim Preston said she'd gone to a private psychiatric facility for children, I'd had visions of Chloe in a straitjacket tied to a metal bed and a policeman guarding the door.

'Why would I tell you? It's none of your business. It's Chloe's story to tell. Her mother died, Chloe was stuck alone with her for hours. Can you imagine what that does to a child?'

'But you told me she went to a private boarding school immediately after the accident.'

'No I didn't, Joanne. You just assumed.' He folds a shirt carefully on the bed. 'She was in shock. She needed therapy, a lot of therapy. It was a terrible time. How do you know about that anyway?'

'It doesn't matter how.' God, if Richard found out I tracked down the journalist who covered the story, I don't think he'd ever forgive me.

I decide to change tack. 'Why did she say there was an intruder in the house if it wasn't true?'

He stares at me, his gorgeous eyebrows furrowed together in confusion. 'She told you that?'

'It was in the article. My question is, why did she change her mind about that? Why did she say there was an intruder and then say there wasn't?'

'She was confused. We had security cameras all around the perimeter of the house. Nobody came to our house that day.'

'So she made it up.'

'No, she was confused. She understood there couldn't have been an intruder. The evidence showed that.'

'And you don't think that's strange? If your mother died and you were certain you'd heard someone in the house, why change your story? Security cameras or not? You don't think that's odd?'

'No, I don't.' He rakes his hand through his hair. 'Can you please stop this madness? Because I really can't deal with this anymore.'

'Look at me, Richard.' I take his face in my hands. 'Look me in the eyes and tell me you believe from the bottom of your heart that Diane's death was suicide.'

'What are you saying?'

'Just say it.'

'Diane killed herself! What are you doing?'

'What about Sophie?'

'What?'

'What happened to Sophie? You don't think Chloe had anything to do with Sophie's death? Say it, Richard.'

The shock on his face makes me waver. He takes my wrists and pushes my arms away. 'I can't believe you just said that.'

'Just say it. I want to see it in your eyes, that you don't have the slightest doubt. Just say it.'

'What the hell are you suggesting?'

'You can't even say it. What are you not telling me, Richard?'

'You have no idea what you're talking about!'

'I know there's something, I know it, tell me! I know something isn't right with Chloe and I'm getting very worried about her, Richard. I'm very worried about having her in the house right now, so tell me the truth!'

'She didn't have anything to do with Sophie's death, for Christ's sake. She wasn't even there!'

I freeze. 'She wasn't?'

'Chloe was staying with her grandparents, Diane's

parents, when Sophie died. She wasn't anywhere near her sister.'

I sit down on the edge of the bed. I try to make sense of what he just said.

'What's going on, Jo? You seriously think Chloe would hurt her little sister? Do you realise how insane that sounds?'

'I'm sorry, I…'

'How could you think such a thing?' He narrows his eyes at me. 'Have you been taking your medication?'

My medication. He means the anti-anxiety medication Dr Fletcher prescribed for me. 'This has nothing to do with that, okay?'

'Doesn't it?'

'No. It doesn't.' But suddenly I'm not so sure. Moments ago I was dead certain Chloe had smothered her baby sister out of jealousy and she was planning on doing the same to Evie. Now I find out she wasn't even there when Sophie died. So what does that make me?

'Oh, Jo…' Richard looks like he's going to cry. Suddenly this conversation feels eerily familiar. 'You haven't been taking your medication.'

'I... I forgot to take them.'

'You forgot to take them? Joanne! How can I trust you to look after our daughter, and after Chloe, if you can't even look after yourself? How do I know what's happening with you? What did the doctor say?'

I wring my hands together. 'The doctor?'

'The specialist you saw today! Did you tell him you're paranoid like your mother? That you suspect my daughter of the worst crimes imaginable? That you think she killed her own mother? And her baby sister?'

'I'm not imagining things, Richard,' I say, biting on a fingernail.

'You're sure about that?'

But suddenly I remember. 'I have to show you something.' I scramble for my phone, then realise I left it downstairs. 'I'll be right back.' I run down the stairs and find it on the coffee table in the living room, which is odd because I don't remember leaving it there.

I'm breathless when I get back upstairs.

'Take a look at this.' I tap on the security app and scroll through the videos until I find the one I want, the one with Chloe crouched in the corner of the nursery.

Richard peers over my shoulder. 'What the hell is this?'

'It's the security app. I want to show you this video, and then you'll see.'

'I thought you'd deleted this app from your phone?'

'I downloaded it again.'

'For Christ's sake, Joanne! Why?'

'Just hang on a sec, I'll show you.'

But I can't find the video anymore. I look and look, scroll back and forth, check the dates, but it's gone. 'Chloe,' I whisper.

'What has she done now?'

'She got my passcode the other day. She must have gone through my phone and deleted it.'

Richard raises his hands and lets them drop. 'Or maybe it was never there! Have you thought about that?'

'It was there! She deleted it!'

'No, Joanne! She didn't. This is all in your head! You are using a tragedy from my past to paint Chloe as an evil force who wants to harm Evie. Can't you see how crazy you sound? Can't you see the pattern? Can't you see you're behaving the same—'

He stops abruptly. But that's okay, I can finish the sentence for him. *The same as your mother.* A dim and distant memory comes to me from when I was little: my grandmother crying, telling my mother that it wasn't real. I can hear her voice just now, as clear as a bell. *It's not real. It's not happening. It's in your head.*

'I'm not crazy, Richard,' I mumble.

'Aren't you?' He disappears into his walk-in closet, comes back out with a couple of T-shirts that he throws on the bed.

'Chloe didn't kill her mother. She didn't kill her sister. It's all in your head. Chloe is spoiled, yes. She probably is a little over-possessive of her father, yes. I'll admit that, but that's not a crime. But what you're doing, it's criminal. These sick accusations you're levelling at her, she's barely twenty-one. Still a child, really. It's horrible what you're doing, and frankly I don't know if I can leave my children with you in this house.'

I'm on my feet. 'Does that mean you won't go on your trip?'

'I'm thinking of taking the girls away. We can stay in a hotel while you get some help.'

'But that's crazy! Why would you even say something like that?'

He narrows his eyes at me. 'Because I don't know if I can trust you. I don't know what you're doing.'

My head hurts. If it wasn't for Jim Preston, I probably would start to wonder if I'm the problem here. 'She's trying to…'

'What, Joanne? What is she trying to do?'

I was going to say, *drive a wedge between us,* but that would perpetuate the argument for eternity. He will never believe me, and of course at some point, Chloe will whip up the fake photo of Simon and me, like a rabbit out of a hat. Would Richard believe what he sees? Of course he will. *I don't know if I can trust you.*

I sit down on the edge of the bed and press two fingers against my eyelids. 'I'm sorry, I really am. I don't know what's wrong with me.' I look down at my phone, at the missing video. God, she's good.

'I'm not like my mother,' I say in a small voice. 'I'm just tired, that's all. I'll be better tomorrow.'

'You're scaring me, my love, you really are.'

'I know. But it will be all right.'

Chapter Thirty-Three

'Do you want to call Dr Fletcher?' Richard asks. 'I'm sure she would give you a referral if you wanted to go to Hopevale for a few days. You could have a nice rest.'

'To Hopevale? You mean, to the hospital? No! Richard, of course not. And what about Evie?'

Oh god, please don't say Chloe will look after Evie.

'I'll stay here with Evie of course. You don't think it would do you good?'

'Absolutely not.'

He sits down heavily next to me. 'Maybe I shouldn't go.'

'Of course you have to go.' If Richard really thinks he can't leave me alone with Chloe and Evie, I'm one step away from being committed against my will. I have to show him I'm completely rational and that there's nothing to worry about.

'You cannot cancel your trip. You're giving a keynote presentation. It's important that you go.'

He doesn't reply.

I shake my head. 'Look. I know I said some terrible

things. I'm so sorry about that. But you're going on your business trip and the three of us will be absolutely fine.'

The following morning I'm finishing packing for Richard while he goes to say goodbye to Chloe. When I glance out the window I see them strolling outside, his arm around her shoulders. They stop by the pond and Richard pulls out his paper bag of fish flakes and sprinkles them. From the way his lips move, he must be talking to the fish. He points at them, probably telling Chloe their names. She laughs. He gives her the paper bag and she nods, puts it in the pocket of her jacket.

'There you go, all done,' I say when he returns. He glances at me as I close his suitcase, then goes back to checking emails on his phone.

'Why don't you give Robyn a call?' he says. 'She could come over.'

'Why?'

'Because she's your best friend, and you trust her, and it would make me feel better. And somebody needs to talk some sense into you,' he adds with a crooked smile.

I don't mention that Robyn is the one who insists I should trust my instincts. I shake my head. 'Robyn is busy with work. She's got a court case coming up. I don't want to do this to her.'

He rubs his chin. 'What about Roxanne? She could stay in one of the spare bedrooms.'

'Roxanne? Why?'

'Because I don't want you to be alone, Jo, okay? If I'm going to be away, I really would like somebody else here, with you and the girls.'

I think about it. I'm not a big fan of Roxanne, but she lives close by and it's true that I would feel better if Roxanne were here. She'll keep Chloe busy. With a bit of luck they'll lock themselves up in Chloe's room for three days. I'll even deliver meals on a tray if they want. 'Okay, fine. I'll call her,' I say.

'I'll do it.' He still has his phone in his hand. 'What's her number?'

I click my tongue. 'Don't you trust me?'

He smiles, tilting his head a little. I retrieve my own phone from the bedside table and read out the number. Maybe it's better anyway if he calls her. I've got some idea that if I called, she might say no.

He walks to the windows and I listen as he explains about his trip and that Evie isn't sleeping well and he would feel better if she could stay here while he's gone and of course we'll pay her for her time.

'Dad?'

Richard turns to the doorway where Chloe is standing. He holds up one finger, confirms the arrangement with Roxanne before finishing the call.

'I'll be right there, sweetheart. Just give me a moment with Joanne.'

Chloe rolls her eyes and turns to leave.

'Did you see that?' I ask after she's gone. I point at the door.

He frowns. 'What are you talking about?'

'Never mind. What did Roxanne say?'

'She'll be here late afternoon. Does that make you feel better?'

'Yes. Thank you, Richard. It does. Now go. You're going to miss your flight.'

'You promise to look after yourself while I'm away?'

'Yes. I promise,' I say.

'Promise to take your medication?'

'Cross my heart.' I put my arms around his neck. 'Stop worrying. I love you.'

Half an hour later I see the taxi drive up to take Richard to the airport, and my stomach clenches. I don't want him to go. Maybe I should ask him to stay while there's still time. No, that would be silly. Surely I can manage three days with Chloe. Roxanne will be here anyway.

I find him in the living room, talking to Chloe. They're sitting together on the couch, her head on his shoulder. He's talking to her in a low voice while she looks sullen, playing with Richard's phone.

'Your taxi is here,' I say.

Richard looks up. 'I'll be right there.' Chloe drops his phone on his lap and walks past me without a word. It occurs to me she doesn't want to be alone with me for three days either.

A couple of hours later, I'm making myself a cup of tea when Chloe comes in.

'Would you like one?' I ask. I feel guilty that I suspected her of smothering her baby sister when she wasn't even there.

'No, that's okay.' She's about to say something else when my phone rings on the table. We both frown at the screen. It's Solomon, our family solicitor. I pick it up, remembering the snippets of conversation I overheard the other day. I completely forgot to ask Richard about that. I wish Chloe would leave so I could ask Solomon now.

'Aren't you going to answer it?' she says, hoisting herself up on the kitchen counter.

I pick up the call. After we exchange greetings, Solomon asks to speak to Richard.

'He's on a plane,' I say, glancing at my watch.

'Ah, that's why I haven't been able to reach him.'

'He'll be landing shortly,' I say. 'Would you like me to give him a message?'

'I'll try him again, but if you speak to him, he wanted to know when Chloe called about the will. Can you let him know it was the twenty-fourth of November?'

My gaze snaps to Chloe. She tilts her head at me, eyebrows raised, her feet swinging.

I swallow. 'I'll tell him,' I say.

After I hang up, Chloe asks, 'So what did old Solomon want anyway?'

I study her face. 'Something about you calling him about a will? Richard wanted to know when that was.'

She nods slowly, her eyes not leaving mine. 'Interesting. I wonder why Dad didn't ask me directly.' She studies her fingernails. 'So when did I call old fart Solomon?'

I wince at the slur. 'Twenty-fourth of November.'

She nods thoughtfully. 'I'd forgotten it was that long ago. Interesting.'

After a moment's hesitation I ask, 'What's it all about?'

'It's about my half of my mother's estate,' she says, pushing herself off the counter. 'I inherited it the other day.'

'The other day?'

'When I turned twenty-one.'

Later I'm watching Evie playing happily in her little playpen. When I gaze outside I see Chloe standing by the fishpond, looking down, her hands deep inside her pockets, Oscar by her side. I vaguely wonder if she's feeding the fish again, when she crouches down, does something with a stick. My phone rings and I walk away.

Chapter Thirty-Four

It's probably Richard. He must have arrived at the hotel by now. I already miss him so much. I reach for my phone, determined to sound upbeat. I just want to hear his voice.

But it's not Richard. It's Jim Preston. I walk over to stand at the window of the nursery where the mobile reception is best and look down. Chloe is still out there, standing very still, gazing at the pond.

'I said I'd get back to you about the facility where Chloe stayed,' Jim says. 'It was a private psychiatry clinic in Yorkshire called Vincent Gardens. Very expensive and, you might say, exclusive.'

God, I so don't need this right now. 'Thanks, Jim, but I spoke to my husband about it. Richard explained she'd had a few sessions, that's all. Which, under the circumstances, is hardly surprising.'

There's a moment of silence and I pull the phone away, half thinking I lost him. '…months.'

'Sorry, what did you say?'

'I said she was an inpatient there for three months.'

'Three months? No! That can't be right. The way Richard put it to me, it was a handful of visits.'

'Three months and one week,' he says. 'I have the exact dates here. Look I'm not saying it means anything or that there's anything wrong with it, just that I said I'd get back to you.'

I keep looking out the window. Chloe hasn't moved at all. 'But why Yorkshire if they lived in London? Do you know?'

'No idea. It was more discreet, is my guess.'

I shake my head. 'Look, thank you, I appreciate the call, but it doesn't matter now.'

'Can I ask why?'

'Richard told me Chloe wasn't anywhere near Sophie the day she died,' I say primly. 'She was staying with her grandparents. She couldn't have had anything to do with her sister's death.' There. Stick that in your Pulitzer.

'Erm… I don't think that's quite true.'

'Well, it is. I got it from the horse's mouth, so to speak.'

'Chloe was at the house with her parents the night Sophie died.'

My heart is thumping in my throat, like a drum. I swallow. 'She wasn't. Richard told me she wasn't. How would you know that, anyway?'

Just then, Chloe turns around and looks up. When our eyes meet, I get the distinct feeling she knew the whole time I was there, watching her. I smile nervously, feeling guilty I'm talking about her. She doesn't smile back.

'It came up during the investigation into Mrs Atkinson's death,' Jim says. 'Sophie's death was cited as the primary reason for returning the cause of death as suicide. I remember clearly, and it was all documented in the inquest report. The whole family was together in the house when Sophie died, Chloe included. Chloe did go to stay with her grandparents, and she was with them for some time, but that was after little Sophie died. I'm certain of it.'

'So why would Richard say she was with her grandparents that night?'

'Maybe he got confused about the dates. Or maybe, and Joanne I hope you won't mind me saying this, but maybe your husband refuses to admit what's right in front of his face. Maybe that's affecting his recollections of the events.'

He's right on one point. Richard has been in denial about Chloe right from the beginning. Maybe defending Chloe has become a habit so ingrained it's just second nature now. *Chloe is fine, she's great, she's perfect, she's a great kid, she went through a hard time so what do you expect? She's really sweet.*

So why did you send her to a psychiatric ward for three months if she was so sweet? Why did you send her to boarding school so soon afterwards if she was still in shock over her mother's death?

I have so many unanswered questions, and they all point to the same thing. *What are you not telling me?*

I wrap my arms around myself. I'm shivering, but not from the cold.

If only Richard hadn't thrown out those security cameras.

'And that's the other thing about your husband, if you don't mind me saying—'

The cameras. 'Sorry, Jim, I have to go.'

I hang up.

Chapter Thirty-Five

I glance outside one last time and see that Chloe has taken off on a walk towards the gate, Oscar by her side.

My heart is pounding as I run down to the pantry. I dig out the bag with the remaining cameras from where I left it, pushed far under the shelves. I brush it off and check its contents. The three remaining cameras are still there.

I run back upstairs. I put one of them in the nursery and this time I hide it in the cupboard shaped like a gingerbread house. There's a diamond-shaped hole in each door and as the camera would be visible if you happened to open the cupboard, I wrap it inside one of Evie's summer blankets. I pick a crocheted one that has lots of gaps, then position it directly behind the diamond-shaped hole on the right side. It's not perfect, but it's the best I can do. The only way Chloe could find it is if she pulled out those blankets and I don't see why she would.

Unless she was looking for it.

I glance out the window again and see Simon working near the fishpond. Chloe is nowhere to be seen. Evie is awake but happy and I consider leaving her in her cot while I go and speak to Simon, but then I change my mind. I'm not comfortable going out of the house and leaving her alone, even for a few minutes. I bundle her up and take her with me. At this point I'm seriously considering strapping her to my body so she's never away from me.

'Hi, Simon, can I ask you a favour?'

He was cleaning the bottom of the pond with some kind of broom. He stands up straight. That man is never cold. He's only wearing a T-shirt and his biceps are showing even when he's not using them. I immediately think of the doctored photograph my deranged stepdaughter whipped up and feel my cheeks burn.

'Sure, what can I do for you, Mrs Atkinson?'

For some reason, his words make me turn even more beetroot. I cough a little to hide my embarrassment. 'I need to put a lock on the nursery door. The kind you can only open and close with a key. Can you do that?'

He looks at me for a second too long, his eyes clouded with confusion.

'Can you?' I repeat. 'You know the type of lock.' I make a circle with my thumb and index finger. 'About this big.'

'You want a lock on the nursery door?'

'Yes, please.'

He smiles down at Evie. She grins back. 'You're worried Evie will get up and walk out?'

'Ha ha! So can you?'

'Sure, that's no problem. I can go and pick something up tomorrow at the hardware store. I can put it up next Tuesday when I come back.'

'No, no. I need it today.' I shuffle Evie around to my

other hip. 'Can you get it now? Don't worry about the fish.' We look down at the pond.

'They're all dead, Mrs Atkinson.'

I blink at him. 'What did you say?'

'The fish. There's no point worrying about them. They're all dead.'

'What happened?' I ask. He shrugs. I grab his forearm. 'The lock. You have to do it today, now. Can you pick the most discreet one you can find? Also don't say anything to Chloe, if you happen to see her.'

He scratches his head. 'What if she's there when I'm putting up the lock?'

'I'll make sure she won't be. And anyway I'll tell her myself later. When you've bought the lock, come back here but not into the house. Just wait for me in the shed.'

He looks at me like I've grown another head, but I don't care. I rush back inside, up to the nursery where I sit in the rocking chair at the window with Evie on my lap. Simon returns. He parks his old battered pickup truck where he usually parks and walks off towards the shed.

I knock on Chloe's door and pop my head in. She's lying on her unmade bed with her shoes on, tapping on her phone.

'Can you please take my bicycle to ride to the village and buy some nappies for Evie? She's run out. It's kind of urgent.'

'I think I should stay here,' she says.

'Why?'

'I just think I should.'

'Please, Chloe. I'm rather desperate here. It won't take you long. I'd go myself but you know what a production it is going to the shop with Evie.'

'I think I should stay, in case something happens,' she says slowly.

Great. Richard must have spoken to her. He's probably given her instructions. *Whatever you do, don't let Joanne out of your sight.*

'I'm fine, really. And Simon's here!' My ears start to feel hot and I have to resist the urge to put my hands over them.

She hesitates and I wonder what I'll do if she says no, but she swings her legs off her bed.

'Okay, fine.'

'Thank you.'

After she's gone, I smuggle Simon into the house and set him to work. I watch him fumble with his toolbox, my stomach knotted, willing him to go faster.

'I got a good one, Mrs Atkinson. See?' He holds up the lock for me to see. It means nothing to me. It's just a lock. He must mistake my anxiety for scepticism because he adds, 'I know, it doesn't look like much, but trust me. Top brand. Heavy steel. Evie's not going anywhere.' He chuckles.

'Sorry, Simon, but I'm in a bit of a hurry.'

'It won't take long.'

Fifteen minutes later and the result is perfect. A simple silver circle at about eye height. In fact, it looks like it's always been there, which is what I'm going to say if either Richard or Chloe or even Roxanne should ask. It's always been there. I'm surprised you've never noticed it before.

A floorboard creaks above us. I grab Simon's arm. 'Did you hear that?'

'Hear what, Mrs Atkinson?'

'Someone's up there.'

I should have known. Chloe didn't go to the village, she's hiding somewhere, spying on me.

We both listen for a few seconds. Silence. 'This house creaks, Mrs Atkinson. I wouldn't worry about it. You want me to go up there and take a look?'

'Yes, please. Thank you.'

While he's gone I hide the key in the pocket of my dressing gown that hangs behind my bedroom door. Simon comes back a few minutes later. 'Nothing up there, Mrs Atkinson. Just an open window. I closed it. Was there anything else?'

'No, thank you.' I almost push him out of the house. Five minutes later Chloe arrives. She hands me a packet of nappies. 'You want me to change her?'

'Were you in the village all this time?' I ask. I try to sound innocent, unbothered. What I really want to ask is, *Was that you upstairs? Did you* actually *go to the village?*

She raises an eyebrow. 'Yeah, so do you want me to change her?'

I study her face. She is such a good liar, it's scary. I take the packet of nappies from her and look at it closely. Is that one of mine? I have spare packets in the cupboard in the nursery. Could she have found them? Did she grab one while I went to fetch Simon?

'No, thank you. I'll do it.'

But I don't. I wait for her to shut herself up in her room, then run around the house like a mad woman with my bag of cameras in one hand and the baby monitor in the other.

I stick one camera on the top of the wall light sconce in the first-floor corridor. It sinks about halfway, so I lift it and stand on my toes and see that there's no bulb in that light. Just the socket. It must have blown, which would explain why Richard took it out, but he didn't remember to put a new one in. Too bad. I leave the camera there. In a way it's even better that way. Less visible but enough to get a good view. I hurry downstairs, my eye trained on the monitor. Everything is fine up there. Evie is fine. I put another camera in the hall on the console table, behind the vase. There's a small pile of papers, a couple of receipts and a gardening catalogue. I prop them up on either side of the camera, just to try to make it blend in. Again, not ideal, but at this point, it's the best I can do.

I turn around to get my phone so I can check the vision on my camera app, but it's not there. What did I do with it? I had it in my hand. I put it down somewhere. Did I leave it upstairs?

The floorboards creak above me.

I check the baby monitor. Nothing unusual, just Evie in her cot trying to grasp the woodland animals on the mobile above her head. I quickly go back up the stairs. I can smell something, something chemical and out of place. I retrace my steps, trying to identify the smell when I glance at the monitor and almost scream.

Chloe is in the nursery, facing the window. Evie isn't in her cot.

'What are you doing?' I cry, running to the door. Chloe turns her head. She's holding Evie in her arms. Evie looks content, happy, as she grasps strands of Chloe's hair.

'You need to be careful, Joanne,' Chloe says in a chillingly deadpan voice.

'Careful of what? Please don't do that. I said I'd change her. Put Evie back down, please.'

'I'm sorry, I can't do that.'

'Why not?'

'You have to leave.'

'Leave?'

'I'm going to put Evie in the basement.'

'Oh my god. Please give me my baby! Please, Chloe, give her to me now.'

'I can't do that, Joanne. I have to hide her.'

'Hide her?'

'Before he comes back.'

'Who?'

She turns to look at me, her eyes wide like saucers. 'The big bad man,' she breathes.

Oh my god. She's insane. I open my mouth and scream.

'Simon!'

Chapter Thirty-Six

I take a step forward and crane my neck, scanning the gardens for Simon's truck, but it's gone. It's just Chloe and me in the house now and I don't know where my phone is. I put my hands out. They're shaking uncontrollably.

'She's just a baby. She's not a threat to you. Your father loves you!'

'My father?' She sneers. 'My father doesn't love me. My father doesn't give a shit about me.'

'Oh god, Chloe, you're so wrong about that.'

'I'm not. Trust me on this one.' She opens the window with her free hand.

'What are you doing? Please, Chloe, I'm begging you. Give her to me.'

'We don't have a lot of time. The sun is going down.'

'What does that mean?'

'He's not who you think he is.'

'Who?'

'My dad, your *husband*.'

'Of course he is. He's a wonderful man and he loves you so much. Please get away from the window.'

'No, he's not, Joanne. He's evil, and he's going to come back. Oh, and you and Evie are going to die.'

The floor shifts under me. Oh god, Richard. Why hasn't he called? Or maybe he has and I didn't hear it because I don't have my phone. But why hasn't he called the landline? He'd be at the hotel by now. He must be getting worried. I eye the receiver in the corner. If I could reach it I could call the police.

'Listen, honey, we're going to get you some help, your father and I. I promise you. We're going to look after you.'

She's still staring outside. 'You should leave if you don't want to die.'

I've got to keep her calm. She could drop Evie any second. I inch my way towards the phone. 'I know it's not easy having a baby sister when you've been the centre of your father's world.'

'Hardly,' she says.

'And I know that when Sophie was born it was difficult for you. But it doesn't have to be this way. Evie and I, we could move away, leave your dad. You could stay with him here. Please close the window, Chloe.'

'The sun is setting. Do you see that?'

'Yes, please close it. Evie will be cold.'

She turns around. 'What did you say about Sophie just now?'

'I know it was hard for you when she was born.'

'It wasn't hard. You have no idea what you're talking about.'

'With your mum being so focused on another baby, I think it's perfectly natural. All siblings feel some degree of jealousy.'

'Is that what he told you?'

Evie is sucking her thumb, her head against Chloe's chest. She looks up at me. I extend my arms. 'Give Evie to me.' Evie turns away from me, buries her face in Chloe's neck.

'I loved my baby sister. I loved her more than anything in the world,' she says, clutching Evie.

Oh god. 'Let me hold her.'

'I can't. If I give her to you, you'll call the police.'

'We'll get you some help.'

'And if you call the police, you're going to die. You and Evie.'

'Oh my god. You're insane. Oh thank god.' My hand flies to my mouth. Out there, in the distance, is Simon's truck. He's coming back.

I rush to the window, my hand already raised. She grabs my wrist and pulls it down.

'I'm not insane, Joanne. This is all his fault, okay?'

'If you give her to me, I won't say anything to Richard. I promise you.' I look back to the window. Simon is almost here.

'Listen to me. My dad killed Soph, and then he killed my mother. He's doing it again. He's going to do the same to you and Evie, and I can't let it happen again.'

I can't even make sense of what she's saying.

'I'm doing this to help you and Evie. I know you don't believe me right now, but trust me, you will.'

Simon gets out of the truck and picks up… what is it? A shovel? He throws it in the back.

'Simon!' I shout.

Chloe closes the window and glares at me. 'What the fuck are you doing?'

'Nothing! Oh god, please give her to me, Chloe.'

'No!' She holds Evie tighter. 'I told you. I can't do that.'

My heart sinks. I look at Chloe. She's staring out the window again and I'm looking at the back of her head. I want to cup my hands around my mouth and scream

Simon's name, but it's no use. Not while she's holding onto Evie like that.

She's still distracted and I use the moment to inch my way to the landline. I pick it up, slowly, and bring the receiver to my ear. No dial tone. Nothing. The line is dead. I drop the receiver and it lands with a clank on the table. I bring my hands to my skull. 'What did you do?' I wail.

'I told you. He's coming back, and if you don't do as I say, you're going to die.'

'You're sick! You have to stop this now!'

Simon is looking for something on the ground near the pickup. If only he'd look up, maybe I could get his attention. If I could … what could I do? Raise my hand while Chloe isn't looking? Would that even work?

'I'm not sick. Didn't my dad tell you that? There's nothing wrong with me.'

'Because he doesn't want to admit it. But he sent you to a psychiatric hospital for three months, didn't he?'

'Yes,' she says calmly. 'That's true. He put me there. He said that if I kept telling everyone there was someone in the house that night, I'd never get out.'

Simon walks back to the pickup. My heart is thumping in my chest. And then, a miracle. He turns around and looks up, waves. I raise my hand behind Chloe but I don't think he can see me. Just her. It's too dark already and I'm too far away from the window.

I come to stand closer to Chloe. She doesn't object, doesn't look at me. She waves back at Simon. 'Listen to me carefully, Joanne. Don't call the police. Don't try and get Simon to come in here. Dad never went to the conference in Spain. He just pretended to and then snuck back into the house and pushed my mother off the third-floor landing.'

'No! Chloe, no such thing happened, I promise you.

There were security cameras all around the perimeter of your house. He would have been seen.'

'Cameras have blind spots. At least ours did. He made sure of that, and he knew exactly where those blind spots were. It took me years to figure out how he did it. He drove his car to the airport and left it there, then came back. You gonna wave goodbye to Simon or what? He's waiting.' She bounces Evie in her arms.

'He would have been picked up by the police. The police would have checked that he was at the conference.'

'You don't get it. My dad got someone else to go and pretend to be him, and that man is dead.'

'What? Who?'

She hesitates.

'Tell me!'

'Alfred Butterworth was his name. He was my dad's business partner back then. Wave goodbye, Joanne. Simon is starting to think something is wrong.' She holds up Evie's hand and makes her wave.

I bite my bottom lip and raise my hand. Simon nods and gets back in the pickup, then does a U-turn.

'You're insane.'

She turns back to me. 'Their business was going under. They'd been operating when they knew they couldn't honour their debts. How do you think Dad buys you all these nice things all the time? How do you think he can afford this house?'

'He runs a successful business. You know that.'

'They were going bankrupt. He told his business partner he could wipe out the debts, all he had to do was go to the conference as my dad, wear his clothes and be seen, but not ask questions.'

'I don't believe a word you say,' I whine.

'Think about it. Don't you think it's strange that there

was no mention of my mother's death in the tabloids? On TV? It's not like women throw themselves off balustrades every day in million-pound homes, is it? You know why? He paid people off. He kept the news out of the papers as much as he could. He sent me off to the nuthouse to keep me quiet. But his business partner figured it out eventually. You see, that money to wipe out all those debts came from the life insurance my father took out on my mother, plus he inherited half her money. She was very rich, by the way.' She tilts her head at me. 'Are you rich, Joanne?'

'What did you say happened to that man? Alfred Butterworth?'

Evie grouses. Chloe rocks her gently. 'He threw himself in front of a train at Victoria Station during rush hour. Nobody saw how it happened.'

'How do you even know all this?'

'It doesn't matter.'

'It does.'

'I spoke to his widow. Got bits of the story and put it together. At some point, her husband must have figured out he'd been used. Which is why he had to die.'

'So why didn't you go to the police?'

'Are you nuts? My dad had me committed to a psych ward. He threatened to leave me there forever if I didn't stop saying that someone was there that night. You see, I was supposed to be asleep when it happened. He thought he could sneak in, kill my mother and sneak out again and that I'd wake up the next morning and find her dead. He thought it would be over in a flash, but it wasn't. My mother fought back. I heard them arguing and woke up.'

'So why didn't he kill you too, if he's the monster you claim he is?'

'Because he wanted to make it look like suicide. He didn't

want a big investigation, just an open-and-shut case. But he's going to kill me now. After he's killed you and Evie. Then he's going to make it look like I did it before killing myself.'

She's completely insane. I swallow the lump in my throat. 'Why would he do that?'

'Money, of course. It's always about money with my dad.'

'You're lying. I don't believe a word you say. Give me my baby!'

'I can't give her to you. That's final. I have to protect her and I can't do that if I give her to you.'

I crack a sob. 'Roxanne is coming later, okay? She'll be here any minute.'

'Roxanne isn't coming.'

'She is. Your dad called her and asked her to come and stay. She'll be here soon. Please just stop this madness while there's still time and give me back my baby.'

'He didn't call her. He just pretended. This is all part of his plan to make you feel secure. Nobody is coming to save you.' She leans forward a little. Like she's going to tell me a secret. 'I'll kill him this time. He won't get away with it. Evie will be safe. I know you don't believe me, but that's okay. Trust me. You will.'

That smell again. I freeze. 'What is it?'

'What?' she asks.

'That smell.'

'What smell?'

'Oh my god. It's petrol.'

'He's here,' she says.

'What have you done, Chloe? What the hell have you done?'

'Joanne?'

'Oh, thank god, Richard!' I run out of the room and slam into my husband.

He takes my shoulders, holds me at arm's length. 'What's happened?'

'She's insane!'

Chapter Thirty-Seven

'She's crazy! You have to do something! She's got Evie!'

'Okay. Calm down. What the hell is going on here?'

'Hey, Dad.'

'Chloe. Sweetheart. What are you doing?'

'Here we go again, right, Daddy? Just like old times. Well, not quite. This time I'm prepared, but you know what I mean.'

'Richard?'

He turns to me. 'Joanne, I'm so sorry. I got all the way there and I had a message from Solomon and I had to come back. I'm so sorry about everything.'

'I know what you're doing, Dad.'

'Give Evie to me, sweetheart, please.'

'I'm not going to hurt her, but you already know that.'

'I should never have left. Where's Roxanne?'

'I don't know!' I shriek. 'And I can't find my phone!' I point a finger at Chloe. 'She stole my phone! And the land-line is dead! We have to call the police!'

Richard pushes me gently to the side. 'Give me the baby, Chloe sweetheart.'

Chloe leans forward slightly. 'If you try to lay a hand on her, I swear to God, I will kill you.'

'Oh god.'

'How do you propose to do that, sweetheart?'

I stare at him, confused by his tone. 'Do something!' I hiss.

'What do you want me to do?' he says.

'Get Evie away from her!'

He grips my arm and frowns at me. 'And I will. But you need to calm down. I can handle this. Do you want to wait for me downstairs?'

'Are you out of your mind?' I cry. 'I'm not going anywhere! I'm staying right here!'

Suddenly the door of the bathroom slams shut, followed by the sound of the lock turning.

I run to the door. 'Chloe! Open the door!'

Richard bangs on it with his closed fist. 'Open the door, Chloe!'

The noise has brought Oscar up here. He starts barking.

'Shut up!' Richard snaps and for a moment I think he's talking to me, but he's trying to move Oscar out of the way with his foot.

'We have to call the police,' I say.

He puts his hand on my shoulder. 'I've got this. Why don't you go and find out what the smell is?'

'I know what it is, Richard! It's petrol! She's poured petrol out there somewhere!'

'Exactly. And we must find out where it's been spilt because if she gets out, she's going to set it alight. We need to know exactly where she's poured petrol so we know the safest way to get out if we have to.'

'Oh god, you're right. You're so right. Do you think she's going to get out and run?'

'I don't think so. I think I can talk her into ending this whole mess, but we must be prepared. Just in case.'

'Okay.' I nod, wringing my hands together. 'I'll go and see what I can find.'

He squeezes my shoulder. 'It's going to be okay. Just go and find out where it's coming from.' He turns back to the door. 'Listen to me, sweetheart, it's going to be all right. Whatever you've done, it's going to be all right, I promise. Just open the door.'

I run out of the room.

Chapter Thirty-Eight

Every time Richard slams his shoulder into the bathroom door, an enormous boom reverberates, accompanied by Oscar's barks. I try not to picture a terrified Evie on the other side, but she's screaming so loudly it's breaking my heart. I try not to think what Chloe might do to her if she feels cornered. I have to trust Richard knows what he's doing and that he knows how to reach her, both literally and figuratively.

I flick the switch in the corridor, but nothing happens. The bulbs must have blown. No, wait, there are five sconces on each side of the passage. They haven't all blown at once, have they? I stand on my toes and look into one of the lights. My throat constricts. There's no lightbulb—just the naked socket.

I walk up and down the corridor, trying to find the source of the petrol scent. It's so intense that it's hard to pinpoint where it's coming from. I feel the carpet with my fingers to see if it's wet. I open the door to my office. Could Chloe have drenched my office in petrol? Absolutely. In fact I'd be surprised if she didn't, but the smell is not as strong here. I keep going, then retrace my steps, opening each door as I pass them: guest bedrooms, guest bathrooms, Chloe's bedroom.

I'm about to close the door again when I hear a phone buzzing. It's coming from the dresser. I flick on the switch but again nothing happens. Is that Chloe's phone? Oh god, if that's her phone, then I can use it to call the police! I sprint to the dresser and open the top drawer. The phone is still buzzing amongst her crumpled T-shirts.

I grab it, slide my thumb across the screen. 'Hello?'

Silence.

'Hello?'

'Hey, it's Ro.' The voice sounds like a robot. It's the reception, it's terrible up here. 'Hello?' I hiss.

Crackle. '....hang out?'

Roxanne. 'Roxanne! It's Joanne! Where are you?'

'Mrs A? I was … Chloe.'

'But why aren't you here?'

'…Should I be?'

'Yes! Richard called you this morning, remember? You're staying a couple of nights? You said you'd be here! You're coming? Oh god, something terrible has happened. Hello? You're there?'

More crackling sounds. I go to the window. The line becomes clearer. 'He cancelled.'

'He cancelled?'

'Yes. He said I wasn't needed after all.'

This can't be right. It can't be right, because if it is, it means that Chloe was telling the truth. *He didn't call her. He just pretended. Nobody is coming to save you.* Except in this case, he did call. And then he called back and cancelled.

'Hello? Roxanne? Listen to me—'

'Jo? What are you doing?'

Richard's voice behind me makes me gasp. When I pull the phone away from my ear, Roxanne is gone.

I feel like I'm going to throw up, and not just from the horrible smell.

I drop to the ground, feel the carpet in the dark, my heart thumping in my throat. 'I'm looking, I thought she'd poured petrol in here.' I should tell him the truth. I should show him the phone. *Look what I found. It must be Chloe's.* Then it vibrates again in my hand and the word *Ro* flashes on the screen.

'Give me that.' Richard's hand has reached over me to snatch the phone from my grasp. 'Where the hell did you find this?'

'In the dresser. Shouldn't you answer it? It's Roxanne! Hurry! You'll miss it!'

He flicks his thumb over the screen and brings the phone to his ear. 'Hello?' He pulls the phone away. 'There's no reception in here.' He shoves the phone in his pocket. 'I can't smell anything in here,' he says. 'You're wasting your time.'

I stare at him. I'm so confused right now. I stand up, brush my knees. 'What's happening?' I ask. Evie has stopped screaming. 'Where's Chloe?'

'She won't come out. I'm going to get an axe from the shed and break the door down.'

I gasp. 'An axe?'

'I won't be long. Oh and I found your phone.'

'You did? Where?'

'In your office just now. On your desk. You must have left it there.'

'Why were you in my office?'

Richard looks at me with sad eyes. 'I'm sorry I didn't believe you, sweetheart. Chloe isn't well. I should have known, but I was just…' He runs his hand through his hair.

'You know how it is. When it's your own child, you never want to believe there's something wrong with them.'

I don't know what's going on anymore. I raise my phone. 'I'm going to call the police.'

'There's no need. I've got this.'

'But we have to call the police!'

He takes my shoulders. 'I don't want to call the police. Not yet.'

'Why not?' I shriek. 'She's got Evie! We have to call the police! We have to do it now!'

'I can resolve this without involving the police. If the police get involved, she will go to prison. You see that, don't you?'

'Yes! Good! I hope she does! I hope she goes to prison forever!'

He puts his hand on my cheek. 'Sweetheart, I'm so sorry about all this. Let me handle this my way. It will be all right, I promise. You go back in there and see if you can talk her out. I'll get this door opened one way or the other.'

I look into his eyes. 'But what if it's too late?'

'It won't be. Go back in there. I'll be right back.'

He runs down the stairs without even flicking the light switch on. Is that because he knows the lights don't work? I walk the few steps to the top of the stairs. 'Richard?'

He turns around. 'What is it?'

'You called Roxanne, didn't you?'

'You know I did. You were there. Why?'

Why? Isn't that obvious? 'So why isn't she here?'

'I don't know! Chloe probably told her not to come. Can you please go back in there in case Chloe comes out? Don't go anywhere, okay? Wait for me.'

I nod. 'Okay.' He doesn't move, just stares at me.

'Get back in there!' he snaps.

I run back to the nursery. Oscar is lying on his side, panting. What on earth is wrong with him? I stretch my hand out and he whimpers. I can't worry about that right now. I crouch at the door so I can speak through the lock. 'Chloe, it's me. Open the door.'

No answer.

'Chloe. I believe you.'

I'm pretty sure I hear her sigh. 'Right. Nice try, Joanne.'

'Listen, I found your phone in your room and I spoke to Roxanne, she said Richard told her not to come.'

A beat. 'I told you so.'

'I know.'

'So you believe me now?'

Oh god. I bite the knuckle of my thumb. 'I think so.'

'Do you have my phone with you?'

I bite my bottom lip. 'He took it.'

'You can't trust him, Joanne. You can't believe a word he says. He's isolating us. He cut off the landline, just like he did at our old house. He went to the airport, parked his car, and somehow got himself back here. He must have been back for hours waiting somewhere inside the house for it to get dark.'

I think of the noises I heard earlier in the house, the sounds of someone creeping around. I thought it was Chloe. Is she telling me it was Richard this whole time?

'But he gave my phone back. Why would he do that if he wants to isolate us?'

'Have you checked it? Is it charged? Does it have a SIM card?'

I look down at it. That's when I see the message on the screen. *Insert SIM card.*

My hand flies to my mouth. 'The SIM card is missing.'

She sighs audibly. 'I told you so.'

I'm so frightened. I don't know who to believe any more. 'How did you know?'

'How do you think? He did the same to us last time.'

'Oh, god.' I grab a fistful of hair. 'He's going to be back any second. Open the door, Chloe!'

She unlocks the door of the bathroom so fast I stumble forward. She's still holding Evie against her chest as she grabs my hand and pulls me up. Evie grins at me. She thinks we're playing peek-a-boo or hide and seek.

I guess we are.

'Can I take her now?'

'No.'

'Why not?'

'I don't trust you.'

The front door creaks open.

'He's here!' I hiss. I drag her out of the nursery and push her in my bedroom. 'You hide in here with Evie. I'm going to stop him.'

'How?'

I fumble with my bathrobe hanging behind the door and find the key. 'I had a lock put on the door of the nursery.'

I crouch across the landing just as the top of Richard's head becomes visible on the stairs. I slip back into the nursery and realise the bathroom door is open. I leap to it. I've only just closed it and I'm crouched in front of it when Richard enters, the axe dangling by his side. It's a small one that Simon uses to chop wood for the fireplace, but still. It's big enough.

Oscar gives a frightened yelp.

'What's wrong with Oscar?' I ask.

'Maybe I kicked him,' he says impatiently. 'I don't know. He got in my way. I just meant to push him away, that's all.'

'You kicked him?'

'If I did it was only a little bit.'

'I can't believe you did that.' I put my hand out to pat

Oscar as Richard takes two strides towards me, raises the axe over one shoulder. I open my mouth to scream, my arms in front of my face.

'For Christ's sake, Jo! Get out of the way!' He's looking at me like I'm an imbecile, while holding the axe high above his shoulder.

I scramble away. The first blow hits just as I slip out of the nursery. *Crack!* I close the door and I'm struggling to put the key in the lock because my fingers are shaking so much. All I can think about is Evie. I need to hold Evie in my arms and get us out of here. Finally I get the key in but it's stuck. *Oh god. Please god.* Another loud crack, like a thunderclap. The sound of wood splintering. How can he not realise that Evie isn't in there? She's not even crying.

Well, he's going to work it out any second now. An even louder crack this time, almost like an explosion. Timber breaking. He must be kicking the door down.

I jiggle the key and this time it turns.

'Where the hell is she?' he roars.

I run back to my bedroom.

'That door is heavier but we won't have much time before he gets out. We have to get out of here.'

'Joanne!' Richard shouts, banging on the nursery door. 'What the hell is going on? This door is locked!'

Evie is sucking on her thumb. Her eyes are wide with curiosity. She doesn't seem frightened. Whatever noise is going on doesn't seem to worry her at all.

'So what do we now?' Chloe asks.

'Let me take Evie,' I say. There's a split second where our eyes lock, where we're both trying to figure out if the other can be trusted. The sound of Richard hitting the door makes us jump.

'No.'

'Why?'

'I'm going to save you both, that's why.'

Chapter Thirty-Nine

I have no choice. I mean, it's not like I can wrestle Evie out of her arms. And I believe her. I really do. I don't think she'd hurt Evie right now. But then, as we tip-toe across the landing toward the stairs, Evie pops her head up and points at the nursery.

'Yaya!'

I put my hand gently over her mouth. We hold our breath.

'Jo?'

He heard. Chloe grabs my sleeve and tugs. 'Let's go,' she urges softly.

'Jo, listen to me, sweetheart. I love you. I would never do anything to hurt you or our baby. I don't know what Chloe said to you but she's lying. Please open the door, sweetheart.'

His voice is so gentle, so soothing, so close, that I find myself transfixed by it. Suddenly I long to open the door and fall into his arms, tell him that I'm sorry, that I don't know what I was thinking.

'You're putting your life and our baby's life in danger by listening to her filthy lies. You were right. She's evil. I see that now. Diane tried to tell me, you tried to tell me. I think she killed her mother. She may even have smothered her baby sister.'

I stand there, heart pounding.

His voice cracks. 'You have no idea how sorry, very sorry, I am. And it's not your fault. She's bewitched you. Just like she bewitched me.'

Have I been *bewitched?* I mean, if we were playing a parlour game, say, word association, I don't know that *bewitched* is the first thing that'd pop into my head in response to *Chloe*, but did she convince me, somehow? Did I fall for her filthy lies?

'You can't believe him,' Chloe hisses, still tugging at my sleeve. 'We have to go!'

'I don't know who to believe,' I whisper, just as Richard slams his fist on the door so hard it shakes.

'Open the fucking door!'

Any minute now he's going to take the axe to it. We run down the stairs, which is where the petrol has been poured, I now realise. The carpet is so drenched in places, my feet are sloshing in the stuff. Clearly someone meant to cut my escape route from the first floor.

Even with Evie in her arms, Chloe moves faster than me. She's already at the front door, pulling on it as hard as she can. 'It's locked,' she says, and I think I can hear a note of panic in her voice.

'Oh god. How?'

'What do we do now?' she shrieks.

I have to pull myself together. I have to get us out. 'Back door,' I snap. We run through the passage and into the kitchen. I run from window to window as I pass them but every single one is locked.

'The back door is locked too,' she whimpers. She grabs my arm. 'We have to get down to the basement.'

'The basement? Why?'

'Because it's the best hiding place right now. Because he knows you're terrified of going in there.'

I stand and look down, dizzy as I stare into the abyss. I feel for the light switch. Chloe puts her hand on my arm. 'No.'

'But he might not have taken the light bulbs out here.'

'Exactly. He'll see the light under the door. We can't risk it.'

'Are you crazy? You want me to go down there *in the dark*?'

Boom! This time it sounds like Richard is ramming his shoulder against the door. I can't believe it's still holding. I'm going to give Simon a raise, if I ever see him again.

I swallow the lump in my throat, look down at Evie in Chloe's arms. She grins at me. She thinks this is the funniest adventure ever.

Chloe takes a few steps, then turns around. 'You're coming?'

I take a tentative step.

Boom!

I grab the railing with both hands and take the first step down. My legs feel like jelly.

'There were ten in the bed and the little one said—'

I stop. 'You're singing to her? Now?'

'It keeps her calm. Roll over! Roll over!'

Evie giggles.

'She seems very calm to me.'

'So they all rolled over…' she continues softly.

It's funny, but I used to find her singing creepy as hell, but now I find it unbelievably soothing.

'And one fell out.'

Evie cracks up.

'This is the last step,' Chloe whispers. She takes my hand, and I feel the ground with my toe until I find my footing. It's cold and damp down here and for some reason I think of the plans Richard had to transform the space into a cinema, or was it a pool room? The memory brings a rush of nostalgia.

I am truly losing my mind.

'You okay?'

'Not really.'

'This way. We're going to go straight ahead until we reach the wall.'

'The other end? All the way over there? Behind the concrete wall?'

'It's the safest place to hide if he does come down here.'

'I thought you said he wasn't going to come down here.'

She ignores me. 'Just hold my hand and wave your other arm around.'

'Why?'

'Cobwebs. So they don't hit your face.'

'Oh god.'

'There were nine in the bed and the little one said... Come on, Joanne. It will take your mind off it. Sing with me.'

It's not going to take my mind off *it*, whatever *it* is, but I swallow, put my hand out, palm first and start singing in a trembling whisper.

'Roll over, roll over...' Evie squeals with joy. My baby girl is truly afraid of nothing. 'So they all rolled over and one fell out...'

We sing softly the whole way and make it to the other end.

My hand touches the wall. It's rough under my fingers. 'What if there are rats and spiders crawling around?'

'They're more scared of you than you are of them.'

'Somehow, I doubt that very much.'

I swallow, sit down, and bring my legs in front of me. We can only just hear the thud of the axe hitting the door. 'It won't be long now until he breaks it down,' I say. I look over at Evie. 'Please?'

She hesitates for a moment. 'If I give you Evie, promise me you'll help us get out of here? You'll help me?' She studies my face. 'You can't leave me here with him. He'll kill me. I came here because of you and Evie.'

'Yes. I mean no. I won't leave you behind' I say. I press my lips together, hoping — praying — that she'll believe me. At this point I'll say anything to have Evie back. When she passes her to me, I want to burst into tears. She's safe in my arms. I can finally breathe. I settle her on my lap. 'She's asleep.'

It's incredible, but it looks like our very bad singing has put her to sleep.

'What are we going to do?' I ask.

'We wait. We listen. Somewhere above here is the front door. We should be able to hear if he unlocks it.'

But what if he locks the door after him?'

'Let's wait and see. If he thinks we're already outside, he won't lock it.'

'And then what?'

'Then we run out of here as quickly as we can. He probably took the keys to your car too, but we can hide in the shed. Maybe. We have to last until daybreak. It'll be easier after that.'

'I have the keys to my car.'

'You do?'

'Well, not on me, but I have one hidden under the back wheel. He doesn't know about it, only because I lost them once and he got really annoyed with me. I've been so forgetful lately...'

'Hey, you probably haven't, or nothing out of the ordinary. That's just his MO. He makes you feel like there's something wrong with you and eventually, you start to believe it.' She gives a small, bitter laugh.

I crack a sob.

'You okay?' she asks.

'No,' I wail softly. 'I'm really scared. I hate this.'

She puts something in my hand. It's my phone. 'You dropped it before when we ran out.'

'Thanks,' I wipe my nose with the back of my hand. 'But it's useless, remember?'

'It's got a torch.'

I flick the screen and it lights up. Chloe grabs my arm. 'Don't turn it on yet. You want to save the battery.'

'Wait.' I show her the screen. 'It's still connected to the wi-fi.' We both squint at the tiny little bar. And I mean, tiny, very small, bar. Barely visible to the naked eye.

'Look! I have a text message!' I sit up. Evie stirs. The text is from Jim Preston.

'Who is he?'

'The journalist who wrote about your mum's death back then. I got in touch with him.'

'You did? Why?'

'I wanted to understand what had happened to you. Richard didn't like to talk about it.'

'Yeah,' she snorts. 'I bet he didn't. So what did you find out?'

'Just what was in the papers. And that your father sent you to a mental institution. But look! We can send him a text! He can get help for us!'

'You can't send texts without a SIM card.'

'But there's one from him right here!'

'Your phone still stores old texts, you just can't send or receive new ones.'

But I hadn't read this one before. I open it.

Joanne, I was trying to tell you before. I don't know if this is relevant but regarding your husband's business. There's rumours that he's in trouble. There's talk of a Ponzi scheme. I remembered back then his other business was in trouble too and I don't know. It just raised a red flag for me. Just be careful.

'I knew it,' Chloe says, reading over my shoulder.

'Oh.My.God.'

If I had any doubts left, they've just vanished. What Chloe said about Richard having money troubles, it was all true. Everything is true. The man I married, the man I've been madly in love with all this time, is a monster. Even when Roxanne said he'd told her not to come, I thought – hoped – there'd be an explanation.

Tears stream down my face as I close the text. I squint at the screen, brush my tears away with the back of my hand. 'Oh.'

'What?'

I point to the icon for the security camera app and tap to open it. It takes ages to load and for a moment I think it's no use, there's not enough signal down here, but it finally opens.

The screen shows the vision from the camera in the nursery. It's dark and hard to see through the doors of the cabinet, but you can just make out the outline of Richard's back. We stare at the grainy image. 'What is he doing?' Chloe asks.

I look up and listen. The thudding has stopped. I stare at the screen again. 'I think he's breaking off the timber with his hands.'

'Where is the camera? I thought Dad threw them all out?'

'I had a couple left over. I put them up earlier.' I don't tell her I put them up to keep an eye on her. That I was afraid she might do something crazy.

My eyes have adjusted to the darkness. There's a small square window up the other end of the passage we're in. It's tiny and there are bars so we wouldn't be able to get out that way, but it lets in a sliver of moonlight.

We sit there in silence and watch Richard swing the axe again. I just can't believe what I'm seeing. I don't recognise my husband. Did Chloe really come to this house because she was afraid of what he might do to us? How can that possibly be true? The whole time she's been here with us, she's been awful to me. If she really was afraid for me and Evie, why didn't she say anything sooner? Looking at her profile now -- and let's face it, we've never been this physically close before -- I am struck by how young and vulnerable she looks.

I turn to the screen again. It won't be long now until Richard gets out, and as I hug my sleeping baby, I wonder if we're going to make it out alive.

Chapter Forty

'Why did you Photoshop the picture with Simon?' I ask softly.

Chloe stares down at the screen, the outline of Richard fighting with the door. 'I wanted you to break it off with Dad. I did everything I could think of so you'd leave him. I thought if I kept doing horrible stuff to you, and if I threatened to live with you and Dad forever, you'd walk away and divorce him. Then you'd change your will and cancel your life insurance policy, and you and Evie would be safe.'

'Wait. How did you know about my life insurance policy?'

'I found it in your office. On the first day I got here. Ten million pounds.'

'You went snooping?'

'Yes. Whose idea was it to buy that much life insurance?'

'I don't know. Ours, I guess. I mean, I have the same policy on him. It's pretty standard, isn't it?'

'Ten million pounds? That's not standard. That's a shit load of money.'

'I know. I know. You're right. And yes, it was his idea, but he was thinking about Evie.'

'Yeah, right.' She snorts.

'So how did you know to come here, to this house? How did you know we were in danger?'

'I saw him, at the Connaught. I was working there two nights a week at reception.'

'You were working at the Connaught? You had a job?'

'Yeah, of course I had a job. Why wouldn't I? I have bills to pay.'

'I don't know. I mean, your dad bought you the flat. I imagined you didn't need to work.'

'He didn't buy me a flat. Are you kidding? I wouldn't touch his money in a thousand years. When I saw him come in, I hid in the back and got my colleague to serve him. He went up to a room and didn't come out until the next night. The room was booked by a woman.'

I gasp. 'Isabella?'

'No. Someone else.'

'The supermodel? That was true?' I almost shriek. I mean, I would have, but then Evie would have woken up, so I just hissed it instead.

'No! I made that up. The woman he came to see was in her fifties. I asked my supervisor about her. She's an American, from New York. Very rich, but you could tell that just by looking at her. I knew you guys were married and you'd had Evie, and I just got a really bad feeling. Then I found out the woman was coming to town regularly. Wow, Joanne, don't tell me you're … *crying*?'

'It's just that… I genuinely thought we were happy. It's all such a shock. When things didn't work out with Isabella—'

'Come on. Don't you get it? He met you, he realised how rich you were, he was stealing from his business and about to get caught out. He dumped Isabella for you because you were the bigger fish.'

I snort. 'You've got the wrong idea. I'm not that rich.'

'But you said… about your inheritance?'

'It's only small. Not to me,' I rush to add. 'I mean, compared to how rich your father is.'

'How much is it?'

'Sixty thousand pounds.'

After a short pause, she says, 'He must be more desperate than I thought. But anyway, there's the life insurance. Tell me this, whose idea was it to live out here in the middle of nowhere? You're a long way away from your friends, out here.'

'I thought it would be nice, you know? A big house in the country...'

'Yeah, but did *you* think that? Or did he make you think that's what you wanted?'

I press my fingers between my eyes, try to think. It's true that back when we were looking for a house, every time I took him to see a property I thought would be perfect for us, he'd find fault with it. It was too small, too dark, in the wrong neighbourhood.

I didn't even know he'd been looking at houses so far out of London until he took me to see one.

'Look! It's perfect!' he said when he took me to see it. 'Can you imagine all our beautiful children running around the lawn? And look, there's a fishpond! And we could get a dog, you always said you wanted a dog. Plenty of room for a dog to run around.'

I can't say I immediately shared his enthusiasm. It felt too far away from my friends, from the life I'd started to rebuild in London after living in Chelmsford. I'd moved to Chelmsford for Marc. I didn't make many friends there, just Shelley, really. In London, I felt home again. It's true I was a tiny bit disappointed when he said he wanted to live out here.

'It's so… big. Why do we need such a big house anyway?' I'd said.

'But you told me it was your dream to have a big family, lots of children. Sweetheart! What's wrong? Did you change your mind about that?'

I hadn't. I just didn't think I'd have them all at once, or that I'd have three dozen of them plus a menagerie. But at the same time, I could see the potential. There was a house I'd seen recently that had a glasshouse attached to it where people grew tropical plants. Maybe we could do the same. Open up the kitchen so it would be a lovely big space, but warm too, with a big fireplace.

I wanted Richard to be happy and I made myself see the positives, until eventually, one day, I woke up, and just like that, it was what *I* wanted. That's what he would say to me sometimes. 'It's what you want, isn't it, Joanne? You want this life, this house, this is your dream, isn't it?' And I thought it was. But maybe it was his dream. Maybe he just plonked it into my head and made me think it was mine.

'I really thought you hated me,' I say to Chloe now.

'Well, no offence, Joanne, but I didn't really care about you one way or another. It's when I heard Evie was born that I got a terrible feeling. Then I saw him at the hotel, and I just couldn't live with myself if something happened to Evie. I wanted to come here and get a feel for the situation. But when I saw the life insurance policy, and the way he was with me, you know? The fact he wanted me to stay on as Evie's nanny? I knew. I just knew. You're both going to die, and he's going to pin it on me.'

'You should have said something to me.'

'You're joking, right?'

'You kept saying horrible things to me when he wasn't around.'

'I wanted you to leave him. I thought I'd make your life as miserable as possible until you did.'

'It doesn't work like that.'

'Yeah, well, I did my best.'

'You certainly did.' I roll my eyes, and she smiles. I'm pretty sure this is the first time I've seen her smile. And we had to be hunkering down in a basement with an axe-wielding maniac upstairs for that to happen.

Then I remember something. 'What's this about a phone call you made to Solomon? Richard said he came back because of it.'

'He's trying to muddle you up. When my mum died, my dad got half of Mum's estate. My half of the estate was held in a trust until I turned twenty-one.'

'So …'

'I've just become very rich, yes. I called the solicitor to make a will. Right now, if anything happens to me, Dad gets the lot. I never got around to doing the will, but I tell you what, it's interesting my dad and Solomon are having a conversation about it, wouldn't you say?'

I sigh. 'It does look like it.'

'You see why he doesn't want me to live? After he kills you and Evie, he'll kill me. Then he'll sneak off back to Amsterdam and return in a few days to find that I massacred his family – again -- but this time I killed myself too. Or something along those lines.' She sighs. 'Trust me. I've been there.'

I'm going to be sick. 'I thought you adored him,' I say. But then I remember that time in the kitchen when Richard was feeding Evie, and the look of pure hatred on Chloe's face as she looked on. I'd thought it was for Evie, but it must have been for Richard.

'I couldn't let him guess how I really felt, or he would have known why I'd come. He would have known I was up to something. I had to make him think I was desperate to be in his life again. All these years ago I'd managed to convince him that I was mistaken about someone being there that night. I mean, I knew it was him, I'd heard him arguing with my mum. I was afraid of him, that's why I said it was a stranger in the house. I wanted the police to figure it out, but they never did.'

I can't begin to imagine what it must have been like, knowing your father killed your mother and being unable to do anything about it. 'I'm so sorry, Chloe.'

'Whatever.' She grabs my arm. 'Joanne, look.'

Richard has lifted his leg through the hole in the door and disappears on the other side.

'Oh god. He's out.' I flick the app to the camera in the corridor. We watch in horror as Richard's dark shape slowly walks down the hallway, opening doors as he walks past. 'Joanne! Darling! Answer me!'

I can barely breathe.

'Listen, Jo, I'm not angry, okay? I just want you to be safe. You won't be safe as long as you're with her, you understand? So just come out from where you're hiding, sweetheart. Remember, she's crazy and she's a liar. You can't believe a word she says. It's my fault, I know that. You were right all along. She's unhinged and I didn't want to see it. I love you, Joanne. I love you so much.'

You can barely see a thing but I can hear a strange sound, like a whack, with every step he takes. I squint at the shadowy figure and when I figure it out I gasp and clasp my fingers against my mouth. Richard is slapping the flat of the axe against the palm of his hand, as if weighing up how good the blade is. All the while insisting he loves me *so much*.

'I'm going to be sick.'

'No, this is great. Do you have cameras downstairs? Can we see when he goes outside?'

'There's one in the living room. And one on the little table in the hall.'

Richard is downstairs now, still calling out to us. The vision is slightly better because there's more moonlight filtering down there. We watch him go into his study. When he comes out he's not holding the axe anymore. He's holding something else. I squint again at the grainy image.

'What is it?' I ask.

'The shotgun.'

'Oh god, no.'

'Come out, Chloe! You evil little psycho! I'll find you eventually!'

'Why does he keep calling you that?' I whisper.

'Why do you think? He's trying to convince you that *I'm* the psycho.'

'Right. Makes sense. You still think we should stay here?'

'Yes. I do. It's our best chance.'

We watch as Richard goes back upstairs then walks in and out of rooms, calling my name, calling out to Chloe, calling out to Evie. At one point the camera picks up his face and he looks crazed, his eyes wild, his mouth distorted.

Then he goes up the stairs to the next floor and we can no longer see him. We are silent for a moment, our eyes glued to the screen, waiting for his return. All I can hear is the beating of my heart.

'I thought I saw you one night, crouched in Evie's room.'

She looks up abruptly. 'I've been doing that every night. The moment I entered this house, I knew he'd use the fact that I was there to kill you both and pin it on me. Let me tell you, I was pretty relieved when you decided to keep Evie with you at night, I won't lie. Plus you almost caught me a couple of times.'

'And the Calpol?'

She's silent for a moment. 'I'd just got here and you asked Dad to pick some up, remember? I was afraid he'd put poison in it. That was probably a bit over the top on my part but honestly, I knew he was going to do it while I was here. So I went out on your bike and got another bottle but it was a different one, they didn't have the smaller ones at the chemist in the village. I had to replace the contents.'

I can't believe how wrong I've been all this time. I thought she had come to hurt us. Meanwhile she was trying to save us.

'The journalist who wrote about what happened to your mother told me he thought Richard was afraid of you.'

'The only thing my dad is afraid of is that I know what he did and I'll tell.' She shrugs. 'It didn't matter anyway. I tried, but nobody believed me.'

'But why did you decide to leave? You said you were going back to London next week.'

'I was sick of waiting for him to make his move. But I knew he was going away on this trip and it sounded an awful lot like last time. So I told him I was leaving and watched him squirm. He didn't want me to go. He wanted me to stay because he had it all planned. That's when I knew he was going to make his move.'

'He's back.' I grab her arm. Richard is walking quickly down the stairs, almost running. We can hear him muttering to himself, 'Fucking bitch. You fucking little bitch!' although it's unclear whether he's talking about me or Chloe. Still, it's like watching a horror movie. I've seen Richard lose his temper before but not like this. Never like this. It's terrifying. He races down the next flight of stairs and I switch to the living room camera.

The sound of the front door opening.

Chloe grabs my arm. 'He's going outside. Let's go.'

Chapter Forty-One

We make a run for it, or in my case, a kind of fast walk so as not to wake Evie. Suddenly I don't care about spider webs even as I smash my face into them. Chloe is in front of me and she runs up the stairs and opens the door. We cross the tiled hall.

The front door is wide open. I'm about to run through it but she stops me with one arm.

'Wait.'

She peers around the door, slowly. I get it. Maybe it's a trap. And if it is, it's a good one.

I lean back against the wall by the door and catch my breath. Miraculously, Evie has not woken up. Chloe motions with her head. I peer outside.

Richard is standing in front of my car, the shotgun sitting loosely over one shoulder.

I want to burst into tears. 'Let's just wait here,' I whisper. 'He'll walk away at some point. That's when we'll make a run for it.'

She shakes her head. 'We'll never make it to the car, get the key. He'll shoot us before we get in the door.'

'How would he explain that to the police?'

'He'll say I shot you and Evie and he grabbed the gun from me and shot me.'

'Wow, you're really on top of this, aren't you?'

'Just assume the worst, Joanne. That's what I do.'

She looks around the room. For a hiding place maybe? 'There's the coat room over there.'

'I have an idea,' she says.

Richard walks around the side of the house, or that's what it sounds like. 'Come out, Chloe! Come on out, baby, from wherever you are, you fucking little PSYCHO!'

Evie stirs. We've slipped inside the coat room and we're crouched on the floor, the door ajar. There's barely a sliver of moonlight. I think I'm sitting on a pair of heavy outdoor boots. It's supremely uncomfortable. When Chloe speaks, she sounds like she's talking through layers of tweed.

'I'm going to go upstairs and make some noise,' Chloe whispers. 'That way he'll think we're up there. Meanwhile you—'

'No.'

'—get Evie in the car and get out.'

'Absolutely not. I am not leaving you here alone with this monster.'

'But once you're out there, you'll get help!'

'I'm not leaving you here, Chloe.'

She clicks her tongue. 'We don't have a choice. We don't have time. It's your only shot.'

'No.'

There's movement, coats being shoved about, then she grabs the collar of my shirt. 'It's Evie's only shot!'

I look down at Evie. If only I could protect them both. If only I had a gun, I'd leave Evie with Chloe and go out and shoot him myself.

But I don't have a gun. 'You go,' I say. 'The key is above

the left back tyre. It's stuck there with a magnet. The nearest neighbours are the Thomsons about half a mile down the road. I'll stay here and distract him.'

'You forgot something.'

'What? Oh right. You can't drive. You could take Evie and run there, though, it's not that far.'

'No way. He'll come after us. He's got a gun, remember?' She gets up. Peers around the door. We can still hear Richard ranting and raving outside. 'Wait here, stay hidden until the coast is clear.'

Before I have a chance to object, she's grabbed one of the umbrellas. Something falls from her pocket. She snatches it and shoves it back in.

'What is it?'

'Worst case scenario,' she whispers.

'What does that mean?'

'I took the matches from the kitchen drawer when we tried to get out that way. Once he's up there, I'll make sure he can't get back down so you'll have some time to get away.'

'No! Chloe it's too dangerous!'

But she's already gone and is running up the stairs. I stand up slowly, Evie still asleep in my arms, oblivious to the drama unfolding around her. I hear someone banging above my head and for a moment I think Richard is back, that he's upstairs. The sound of glass breaking.

Chloe.

She's broken a window upstairs with the umbrella.

I peer through the gap in the door. Richard races back inside, slams the door shut and raises his shotgun to his shoulder.

Chapter Forty-Two

My heart sinks when I get out and glance up at Chloe at the window. She looks terrified. And yet, when she opens her mouth to scream, she isn't thinking about her own safety. She doesn't cry out for me to help her. No. What she screams at the top of her lungs is, *RUN!*

I get in the car but I don't go far. The sight of Chloe at the window with smoke rising behind her is still imprinted on my retinas. I don't start the Range Rover because I don't want to alert him. Fortunately, our driveway is on a slight incline, so I put the car into drive and let it roll. I'll start the motor once I'm further away from the house.

But I can't get Chloe's face out of my mind, that look of sheer terror, so I veer left and let the car roll to a stop beside a hedge.

Of course, she's terrified. I left her behind trapped in the house with a shotgun-waving maniac. *You can't leave me alone here with him. He'll kill me. Promise me.*

I have to go back. I made a promise in that basement and

I'm going to stick to it. I turn around to check on Evie. She's awake, studying the roof of the car like it's the most interesting thing she's ever seen.

'There's no way we'll get help in time.' She looks at me, then back at the ceiling. I open my door softly.

'I'll be right back, okay?'

But I don't know if I'm going to make it in time. Can I get to Chloe before he shoots her? Can I protect her? I have no idea but I'm going to give it my best shot.

I lock the car and run back to the house.

I'm not thinking straight. I just want to get up there and somehow find a way to stop him, if it's not too late. Only when I push the door open does it dawn on me that I have no weapon. I have nothing. What am I thinking? That I'll tackle Richard to the ground?

I can hear him shouting up there. 'You thought you could outrun me? You thought I wouldn't catch you this time?' Then he laughs. A maniacal, evil, demented kind of laugh. 'Get out here! Come on out! Or do you just want to burn alive?'

So he hasn't found her yet. I have to get up there. I have to find her, get her out while there's still time. The flames have taken hold of the carpet that runs along the stone stairs, but there's still space on either side.

I go back to the coat room and look for the largest umbrella I can find. I pick the birdcage one with the wooden handle. I lift it up and weigh it in my hands. It's not great but it will have to do. I carefully go up the stairs, my sweater pulled up over my mouth. There he is, right there, at the top of the stairs, his back to me. He's still shouting, his shotgun in position, a crazy man ready to shoot at the clouds. I lift the umbrella and bring it down with all my strength on his skull.

I expect him to turn around, maybe even shoot me, and I've already retreated a few steps, holding the umbrella like it's a cricket bat. But he just stands very still. It's only a few seconds but it feels like an eternity before one leg buckles and he puts his hand out.

'What the...' He turns around then, a trickle of blood running down the side of his face. He narrows his eyes at me, 'Jo?' before collapsing in a heap.

My chest is heaving with the effort of breathing. He's not moving. Did I kill him? I think maybe I killed him. I should grab the shotgun. I bend down slowly, take hold of the barrel and pull, but he's too heavy and the gun doesn't budge.

I let go and push the door to the nursery, or what's left of it anyway. I try to shout her name but it comes out as a strangled cough. My eyes sting and tears are streaming down my face. I hold my jumper over my nose. I would have turned away but I hear a kind of strangled whimper. It's coming from the bathroom.

'Chloe?'

But the face that appears through the hole Richard made in the door before he realised the bathroom was empty doesn't belong to Chloe. It belongs to Oscar.

'Oscar!' I guess he was too weak, or too frightened to get out by himself. He tries to jump on me and lets out a yelp of pain.

'Just wait for me here,' I say. I run up the corridor, shouting Chloe's name into empty rooms, but she doesn't come out. Did she manage to get out? I have to get back downstairs now or I'll get trapped up here. I run back to the other end of the corridor. Oscar is going crazy. He's barking at Richard's slumped body and then turning around and around, backing away from the flames. There's no way he's going to go down there on his own.

There's only one room I haven't checked and that's my

office. I step over Richard, open the door, and there she is, sitting under my desk, her hands over her head.

'Chloe, sweetie.'

She looks up, her eyes wide with terror. 'You came back.' She cracks a sob. 'Is he still out there?'

'He's out cold.'

I help her up. On the landing Oscar isn't barking anymore, he's just running around in circles. I try to coax him to go down the stairs but that's not going to happen. He just gets further away from the flames, throwing me looks of desperation.

I pick him up in my arms and he whimpers. I almost stumble under his weight and Chloe grabs me so I can right myself.

'I've got him. Now go,' I whisper. She sees the shotgun and tries to yank it out from under him, just like I did, but she doesn't have any more luck than me.

'We can't waste any more time. Come on. Stay along this side of the stairs.' I point to the opposite side from the wall. Then, with a terrified Oscar trying to wriggle out of my arms, I step over Richard.

A hand grips my ankle.

Chapter Forty-Three

I try to scream but I can't breathe and my voice is strangled by the thick smoke. Richard's fingers are digging into my flesh and in that moment I realise I'm going to die. I think of Evie locked inside the car and I don't know if any of us are going to make it out alive.

And then he moans. 'I… don't… tell her.'

Don't tell her what? That you're a total psycho? I think she knows by now.

'Let me go!'

I glance down at the stairs where the flames are getting higher. I kick my leg but that just makes him hold on tighter.

Then suddenly Chloe is there, kicking his arm with the heel of her foot, but still he doesn't let go. She stomps on his shoulder, then on his leg and he cries out in pain and finally releases me.

'You fucking bitch,' he moans. He's on his knees, arm outstretched, his fingers like claws as he tries to grab my leg again. I don't know if I'm going to make it. I'm feeling dizzy from trying to hold my breath, from the heat, from the fear that is gripping me, but the effort of speaking has brought on a coughing fit and Richard holds his chest.

We run down the stairs. I don't know how we do it with Oscar in my arms and the flames reaching to our knees, the smoke making it impossible to breathe, but we do it.

The moment we're outside I let go of Oscar and he takes off.

'Where's the car?' Chloe asks between coughs.

'This way.' My throat is burning, my voice sounds strange. I point to the side of the house. You can hear Evie crying from here. I reach into my pocket for the key and for a second I can't find it. Behind us I can hear growls of pain, and when I turn around I see a shadow looming in the doorway, silhouetted by the light from the fire. A wave of panic engulfs me. 'I can't find the key!' I cry, panic strangling my voice, then my fingers brush against it. 'Oh thank god.' I unlock the car and Chloe immediately slides onto the back seat and whispers to Evie. 'It's okay. It's okay.' It's not okay, not by a long shot. We are nowhere near okay, but I'm grateful for how she's keeping it together and that her first concern is for Evie.

'What about Oscar?' she says, winding down the windows.

'Oscar!' I shout, even as I press my foot down on the accelerator. 'Oscar!'

But Oscar is gone and I have to trust that he will be okay now that he's out of the house and away from Richard. I have to get Evie and Chloe out of here to safety.

I turn the corner to get back on the driveway.

'The gate!' Chloe cries. 'It's closed!'

'It's all right.' I glance in the rear-view mirror. No sign of Richard, just the house glowing red. I get out of the car and run up to the number pad. I punch in the numbers to open the gate.

Nothing. The gate doesn't budge. I must have done it wrong. My fingers are shaking too much.

'Why isn't it opening?' Chloe whines.

'Just give me a minute.' I try again. It's only four digits, for Christ's sake.

'He's here!' Chloe screams.

I look back down the driveway.

'Jo! Wait!' Richard yells. He raises a hand. He's dragging his left leg, the one Chloe stomped on. I wonder if she broke it. The left side of his face is completely covered in blood.

'I'm going to try and stop him.' I grab the key from the ignition and throw it at her. 'Lock the doors.'

'What are you going to do?'

I don't answer. I listen for the sound of the doors locking behind me, but it doesn't come. Richard raises the gun and aims it at the car.

'Let them go,' I say. 'They're children. They're your children. They haven't done anything to deserve this.'

'You just don't get it, Jo.'

Chloe is screaming and I'm yelling at her to get down, get Evie down and that's when I see him. He's running so hard, so fast, it takes me a moment to realise that it's Oscar. He jumps through the air and lands on Richard's left buttock. Richard cries out in pain, drops the shotgun and falls to his knees. He's screaming but Oscar is not done with him. He takes another jump, locks his jaws around Richard's left elbow.

I plunge, grab the shotgun, and aim it at him. 'Open the gate, Richard.'

Richard lets out a whimper. 'Don't shoot me! Joanne, please! Listen to me!'

'Open the gate!'

'I love you, Jo! It was Chloe I was trying to stop! Not you! I love you!'

God, I wish he'd give it up. It's excruciating. 'Open the gate or I'll shoot you.'

Then suddenly the gun is yanked off me. I turn to Chloe who is standing there, her face like a mask. 'What are you doing?'

But she's not looking at me. She whips out something from her back pocket. 'Hey, Dad?'

He looks up, his eyes pleading. 'I never told her.'

'Look at this, Dad!'

He fixes his gaze on her. 'Why did you come? Why didn't you leave us alone?'

'You want to know why I came? Here! Take it. Look at it!' She's waving the baby photo of Sophie in his face. He takes it from her with shaking hands.

'That's why I came, Daddy. Remember her? Take a good look at her!' She slaps the photo. It falls out of Richard's hands. She picks it up and pushes it back into his hands. 'Remember her? Do you? Or don't you even care anymore?'

His face is covered in soot and blood, his features distorted. His piercing blue eyes slowly move and gaze at me. 'Help me…'

'People like you don't deserve to be helped. Mum's dead, Sophie's dead, and it's all your fucking fault, Daddy! And now Joanne? And Evie? Really, Dad? Evie?'

'Chloe, baby, I've always loved you more than life itself.'

'You're such a fucking liar.'

The noise is like a thunderclap. It seems to echo around us for a long time. Evie is screaming. I put my hands over my ears. Richard is lying on his back. He no longer has a face.

I claw at my skull. 'What did you do? Chloe? What did you do? He wasn't going anywhere!'

'Payback.'

My hands are clasped over my mouth. She turns to me. 'You don't get it, do you?'

I let my hands fall. 'Of course I do. For your mum. For Sophie.'

She nods. 'And for you, and for Evie. For everything,' she says.

I just make it to the side of the road and throw up, although not much comes out. Just bile. My legs are jelly when I walk to the pad and punch the numbers again. This time the gate shudders.

I guess I did it wrong last time.

I hear the shotgun reload behind me. When I turn back to Chloe, she looks in a trance.

And she's pointing the gun at me.

'What are you doing?'

The gates have completely opened now. They stop with a loud clank. The noise seems to wake Chloe. She shakes her head. Drops the gun. 'Sorry. I don't know what I was thinking.'

I put my hand on my chest. My heart is thumping. 'Oh god, I thought…'

'Let's get out of here.'

Chapter Forty-Four

We told the police that Chloe wrestled the gun from Richard, that it was literally a fight to the death, that it was him or us and that the gun went off accidentally. Technically, when she shot him, he was no longer an immediate threat. I mean, by then he was on his knees, sobbing over Sophie's baby photo and begging for his life. Also, Oscar had helped himself to a pound of flesh and then some. Richard was not going anywhere. But Chloe needed closure.

I can understand that.

It's been two months, and every day I remind myself I'm lucky to be alive. If it hadn't been for Chloe, I'd be dead and so would Evie. Would Richard have gotten away with killing his family, again? It's hard to believe, but as Chloe said, he would have pinned it on her, then he would have said she was responsible for Diane's death all along, he just hadn't wanted to admit it, and Chloe would be dead too, so there'd be no one left to tell the truth of what really happened.

The one good thing to come out of all this is my relationship with Chloe. In this short amount of time, she has blossomed into a happy young woman full of hope for the future. She lives with me now. I'm renting a small house in Islington, and you could say I am like an older sister to her, which I guess is what I always hoped for. She's going back to college to finish her studies and has taken a part-time job at the local pub.

But there's still so much to unravel.

Richard's business was certainly unravelling. He had created new portfolios but none of the investors he'd tried to convince to sign up had done so. His business partners bailed months ago, which Richard never told me about.

There's no record of him staying at the Connaught. But there wouldn't be, of course. He wasn't going to advertise the fact he was having an affair. I've hired a private detective to track down the woman Richard was seeing there but so far we haven't had any luck because she checked in under a false name.

'Dad was very good at covering his tracks, Jo.' Chloe calls me *Jo* now. 'He was always ten steps ahead of everyone else.'

But it's not enough for me. There's so much I want to know.

I want closure too.

Today is a beautiful, warm blue spring day and we're standing at Diane's and Sophie's graves. Chloe bought violets in a pretty clay pot. 'Mum loved violets,' she explains. She puts them down carefully while I wipe leaves away and brush dirt off the stone. Diane's mother Helen would have come too, but it's too much for her these days. So we are going there for tea and scones, and I am thrilled to be meeting her for the first time.

'I love you, Mum,' Chloe whispers and wipes her cheeks

with her fingers. I wait quietly. Then she gets up and brushes down the skirt of her dress. It's a pretty dress I bought her last week, white and yellow with large flowers, sleeveless and secured at the shoulders with a bowknot tie. It really suits her. I've been wanting to do things like that, buy her clothes, so she doesn't have to spend her money and she can limit the hours that she works at the pub. I prefer for her to concentrate on her studies. I left it on her bed and I stood in the doorway when she picked it up.

She looked at me and for a moment I thought I'd done the wrong thing.

'You can change it. I kept the receipt,' I said.

'No… it's not that.'

'What is it?'

'Nobody has ever bought me clothes before. I mean not since…'

'Do you like it?' I pushed a strand of hair off her face. 'You don't have to, it's just that you do wear a lot of black.' I tilted my head at her.

She shrugged. 'I like black.'

'Well, I'd hope so. I thought this would look nice on you.'

She held it up and checked herself out in the full-length mirror. Then she smiled. 'Thank you.' And she hugged me.

I laughed. It was the first time she'd done that. 'You're very welcome,' I said. Then I turned away because I didn't want her to see me cry.

I check my watch. 'We should go. We don't want to be late for your Nan,' I say.

Chloe stands up straight and picks up Evie from the pram.

'Okay.' She hooks her arm into mine while I push the empty pram.

'See you next time, Mum,' she says over her shoulder.

Diane's mother Helen lives in a large ground-floor flat in Knightsbridge. She's also very old, older than I'd realised. I'm shocked by how frail and shaky she seems.

'I've got scones,' she says sternly. Okay, maybe not so frail then. 'And I didn't make them, in case you're wondering.'

Certainly not the welcome I'd expected. The way Chloe described her, I assumed she'd be warm and fuzzy, fussing over Chloe and also, if I'm truthful, eager to meet me.

Right now I feel like she can't wait for us to get out of there.

But Chloe doesn't seem to care. She hugs her affectionately, calls her Nan, and clearly knows where everything is as she gets Helen's special china plates and cups from the cupboard.

As I sit down with Evie on my lap in the living room, I spot a number of photo albums on the shelf.

'Are those your family albums?' I ask Helen when she shuffles back to the living room.

'Those belonged to Diane and Richard,' she says. 'I took them after she died.'

'Oh! Really? I'd love to see photos of Chloe when she was little. And photos of Diane, too. I've never seen a photo of Diane, you know.' Other than in the papers, but I don't say that out loud.

She pulls out a photo album from the shelf and as she lowers herself on the couch next to me, I put my hand out to help her. She slaps it.

'I can do it myself,' she growls.

'Sorry. Yes. I can see that.'

I can hear Chloe in the kitchen turning the tap on. Helen glances at Evie on my lap and Evie giggles at her.

'Would you like to hold her?' I ask.

She narrows her eyes. I'm expecting her to scoff but something in her face softens. She nods and puts the photo album on the couch between us. I pass Evie over, settle her on Helen's lap. Evie babbles away, fingering the amber beads on Helen's necklace. Helen smiles.

'Oh, that's … so sweet,' I say, admiring a photo of a young Richard holding a grinning Chloe on his shoulders. I hadn't expected that, I must say. If that was me, I'd have burned all the photos of Richard.

I turn the page. Lots of photos of Richard and Chloe. She was such a happy little girl, grinning from ear to ear. Not so many photos of Chloe and Diane, I notice, probably because Diane was the one taking them.

Helen points her chin at Richard. 'He came to see me often. Even after you were married.'

Am I hearing this right? She almost sounds like she misses him.

'Are we ready for tea?' Chloe says, bouncing in with a stack of small plates and cups on a tray.

'Chloe, can you run to the shops and get some strawberry jam? I forgot to buy some.'

'We don't need jam, Nan. I'm sure Jo won't mind.'

'I don't mind,' I say.

'Of course we need jam,' Helen snaps. 'Off you go. You can take my purse. It's on the console table in the hall.'

'Okay, Nan! I'll be right back.'

After she's gone, Helen points a finger at a picture of young Chloe. 'She's very bright, that one.'

I smile. 'Yes. She certainly is.'

'Always was,' she continues. 'Always an answer for everything. That's what Diane used to say. She's got an answer for everything. Barking mad, of course. Always telling lies.

Wicked, wicked lies. But very clever. That's how she got away with it.'

I frown, confused. Stare at the photos on the page. 'Who?'

'Her.' She narrows her eyes at the door. 'Criminally insane. I told Richard never to let her out of the psychiatric ward, but he wouldn't listen. He wanted to believe the best of her, no matter the evidence right in front of his face. Always did. But I know he felt guilty because he was at work all the time. He thought Diane wasn't coping. She tried to tell him but he wouldn't believe it.' Evie pulls at the necklace, and Helen gently pries her fingers open.

Oh god. Now I get it. All these years, Richard has been feeding Helen the same lies he fed me. On the surface making out like he adored Chloe, he only saw the best in her, but at the same time planting the seed that she's crazy and probably killed her own mother.

I really, really don't want to have this conversation with Helen.

I turn the page. Helen points to a photo of Richard with another man. They have their arms around each other's shoulders. 'You should talk to him,' she says. 'He'll tell you.'

'Tell me what?'

'That Richard couldn't have done the things they're accusing him of.'

I swallow a sigh. 'Who is he?' I ask. More to kill time until Chloe returns than because I really want to know.

'He was Richard's business partner back then. Alfred is his name.'

'Alfred Butterworth?'

'Yes. That's him.'

I realise with a start that she is probably suffering from dementia. In fact, it wouldn't surprise me if she didn't know who I was. I resolve to discuss it with Chloe later. No wonder she's confused about Richard.

'I'm sorry, Helen.' I put my hand on her forearm. Is it really my place to tell her that Alfred Butterworth is dead? Maybe I should just agree with everything she says and talk to Chloe later.

'Were you close to Alfred?' I ask.

She nods. 'He's a nice man. He was very close to Richard until they had a falling out.'

Which is one way of putting it, I guess.

'He came to see me the other day. He comes to see me often.'

'The other day? No.' It comes out of me before I have time to stop myself. 'Alfred Butterworth passed away many years ago. I'm so sorry.' Also Richard killed him, but maybe let's not go there.

'Alfred? Don't be ridiculous. He lives down the road! Go talk to him. He'll tell you.'

'Down the road? No. That's not possible. And what would he tell me?'

She raises her eyebrows. 'That she's mad! She did this. She did all of them. She comes to see me because she wants me to put her in my will. She thinks she's in there. As if. I have no choice but tolerate her because if I tell her to go to hell, she'll come back and kill me in my sleep! She's capable of it, you know. She's completely barking mad.'

Wow. This is so much worse than I'd thought. I really hope Chloe comes back soon, so we can have our scones and tea and get out of here.

I continue turning the pages. Anything to change the topic. I point to a photo of Sophie lying on her back, grinning. 'Sophie looks adorable.'

Helen nods. A tear rolls down her cheek. She hugs Evie a little closer. I turn the page, hoping for photos that won't bring back more sad memories. A gondola in Venice? The Eiffel Tower? The Parthenon?

Unfortunately, I land on more photos of Richard with Sophie. Chloe is there too, in the background. Helen points to one where she's got her arms crossed over her chest and she's scowling. 'He called it her little angry face. "Where's my little angry face?" he'd say. He thought it was amusing, the way she did that. He didn't understand.'

Now that I look more closely, there is something strange about those photos. I swallow, look at more photographs, my heart racing. I turn the pages faster and faster. In all the photos that have both baby Sophie and Chloe together, Chloe is narrowing her eyes at little Sophie. In one of them, she's looking at Sophie with pure hate.

'She wouldn't let anyone else near her father. In front of him, she was the perfect child, but the moment he had his back turned, she turned into a wicked little girl. She was jealous of everyone close to him. Of Sophie, of Diane… Everyone could see it, but him. I always told him there was something not right about this child. And look what's happened now.'

'Why did he send her to the psychiatric hospital? If he didn't think there was anything wrong with her?'

'Because she told him.'

'Told him what?'

'That she did it.'

Chapter Forty-Five

Blood is roaring in my ears.

'He rang me one day,' she continues. 'Told me Chloe was delirious, he didn't know what to do. Apparently, she'd said to him, "I did it, Daddy. I pushed her. We can be together now. Just you and me. Isn't it better when it's just you and me?" And then she said, "I know you didn't love Mummy. I know you never wanted another baby. I took care of it, Daddy. It's just you and me now."

He thought she was in shock because she was there when Diane died. I told him, she's not in shock, Richard, for Christ's sake. What's it going to take? She's telling you the truth. But he couldn't admit that. He got very angry with me for suggesting it. He kept saying she was having a nervous breakdown or survivor's guilt or some such nonsense. He couldn't handle the truth. It was easier to tell himself she was having a nervous breakdown. And as the police were involved, he didn't want them to hear what she was claiming. So he sent her to that place, Vincent Gardens. By the time she came out, she said she'd made it up. It was just a dream, she said. As if you can have those kinds of dreams and not call them nightmares.'

'Maybe he lied,' I try, my heart pounding. 'Maybe she never said those words, maybe she knew it was him. I mean, that's what she's been telling me.'

She squints her watery eyes at me. 'Why would he do such a thing? He loved his family.'

'For money?' I suggest, my lips trembling.

She scoffs. 'He had a good, kind heart, but he was a terrible businessman. He just didn't have that kind of brain. He should have given it up but his father was a successful financier and he wanted to continue in his footsteps. He tried too hard. He was always away working, but he was hopeless with money. Even buying Chloe a million-pound flat. Such a waste.'

'Chloe says Richard didn't buy her a flat,' I say. 'She says he lied about that.'

She looks at me like I've just dropped the photo album on my head.

'Of course he did. He bought her a nice flat in Primrose Hill. I went there with him.'

Primrose Hill. The words trigger a memory. Richard and I went there together. I was eight months pregnant with Evie, and I felt like a house. We'd spent a Saturday shopping for more baby things and Robyn had recommended a shop on Winchester Road that sold furniture and whatnot for the nursery. We bought lots of things, all to be delivered the following week, and when we came outside Richard stopped abruptly.

'Everything okay?' I'd asked.

He didn't reply, just kept his gaze fixed in the distance. Then he shook his head. 'Sorry. I thought I saw someone.'

'Who?'

'Nobody.'

He looked preoccupied for the rest of the day, and I knew it had to do with whomever he'd seen. When I tried to ask him again, he shook his head and changed the conversation.

Could it have been Chloe he saw that day? My stomach is clenched tight. My heart is thumping. I turn a page and I recognise the photo of Sophie, the one Chloe kept in her suitcase.

The one she shoved into Richard's face before she shot him.

'Chloe loved Sophie,' I say like I've just grabbed hold of a life raft. 'You're wrong about that, Helen. Chloe carried this photo of her everywhere. I've seen it. She adored her little sister.'

'That's not Sophie. That's Chloe.'

I shake my head. 'No. She had this photograph with her. She showed it to me. That's Sophie.'

She leans across, holding Evie with one hand, and turns the pages until she finds the photograph she's looking for. She points to a baby photo.

'*That's* Sophie. Around the same age.'

I pull it out and turn back to the photo Chloe carried with her, put them side by side.

'Even as babies they looked nothing alike,' Helen says. 'When Sophie was born, Chloe really changed. She hated him for having another baby. She hated her mother too, but she'd always hated Diane. Always. She hated anyone who loved her father and anyone her father loved. She wanted her father to herself, and that was that.'

The fish. Richard loved those fish. He gave them names and he treated them like favourite pets. He took Chloe to the pond and showed her how to feed them.

And now they're all dead.

I think back to the moment when Chloe shoved that

photo in Richard's face. *Remember her? Do you?* She wasn't talking about Sophie. She was talking about herself as a baby. *Mum's dead, Sophie's dead, it's all your fault. And now Joanne? And Evie? Really, Daddy?*

Helen caresses Evie's head. 'I don't think he ever told her about Evie. He said he was going to, but he wanted to wait until after she was born. He kept making excuses but I could tell, for all his blustering about Chloe being a perfect child that he knew, deep down, that she wasn't right in the head. He just couldn't admit it to himself. It was too horrific to contemplate. But a part of him knew it, and that part of him didn't want her to know about Evie.'

Richard's strange words as he kneeled on the ground begging for his life come back to me. I didn't understand them at the time. I didn't think they were addressed to me. I thought they were addressed to Chloe.

I never told her.

I pull out my phone. 'Excuse me for a moment, Helen. I really need to make this call.' Helen frowns at me but Evie puts her hands on Helen's face and she smiles again.

I swipe the screen with shaking hands and call our solicitor, Solomon. He answers on the first ring.

'Joanne. How—'

'Why did you call Richard that day?' I blurt. 'The day he died. You called me, then you called him. About Chloe.'

He clears his throat. 'Chloe got in touch with me about Richard's will. She wanted to know if she was still in it and if the new baby would be in it too.'

'She didn't call about her share of her mother's estate? That she would inherit when she turned twenty-one?'

'Her mother's estate was settled when she died, and it all went to Richard.'

I'm going to throw up all over the Chesterfield.

Solomon continues. 'I told Chloe to ask her father

directly, and I didn't think of it until Richard mentioned months later that she was staying with you.'

She's just being nosy. I'm sure it's nothing.

'And she called you about her father's will in late November?'

'That's right.'

'And she knew about Evie?'

'Yes. That's why she'd called.'

I end the call and try to think. Evie was born on the fifteenth of November. By the twenty-seventh, I am absolutely certain Richard had not told Chloe about her. We were still discussing how to do that weeks later. I was surprised she knew about Evie when she wrote to Richard in February.

Richard hadn't told her. And if he was surprised that she knew, he never said it to me.

But she knew because she saw us, six weeks before she called Solomon to ask about the will. She saw us coming out of the baby furniture shop in Primrose Hill. And Richard saw her too. Even without the fact it was a baby shop, Chloe could not miss that we were about to have one. I was the size of a house by that stage. She waited six weeks and called Richard's solicitor.

Why now? Why did you come now?

She told me some story about her mother's estate going to her when she turned twenty-one, but according to Solomon, that's a lie.

Why now?

Because she knew her father had had another baby. That's all.

Everything that happened over the three weeks she was in the house comes back to me, playing in sequence like a home movie.

Chloe about to put something in the bottle of Calpol. I got the real one tested, the one she dropped to the floor. The other one? The supposedly larger bottle she got from the pharmacy? I've never seen it again.

'Did you think Chloe had something to do with Sophie's death?' I blurt now.

'There was an autopsy.'

I grab her arm. 'And?'

'There were traces of paracetamol in her stomach. But Diane told me she didn't give her any that night.'

'Oh god,' I whimper.

'Richard said she must have been mistaken. She was always so tired. And it wasn't enough to kill Sophie.' She narrows her eyes at me. 'But it was enough to make her sleepy. Enough to make sure she didn't cry if someone pressed her face against the mattress so she wouldn't be able to breathe.'

I start to shake. It was all there, right in front of me. I think of Chloe saying she wanted me and Evie to leave. Now she says it was to protect me. How could I have been so stupid? She was literally saying she wanted her father to herself and Evie and I should go.

I still have the phone in my hand. This time I call Roxanne. Her number is still in my contacts.

'Mrs A?' She sounds surprised.

'Roxanne, this is really important. You were going to come and stay with us that night.' I don't need to clarify what that night refers to.

'Uh huh?'

'You said that Richard called again to cancel. Is that right?'

'Not called, Mrs A. He texted me.'

'He texted? When?'

'I can't remember exactly, but not long. Like, maybe an hour later?'

I hang up, press my hands against my eyes. Chloe had

come for her father when he was on the phone to Roxanne. She overheard that conversation. Then later they were on the couch together and she was sulky, playing with his phone.

It was her who texted Roxanne and told her not to come. Literally under his nose.

It was her who took my phone and pulled the SIM card out. I asked her how she guessed he'd done that. Because that's what he did last time. But it was the fixed line phones that were unplugged. Did they even have mobile phones back then? Maybe, but Chloe could have simply plugged one of the fixed phones back in.

It was her who poured the petrol on the stairs. She had the matches in her pocket. They fell out when she was coming out of the coat room. 'I grabbed them from the kitchen drawer,' she'd said. But I was with her when we ran through the kitchen to the back door and she didn't stop, did she? I don't think she did. I'm sure she didn't. And the doors being locked, the front door, the back door… I just took her word for it. I never tried them myself.

She was going to kill us that night. But when Solomon called with the message for Richard, she realised he would figure it out. She knew he'd come back. He wouldn't take that chance a second time.

I never told her.

She realised he would finally admit the unthinkable: that it had been her all along.

So why did she let me go, me and Evie?

Because Richard coming back was never part of the plan. She had to change tack. If she'd killed the three of us and she'd survived, they'd never believe whatever tale she would have drummed up this time. She'd go to jail forever and she knew it. So she brought me on board. She convinced me that he was the monster, not her, so I would testify to that, and that Chloe was doing what she could to save Evie and me. It was better for her if I stayed alive and backed her up.

Payback, she'd said.

For your mum, for Sophie, I'd said.

And for you, she'd said. And for Evie. *Payback for marrying you. Payback for having another baby.*

'Strawberry jam delivery!' Chloe sings out from the hall. 'I'll get everything ready and bring it out, Nan. I won't be long.'

My heart is pounding in my chest. I glance down at Evie on Helen's lap, then at Helen. 'What am I going to do?' I whisper.

Chloe bursts out laughing in the kitchen. 'Silly Nan! You've got loads of strawberry jam!'

Helen grips my wrist. 'She lives with you, you said?'

I nod, my gaze landing on a photo of Diane. She's smiling but her eyes look so sad. Like her heart is broken.

Helen's fingernails dig into my skin. 'Don't let her stay.'
